# SLEIGH BELLS ON CAPTIVA

## CAPTIVA ISLAND
### BOOK FOURTEEN

## ANNIE CABOT

CABOT PUBLISHING GROUP

ISBN ebook, 978-1-966363-00-2

ISBN paperback, 978-1-966363-01-9

# CHAPTER 1

$\mathcal{M}$aggie Moretti's fingers paused on the ribbon she was tying around a gift, the sound of a knock at the door breaking the quiet rhythm of Christmas morning.

It was still early, and she had expected the day to begin with the familiar sounds of her family stirring upstairs, not the arrival of an unexpected guest. The knock was steady, deliberate—not urgent, but carrying a certain weight that immediately put her on edge.

"Who could be here at this hour?" she muttered to herself, her gaze flicking to the clock on the mantel. It wasn't yet seven.

Paolo, who had been adjusting the holiday decorations in the hallway, looked up and met her eyes.

"Maybe it's Sarah and Trevor, surprising us by coming early."

Maggie nodded, but something about the knock didn't sit right with her. Years of managing the inn and her large, lively family had taught her to trust her instincts, and they were telling her this visit was more than just a simple drop-in.

"I'll get it," she said, her voice calm as she moved toward the door. Behind her, the inn was beginning to come to life; she could hear her grandchildren's laughter echoing down the stairs, and the rich aroma of coffee brewed by Oliver in the kitchen was filling the air.

Maggie opened the door, and the sight of the man standing on the doorstep made her breath catch. He was tall, with dark hair that curled slightly at the ends, and his eyes—though warm—held a guarded look that immediately caught her attention.

"Good morning," he said, his voice deep but soft. "I'm looking for Oliver Laurier. I was told he might be staying here."

Maggie narrowed her eyes slightly, trying to place the familiarity in his face. He was well-dressed, though not in an ostentatious way—more like someone who knew how to make a good impression without drawing too much attention. A small suitcase sat beside him, signaling that he wasn't just passing through.

"May I ask who's looking for him?" Maggie's tone was polite, but there was an edge of caution in her voice.

"My name is Philippe Laurier," he replied, holding her gaze. "I'm Oliver's brother."

The words hit Maggie with a jolt. Oliver had never mentioned having a brother. In all the time he had been at the inn, he had shared very little about his life growing up, and what he did share had been tinged with loss and pain.

"Please, come in," Maggie said, stepping aside to let him enter, her mind racing with questions. As he walked past her into the inn, she couldn't help but wonder what had brought him here, and why now.

Philippe entered the sitting room, his eyes taking in the warm, cozy space. The fire crackled in the hearth, casting a soft glow on the holiday decorations that adorned the room. It was a place of comfort and joy, but there was a tension in the air now that hadn't been there before.

"I'll get Oliver," Maggie said, her voice steady, though her thoughts were anything but. She moved toward the kitchen, her mind buzzing with the implications of this unexpected visit. Whatever had brought Philippe here, she had a feeling it wasn't just a friendly reunion.

When Maggie entered the kitchen, she found Oliver at the stove, stirring a pot of something fragrant. He looked up as she approached, and she saw the flicker of concern in his eyes.

"Good morning, Maggie. Are people up already?" he asked.

"Oliver," Maggie began, "there's someone here to see you."

Oliver's hand froze on the spoon, his gaze locking onto hers. "Who?"

"Your brother," she said simply.

Oliver didn't move for a moment, his face unreadable. But in his eyes, Maggie saw a flash of emotion—surprise, and something harder, something that spoke of old wounds not yet healed.

"Philippe," Oliver said, almost to himself. He set the spoon down slowly and wiped his hands on a towel, his movements controlled.

"Did you tell him that I'm here?"

Maggie nodded. "Yes, of course."

She could tell that Oliver didn't want to see his brother, but he didn't come right out and say it.

"I didn't think he'd find me here," he said. "I'll be right out."

Maggie wanted to ask more, to understand the history that lay between these two brothers, but she held back. Oliver was a private man, and she knew he would share when he was ready.

"I've brought him to the sitting room," Maggie said softly. "Take your time."

Oliver nodded, offering her a tight smile. "Thank you, Maggie."

As Oliver left the kitchen, Maggie watched him go, her heart heavy with concern. She couldn't shake the feeling that whatever had brought Philippe to Captiva, it wasn't going to be easy for Oliver to face.

❄

Oliver stood in the doorway of the sitting room, his hand resting on the doorframe as he took in the sight of his brother. Philippe was seated on the edge of the sofa, his back straight, his hands clasped together. When he looked up, their eyes met, and the silence between them was thick with years of unspoken words.

"Oliver," Philippe said, his voice steady but with an undercurrent of emotion. "It's been a long time."

Oliver didn't move from the doorway. "Why are you here, Philippe?"

Philippe sighed, his shoulders relaxing slightly. "I came to see you. To talk."

"Talk?" Oliver's voice was sharp, filled with skepticism. "After all this time?"

"Yes," Philippe replied, his tone sincere. "I know we didn't part on good terms. But I'm here now, and I want to make things right."

Oliver's jaw tightened, his emotions swirling just beneath the surface.

"You think you can just show up and make things right? You don't know what these years have been like for me."

Philippe nodded, acknowledging the truth in Oliver's words.

"You're right. I don't know everything you've been through. But we're brothers, Oliver, and I want to try and fix what's been broken between us."

Oliver's gaze hardened. "It's not just about us, Philippe. It's more than that."

Philippe's expression softened, a knowing look in his eyes. "Father."

The word hung between them, heavy with the weight of old resentments and unresolved conflicts.

"Yes," Oliver said quietly. "Father."

Philippe leaned forward, his hands unclasping as he spoke. "Oliver, he's not well. He's been asking about you."

Oliver's breath caught, the news hitting him harder than he would have expected. Their father had been a central figure in their lives—once admired, later resented. The distance between them had grown over the years, fueled by misunderstandings and stubborn pride.

"Why are you telling me this now?" Oliver asked, his voice strained.

"Because it's not too late," Philippe replied, his voice earnest. "Not too late to try and heal. I know we can't change the past, but we can at least face it together."

Oliver felt a wave of conflicting emotions—anger, sorrow, and a glimmer of hope. He had spent years closing himself off, but now, faced with Philippe's words, he found himself at a crossroads.

Could he allow himself to hope for reconciliation?

"You come here at my place of employment on Christmas morning, and you want me to tell you that everything is fine? That we'll work things out, after years of distance and cruelty? I don't know what you expect of me."

Philippe nodded. "I don't expect anything. I hoped we could at least consider doing things differently going forward. I miss having my little brother in my life. I'd like to think you miss me as well. Besides, you and I soon will be all that's left of our family."

Philippe's words stung. Oliver had lost his wife and two children only a year earlier. Oliver had no idea if his brother knew of the tragedy, but he didn't allow himself to care one way or the other.

"I'm sorry, I didn't mean…" Philippe responded.

Oliver looked him in the eye.

"So you know?"

Philippe nodded. "I'm terribly sorry, Oliver. I don't know what to say."

"I'd like you to leave," Oliver said walking toward the front door.

Philippe turned to leave, stopping just before he walked out of the house.

"Please take some time to think about this. I'm staying at the Marriott at the Sanibel Bridge. I have only a one-way ticket and can stay as long as it takes."

Oliver wanted to tell him to book a flight, but held back, uncertain of his emotions.

As Philippe turned to leave, Oliver found himself speaking again. "Why did you really come here, Philippe?"

Philippe paused, turning back. "I came because I didn't want to lose more time. Life is too short, Oliver. I don't want to live with regrets."

With that, Philippe walked down the stairs and to a waiting car, leaving Oliver alone with his thoughts. The holiday cheer outside felt distant, as Oliver grappled with the emotions stirred by his brother's unexpected arrival. There would never have been a good time for Philippe to look for him, but that he came at Christmas was especially painful. All he could do now was focus on his job and Maggie's family...now his true family.

Maggie watched as Oliver shut the front door. Whatever Philippe said to Oliver, Maggie could tell that this was no casual visit—whatever had brought him to Captiva was serious.

As she returned to the kitchen, her thoughts were with Oliver. She had seen the way he had reacted, the tension in his posture, the controlled expression on his face. Whatever history he shared with Philippe, it was clear that it hadn't been an easy one.

"Maggie?" Paolo's voice pulled her from her thoughts. He was standing by the counter, a cup of coffee in hand, concern etched on his face. "Everything okay?"

Maggie sighed, offering him a small smile. "I'm not sure. That was Oliver's brother at the door."

Paolo raised an eyebrow. "Brother? I didn't know he had a brother."

"Neither did I," Maggie admitted, moving to pour herself a fresh cup of coffee. "He's here to see Oliver, but I think there's more to it than just a visit."

Paolo nodded slowly, sensing the gravity of the situation. "Should we be worried?"

Maggie took a sip of her coffee, her thoughts drifting back to the brief conversation she had overheard. "I don't know. But whatever it is, I think it's something Oliver needs to handle. We just have to be here for him."

As Oliver continued with the Christmas food preparation, Maggie approached him. "Can I help you with anything?" she asked.

Oliver shook his head. "Nope, I've got everything under control. You go back and enjoy the time with your family."

Maggie nodded and forced a smile. She wanted desperately for everything to go well today, and now, with Philippe's arrival, there was a sadness in the air. Even though the inn was soon to be filled with the warmth and noise of a large family gathering, Maggie's mind kept drifting back to Oliver and Philippe.

As the morning continued to unfold, the inn came to life with the sounds of more family arriving. Sarah and Trevor were the first to show up, their children bursting through the door with excitement, followed by the rest of Maggie's children and grandchildren slowly descending the stairs.

Oliver moved through the house with a quiet, focused energy, but there was a tension on his face that hadn't been there before, and Maggie couldn't help but worry about what it meant.

But the day was filled with other distractions—presents to

open, food to prepare, and the joyful chaos of family that demanded her attention. She found herself drawn into the festivities, but always with one eye on Oliver.

It wasn't until later in the day, after the presents had been opened and the children had retreated to play with their new toys, that Maggie found herself alone with him in the kitchen.

"Are you okay?" she asked gently, watching him as he methodically cleaned up after the morning's feast.

Oliver didn't look up, his hands busy with the dishes. "I'm fine."

Maggie frowned, not convinced. "Oliver, you know you can talk to me, right? About anything."

He paused, his shoulders tensing slightly before he let out a long breath.

"It's complicated, Maggie."

"I figured as much," she replied, moving closer. "But you don't have to handle it alone."

Oliver finally looked up, his expression conflicted.

"Philippe's here because of our father. He's not well, and he wants to see me."

Maggie nodded slowly, understanding the weight of what he was saying.

"And you're not sure if you want to see him."

Oliver's jaw tightened, a flash of pain crossing his face.

"Our relationship... it's complicated. There's a lot of history, a lot of hurt."

Maggie reached out, placing a hand on his arm.

"You don't have to decide anything right now. Just take your time."

Oliver looked at her, his eyes reflecting the turmoil he was feeling.

"Thank you, Maggie. For everything."

She squeezed his arm gently, offering him a reassuring smile.

"You're part of our family, Oliver. We're here for you, no matter what."

Oliver gave her a small, grateful smile before turning back to the dishes. Maggie watched him for a moment longer, her heart heavy with concern. She knew this wasn't something that could be resolved easily, but she hoped that, in time, Oliver would find the peace he needed.

# CHAPTER 2

*M*aggie spent the entire morning juggling the demands of her large family while keeping a close eye on Oliver, who had remained largely out of sight after the tense exchange with his brother. As much as she wanted to help Oliver navigate this unexpected family reunion, Maggie knew that Christmas Day was about her own family, too.

Her grandchildren, filled with the energy only a holiday could bring, had kept her busy with their constant requests to play games, show off their new toys, or simply cuddle on the couch. But now, as the day wore on, the frenzy had started to fade, replaced by the soft contentment that comes with a day well spent.

In the living room, Maggie found herself surrounded by her children. Michael was deep in conversation with his brother-in-law Gabriel, while Lauren and Jeff were nestled on the couch, their newborn son, Daniel, sleeping soundly in Lauren's arms. Across the room, Becca was quietly talking to Beth, her hand resting protectively on her growing belly, while Sarah kept an eye on her children as they played in the corner.

Maggie felt a pang of pride as she watched her children and

their families, each one flourishing in their own way. But there was a bittersweetness to it, too—she knew that in just a few days, the inn would be quiet again as they all returned to their lives.

She was drawn out of her thoughts by the sound of Paolo's voice behind her. "How is my beautiful wife holding up?"

Maggie smiled up at him, grateful for his steady presence.

"I'm doing all right. It's just a lot, you know? But it's a good kind of busy."

Paolo nodded. "You've done an amazing job keeping everything together today. But don't forget to take a moment for yourself, too."

Maggie reached for his hand, squeezing it gently.

"I will. Thank you, honey. For everything."

As the afternoon light began to fade, Maggie noticed Chelsea slipping away from the lively conversations. She followed her friend out to the back porch, where Chelsea stood looking out at the garden and enjoying the sound of the waves in the distance.

"You okay?" Maggie asked, stepping up beside her.

Chelsea turned to her with a soft smile.

"I'm more than okay. I just needed a moment to take it all in. You know how I am—sometimes I need to step back and breathe."

Maggie nodded, understanding all too well.

"I do. It's a lot, especially with everything that's been happening. Where is Steven?"

Chelsea sighed, her gaze drifting back to the ocean. "He had to make a phone call. He's back at my place but will be around later. I've been thinking... about the wedding."

Maggie smiled. "I don't see how you can think about anything else. You're in a lovely place right now, Chelsea. I'm so happy for you. Are you still thinking of doing it soon?"

Chelsea nodded, a determined look in her eyes. "I don't want to wait. Life is unpredictable, and I don't want to waste any more time. Steven and I want something small, just close friends and family. But I'll need your help to pull it all together."

Maggie felt a surge of excitement at the prospect of planning another wedding, especially for someone as dear to her as Chelsea. But there were also the challenges to consider—Chelsea's sisters, the short timeline, and the fact that her children would be leaving soon.

"You must have heard that I know how to put on a good wedding," Maggie teased. "We can make it happen," she said with confidence in her voice. "It might take some creative thinking, but we'll do it. And don't worry about your sisters. We'll figure out how to handle that, too."

Chelsea laughed softly. "That's what I was hoping you'd say. I knew I could count on you. You know what my sisters are like. It won't be easy."

Maggie smiled and put her arm around Chelsea's waist.

"Nothing worth anything ever is."

The two women stood in comfortable silence for a moment, the weight of the day giving way to the anticipation of what was to come.

"Let's go talk with the others," Maggie said finally. "I think we could all use a little girl time on the beach."

"Oh, I'd love that. Let's do it," Chelsea said, as they made their way back inside to gather the rest of the women.

The beach was quiet, save for the gentle sound of the waves and the distant calls of seagulls. The sun had dipped low in the sky, painting the horizon in shades of pink and orange. Maggie, her mother, and the other women had found a secluded spot where they could sit in the sand, their laughter and conversation mingling with the sound of the ocean.

Lauren cradled baby Daniel in her arms, his tiny form

bundled against the cool evening breeze. She breathed in the scent of his soft skin, reveling in the sweet, familiar smell of a newborn. "I'd forgotten how much I missed this," she said softly, smiling down at him.

"It's amazing how quickly you forget the sleepless nights and endless diapers," Sarah chimed in, her eyes twinkling as she glanced at her own children playing nearby. "But then, when you hold them, it's like all of that melts away."

Becca nodded, resting a hand on her belly. "I'm looking forward to it, but I'm also terrified. Being a third-year medical student is hard enough, but adding a baby into the mix…" She trailed off, her eyes wide with the weight of the responsibility ahead.

"You'll manage, Becca," Ciara said reassuringly, her voice gentle but firm. "You're stronger than you think, and you've got all of us here to help. Plus, you've married into a family that knows how to support each other."

Becca smiled at her stepmother's words, feeling a sense of comfort in the support of the women around her. "You and Dad have been wonderful, Ciara. I'm so glad our families have blended the way they have."

Ciara smiled. "Me too, honey."

"I'm just excited to finish school," Brea said, her voice carrying a note of determination. "It's been a long road, but I'm almost there."

"I give you so much credit for going back to school after having children," Beth added. "I don't think I could do it."

"There have been days when I thought I couldn't manage. The brain fog and conversations with only children day after day made me think I couldn't handle it, but I did."

Maggie smiled at her daughter-in-law, proud of the journey Brea had taken to balance raising her children and pursuing her education. "You've done an incredible job, Brea. And you're almost at the finish line. We'll have to have a celebration party."

Lauren laughed. "That's us Wheelers for you, always celebrating every milestone with a party."

Everyone laughed and agreed. The conversation shifted as the women shared their stories, their dreams, and the challenges they faced. They talked about the upcoming year, their plans for the future, and the ways they had grown as individuals and as a family.

"I'm really looking forward to getting the orchard back up and running," Beth said, her voice filled with a quiet determination. "Thomas will be coming to help in the spring, and I think we can really make something of it. It's been too long since that land was put to good use."

Maggie's mother nodded approvingly. "It's good to see you taking that on, Beth. The orchard has so much potential, and it'll be wonderful to see it thriving again."

"And it's a great way to connect with the past," Sarah added. "It's a legacy that can be passed down to future generations."

As the conversation turned to Chelsea's upcoming wedding, the mood shifted slightly, becoming more playful and teasing.

"So, when exactly are you planning to pull off your dream wedding?" Lauren asked, her tone light but curious.

Chelsea laughed, a hint of nervousness in her voice. "I don't know about the dream part, I'm just thrilled to be marrying such a wonderful man. We'd like to do it as soon as possible. Steven and I don't want a big production—just something small, intimate, and meaningful."

"You know your sisters will want to be involved," Maggie's mother pointed out, her tone gentle but firm. "Have you thought about how to handle that?"

Chelsea sighed, leaning back on her hands as she gazed out at the ocean.

"I have, and that's the tricky part. They're not exactly the easiest people to deal with, but they're my sisters. I can't not invite them."

"We'll figure it out," Maggie said, her voice reassuring. "We'll come up with a plan that keeps everyone happy—or at least as close to happy as we can get."

Ciara smiled at Chelsea, her eyes twinkling with mischief. "And if all else fails, you can always elope and avoid the drama entirely."

The group burst into laughter, the tension easing as they imagined the various ways the wedding could play out. Despite the challenges ahead, there was a sense of camaraderie among the women, a shared understanding that whatever came their way, they would face it together.

"I hate that we're all going to run back to Massachusetts just when you're getting married. I mean, it would have been nice to be here for it," Lauren said.

Chelsea smiled. "Then, don't go home. Stay longer...stay as long as it takes to create a last minute wedding."

Maggie looked at Chelsea. "You're serious? How long will they all have to stay? When is this wedding happening?"

Chelsea shrugged. " I don't know. How does in a few days sound? When are you all going home?"

"Oh, for heaven's sake, Chelsea. We can't put a wedding together in three days. Everyone is leaving on Tuesday."

"Why can't we put a wedding together in three days?" Beth asked. "We're all going to be here, and besides with so many of us helping, we can get this show on the road right away."

Chelsea laughed. "When you say it like that, I feel like we're in one of those old movies where the actors pull together a big show in a barn in twenty-four hours, and no one thinks it's a crazy idea."

Maggie chuckled. "Well, I think it's a crazy idea."

"That's because you have no spontaneity," her mother said. "I remember when you were a little girl. When we said we were going somewhere, you always ran back to your bedroom to check your mirror and organize your clothes."

"Oh, quiet over there...I can be spontaneous."

Chelsea waved Maggie away, "It doesn't matter, you don't count. You have to be in my corner no matter what I say or do. That's what best friends and Matron of Honors do."

Maggie didn't realize what Chelsea had said initially, but suddenly, as Chelsea waited for her response, Maggie understood what was being asked of her.

"Oh, Chelsea, really? You want me to be your Matron of Honor?"

Chelsea smiled and nodded. "Let's face it, you're too old for flower girl."

# CHAPTER 3

*O*liver sat on the worn wooden steps of his bungalow, the rhythmic sound of the ocean waves crashing against the shore a few yards away.

The sky above was beginning to darken, the sun sinking low on the horizon, casting the world in shades of orange and pink. It was a view he had grown to appreciate in his time on Captiva Island—a view that had become a balm for his fractured soul.

But tonight, the beauty of the sunset couldn't quiet the storm raging inside him.

Philippe's arrival had shattered the fragile peace Oliver had built for himself over the past year. His brother's sudden appearance had dredged up memories he had long tried to bury—memories of a time before his life had been irrevocably changed by tragedy.

As he stared out at the ocean, Oliver felt the weight of memories pressing down on him. His thoughts drifted back to the years before he met his wife, to the turbulent relationship he'd had with his father and brother. Estrangement had been inevitable—a consequence of choices made, words spoken in anger, and the stubborn pride that ran through the Laurier family like a curse.

His father, Jacques Laurier, had been a man of rigid principles and unyielding expectations. For as long as Oliver could remember, he had struggled to live up to those expectations, always feeling like he fell short. Jacques' disappointment had been a constant, a shadow that darkened every achievement and magnified every misstep.

The rift between father and son had begun in Oliver's late teens, when he announced his decision to pursue a career as a chef. Jacques was furious, viewing it as a betrayal of the family's legacy in finance. Jacques had envisioned his sons following in his footsteps, joining the family business, and upholding the Laurier name in the world of high finance. But Oliver had craved something different—something creative and expressive, a life beyond numbers and ledgers.

Philippe, the eldest son, had always been the golden child, the one who could do no wrong in their father's eyes. He embraced the path laid out for him, excelling in finance and winning their father's pride and approval. Oliver, by contrast, always felt like the outsider, the one who didn't fit the Laurier mold. And when he chose his own path, the distance between him and Philippe grew.

But career choices weren't the only thing that had come between them. There had been a woman—or, more accurately, two women, who complicated their already strained relationship.

The first was Sabrina McGovern, the daughter of one of their father's closest friends. She was beautiful, intelligent, and fiercely ambitious, the kind of woman who captivated both brothers. But it was Oliver who won her heart, much to Philippe's dismay. Despite her affection for Oliver, Sabrina was drawn to wealth and power, values she shared with her own family. Philippe saw this clearly, sensing that her attraction to Oliver was fragile and would falter in time. Patiently, he waited, confident that her true nature would eventually reveal itself and she'd come running to him.

And, in the end, Philippe was right. Although Sabrina loved Oliver, her need for luxury and status pulled her toward Philippe, who represented the world she craved. Slowly, she grew distant, and when she finally left Oliver, she turned to Philippe, more out of ambition than love. For Philippe, Sabrina represented an opportunity to align himself with wealth and prestige, though his feelings for her were always shallow, more admiration than genuine love.

True love for Philippe came later when he met Katherine "Katie" Barden, his best friend's younger sister. Katie was intelligent, graceful, and kind-hearted—everything Sabrina was not. She stirred something real in Philippe, but there was one problem: Katie only had eyes for Oliver. To Oliver, however, Katie was just a girl, someone he'd known since she was a child. He dismissed her interest as an innocent crush, thinking of her as little more than a kid.

It wasn't until a few years later, after the turmoil with Sabrina had settled into a distant, painful memory, that Oliver began to see Katie in a new light. They hadn't seen each other in a while— he had been busy building his career, and she had gone off to college. But when she returned one summer, something about her felt different. She was no longer the shy girl with a quiet crush; instead, she had become a confident, intelligent young woman.

It was during a Laurier family gathering when he first noticed the change. Katie walked into the room with an easy grace that caught his attention, chatting animatedly with friends and laughing at a story someone was telling.

Oliver watched her from across the room, surprised by the shift. Her laughter, bright and uninhibited, filled the room, and he couldn't help but notice the way her eyes sparkled with genuine warmth. She carried herself with a maturity he hadn't seen before, and he felt himself drawn to her in a way he couldn't quite explain.

Later that evening, as the gathering began to wind down, he found himself alone with her on the terrace, the sounds of the evening quiet around them. She was leaning against the railing, gazing up at the stars with a calm expression. He approached her, the familiar feeling of their friendship easing his nervousness.

"Nice to have you back, Katie," he said, smiling. "Feels like forever since we've had a chance to catch up."

She turned to him, her eyes warm and full of a confidence he wasn't used to seeing. "It's good to be back," she replied. "And it's nice to see you, Oliver. I've missed these family gatherings... and I've missed you."

Something in her tone made him pause. There was a sincerity there, an openness that hinted at the depth of her feelings. For the first time, he allowed himself to look at her without the lens of the past, without dismissing her as the "kid" he once knew. She had become someone intriguing, someone whose company he genuinely enjoyed.

As the weeks went by, they found more reasons to spend time together. Oliver started to look forward to their conversations, drawn to her kindness, her wisdom, and the quiet strength she carried.

Katie had a way of listening that made him feel seen, understood, and valued. Her presence became a balm for the wounds of his past, a reminder of the kind of love he had once doubted could exist.

One evening, they went for a walk along the beach, the moon casting a silvery glow over the waves. As they strolled, talking about everything from their dreams to the challenges they'd faced, Oliver felt a warmth bloom in his chest.

He realized that Katie saw him for who he truly was—not the black sheep of the Laurier family, not the outsider, but the man he'd fought to become. And in that moment, he knew he was falling for her.

The realization took him by surprise, but it felt right. Here was a woman who knew him, flaws and all, and still chose to stand by his side. She had loved him from afar, patiently waiting as he found his way to her. And now, standing by her side on that moonlit beach, he knew he wanted nothing more than to spend the rest of his life with her.

Eventually, after months of deepening their bond, Oliver took her hand in his and asked her to be his forever. With tears in her eyes, Katie agreed, and they embraced, both knowing they had finally found the love they'd been searching for all along.

Philippe had never forgiven Oliver for "stealing" Katie, and their father had seen Oliver's choice as another act of rebellion.

When Oliver and Katie had married, his father had disowned him, cutting him off both financially and emotionally. Philippe had sided with their father, and the two had closed ranks, leaving Oliver to forge his own path without the support of his family. It had been a painful break, one that had left deep scars on all sides.

But despite the bitterness and the estrangement, Oliver had found happiness with Katie. They had built a life together, had two beautiful sons, and for a time, Oliver had believed that he had everything he needed. He had even come to terms with the idea that he might never reconcile with his father and brother. He had his own family now, and that was enough.

Until the flood had taken it all away.

The memory of that day was like a knife to his heart. The images flashed through his mind—rushing water, the panicked screams of his children, the desperate struggle to hold on to them. And then, the crushing realization that he had failed to save them.

Survivor's guilt had haunted him ever since, gnawing at him day and night. It had nearly destroyed him in the months that followed, and there were times when he had wished that the water had taken him too. But slowly, with the support of Maggie and her family, and the sense of purpose he found in his work as a chef, Oliver had begun to heal.

And now Philippe was here, bringing with him all the pain and bitterness of the past.

Oliver took a deep breath, trying to steady himself. He had avoided thinking about his father and brother for so long, burying those memories under layers of grief and guilt. But Philippe's arrival had forced him to confront the past, and he knew he couldn't ignore it any longer.

His thoughts drifted back to their last conversation before the estrangement became final. It had been after a particularly heated argument with their father, one in which Oliver had finally stood up for himself, refusing to be controlled any longer.

He had left the family home that night, vowing never to return. Philippe had followed him outside, and in the cold night air, they had exchanged words that could never be taken back.

"You're throwing everything away, Oliver," Philippe had said, his voice filled with both anger and desperation. "Our family, our legacy—don't you care about any of it?"

Oliver had shaken his head, his heart heavy with the decision he knew he had to make. "I care about being true to myself, Philippe. I can't live my life trying to meet Father's expectations. I have to do what makes me happy."

"And what about Katie?" Philippe's voice had been sharp, accusatory. "Is she just another rebellion? Another way to defy Father?"

"She's the woman I love," Oliver had replied, his voice calm but firm. "And she chose me, Philippe. Not you."

Those words had been like a slap to his brother's face. Philippe's eyes had darkened with a mixture of hurt and anger, and he had taken a step back, as if distancing himself physically could somehow lessen the impact of Oliver's decision.

"Then you've made your choice," Philippe had said coldly. "Don't expect us to be there when it all falls apart."

And with that, Philippe had turned and walked away, leaving

Oliver standing alone in the dark, the weight of his choices pressing down on him.

That had been the last time they had spoken. Oliver had tried to reach out to his father after that, but each attempt had been met with silence. Eventually, he had given up, focusing instead on building a life with Katie and their children.

But now, with Philippe showing up at his work, Oliver couldn't help but wonder what his brother's true motives were. Was he here out of genuine concern, or was there something more? And what of his father? Was Jacques Laurier really asking for him, or was this just another manipulation, another attempt to control him from afar?

Oliver didn't know the answers, and that uncertainty gnawed at him. He had spent years building walls to protect himself from the pain of his past, but now those walls were crumbling, and he didn't know if he was strong enough to face what lay beyond them.

As he sat on the porch, the sound of the ocean in his ears, Oliver made an important decision. He couldn't keep running from his past, from the unresolved issues that had haunted him for so long. If he wanted to truly heal, he would have to confront them—no matter how painful it might be.

But he wouldn't do it alone. For the first time in years, Oliver realized that he didn't have to face these demons on his own. He had people who cared about him, people who would stand by him, no matter what.

With a deep breath, Oliver stood up and looked out at the horizon. The sun had set, leaving the sky awash in deep blues and purples. It was a new beginning, a chance to finally lay the past to rest.

And Oliver was ready to take that first step.

Chelsea Marsden sat on the edge of her bed, her phone in hand, staring at the contact names on the screen. The room was quiet, save for the gentle hum of the ceiling fan overhead. She'd rehearsed the conversation in her head a dozen times, but the thought of actually calling her sisters still made her stomach churn.

It wasn't that she didn't love them. Tess, Leah, and Gretchen had always been a big part of her life, but their relationships were complicated, to say the least. Early on, the four sisters had been inseparable, but with their parents' divorce the differences between them had become more pronounced, turning their once-close bond into something more strained.

Chelsea took a deep breath and tapped the screen, initiating a group call. It was better to get it over with all at once, rather than calling each sister individually and repeating the same conversation. The phone rang a few times before the first voice came through.

"Hey, Chels! What's up?" Tess's voice was bright, almost too cheerful, as if she were trying to mask something.

"Hi, Tess," Chelsea replied, trying to keep her tone light. "I have some news, so I wanted to talk to all three of you together. Hang on, let me see if I can make this work," she said, pressing the button once more.

"Hi Chelsea. I'm so glad to hear your voice. How are you?" Leah asked.

"Can you hold on a minute? I'm doing a four-way call. Hang on."

When Gretchen answered, Chelsea hit the button again.

"Okay, I already said to Tess that I've got news to share."

"News? Sounds interesting," Leah chimed in, her tone teasing. "Are you finally going to admit that you miss us and want to move to Key West?"

Chelsea forced a laugh. "Not quite, but it's something exciting."

There was a slight pause before Gretchen's voice joined the call, quieter than the others. "Tell us. What's going on, Chelsea?"

Chelsea could sense the underlying tension in Gretchen's tone, and it only made her more anxious about what she was about to say. But she couldn't back out now.

"Well, I wanted to let you all know that Steven and I have decided to get married. And we're having the wedding in three days, here on Captiva."

The silence on the other end of the line was deafening. Chelsea could almost picture her sisters' faces—Tess's mouth hanging open in surprise, Leah's eyes wide with disbelief, and Gretchen's brow furrowed in concern.

"Three days? Are you serious?" Leah was the first to break the silence.

"Yeah, we've been talking about it for a while, and we just decided that there's no point in waiting," Chelsea explained. "We want something small and intimate, and we'd really love for you all to be here."

Tess let out a low whistle. "Wow, Chels, that's... that's amazing! But three days? That's so soon! Are you sure you want to rush it?"

"We're sure," Chelsea said firmly. "We've been through a lot together, and we're not getting any younger. Why should we have a long engagement at our age? We just want to get married and start our life together. I know it's short notice, but I hope you can all come."

"Of course we'll be there," Gretchen said softly. "You're our sister, and we wouldn't miss it for the world."

Chelsea felt a wave of relief wash over her at Gretchen's words. But before she could respond, Tess jumped back in.

"Three days, huh? Well, I guess we better start packing. Key West to Captiva isn't exactly a quick trip."

"Tess, it's not that far," Leah teased. "We'll be there in no time.

Plus, it'll be fun to see everyone. We can take a little break from all the… business stuff."

Chelsea caught the hesitation in Leah's voice, and it didn't go unnoticed by Gretchen either.

"Right, the business stuff," Gretchen said, her tone tight. "Because that's what we've been focused on lately, isn't it?"

There was a brief, awkward silence before Tess cleared her throat. "Let's not do this now, okay? We're talking about Chelsea's wedding. We'll deal with everything else later."

Chelsea's heart sank. She hadn't realized just how strained things were between her sisters. She knew Gretchen had been feeling unsettled in Key West, but she hadn't understood the full extent of the tension. And now she was asking them all to come together for her wedding, hoping they could put aside their differences for just a few days.

"I really want all of you to be here," Chelsea said, her voice softer now. "But I don't want it to cause any more stress or tension. If it's too much, I understand."

"Don't be silly, Chels," Leah said quickly. "We'll be there, and we'll behave. Right, Tess?"

"Absolutely," Tess agreed. "We'll be on our best behavior. Promise."

Gretchen was silent for a moment before she spoke again, her voice carrying a note of resignation. "We'll be there, Chelsea. Don't worry about us. This is your big day, and we want to support you."

Chelsea smiled, even though they couldn't see it. "Thank you. It means a lot to me. And who knows? Maybe this wedding will be just what we all need to come together again."

"We'll see you soon, Chels," Tess said, her tone upbeat but with an undercurrent of something Chelsea couldn't quite place.

"Yeah, see you soon," Leah echoed.

"Love you, Chelsea," Gretchen added quietly.

"Love you all, too," Chelsea replied, her heart aching with a mix of happiness and worry as she ended the call.

She set the phone down and stared at it for a moment, trying to shake the feeling that she had just opened Pandora's box. Her sisters had promised to behave, but Chelsea knew all too well how quickly things could spiral out of control when old wounds were involved. She only hoped that the wedding would be a time of healing and not another source of tension in their already fragile relationship.

As she stood up and walked to the window, looking out at the ocean, Chelsea took a deep breath and tried to focus on the positive. Her cat Stella rubbed up against her leg. Chelsea picked her up and they both looked out the window.

Her sisters were coming, and they would be there to support her on one of the most important days of her life. Whatever issues they had, they would face them together—just like they always had. But deep down, a small voice whispered that this wedding might be more complicated than she had anticipated.

# CHAPTER 4

"*D*o you ever wonder why some people can't see their own worth?"

Maggie Moretti glanced over at Chelsea, surprised by the sudden question. They were sitting on the beach, their usual spot for heart-to-hearts, but tonight there was a heaviness in the air between them that had nothing to do with the weather.

Chelsea didn't wait for Maggie to answer. She stared out at the darkening horizon, her thoughts clearly miles away.

"It's like no matter how many times you tell someone they deserve better, they just can't believe it for themselves. My sisters... they're all like that, Maggie, especially Gretchen."

Maggie turned to face her fully, her concern growing.

"What's going on, Chels?"

Chelsea let out a long sigh, the tension in her shoulders visible as she tried to find the right words.

"When I talked to my sisters about coming to the wedding, I could tell something was off. Gretchen was always the one I felt closest to, but I'm worried about her. She's been through so much, and I think it's weighing on her more than she lets on."

Maggie nodded, encouraging her to continue.

"You know about her divorce," Chelsea began, her voice tightening. "But what you might not know is that her ex-husband was abusive. Gretchen didn't tell anyone until after she left him. She just... she thought she deserved it. Can you believe that?"

Maggie's heart ached at the revelation. "Oh, Chelsea, I had no idea."

"None of us did," Chelsea admitted, her voice thick with emotion. "She hid it so well, always pretending everything was fine. But when it all came out... I just felt like I failed her. Like I should have known, should have done something. But she wouldn't let me in. And even now, I don't think she believes she deserves better."

Maggie placed a comforting hand on Chelsea's arm.

"You couldn't have known, Chelsea. People who go through that—they get good at hiding it. But you were there for her when she needed you most, and that's what matters."

Chelsea shook her head, frustration evident in her eyes.

"But how do you get someone to see their own worth? How do you make them believe they deserve more than what they've accepted in their lives? I want more for my sisters...not just more, but better."

Maggie paused, considering the question. It was a tough one, and she didn't have an easy answer.

"I don't know if you can make someone believe that, Chelsea. It's something they have to come to on their own. But you can keep reminding them that they're worth it, that they deserve to be happy. Sometimes, just having someone in your corner is enough to start that shift."

"I hope so," Chelsea said, her voice softening. "I just want them to be happy. But with everything going on between Tess, Leah, and Gretchen, I'm worried this visit will bring everything to a head. I've got this wedding to think about, but all I can focus on is how my sisters will get through it without tearing each other apart."

Maggie offered a reassuring smile. "We'll get through this, Chelsea. If anyone can help keep the peace, it's you. And I'll be there with you every step of the way."

Chelsea looked at her friend, gratitude in her eyes, and smiled.

"I have absolutely no idea what I'd do without you. As a matter of fact, I don't know how I got along all those years before the book club. What do they call that thing when people are destined to meet?"

"A collision?" Maggie teased.

"Very funny...no, you know what I mean. Fortuitous, I think. Yeah, that's it. It was a lucky fortune that we became friends. Now, I can't imagine my life without you in it."

"I feel the same way. We've got a lot of adventures to explore, Chelsea Marsden. I plan on being with you for every one of them...well, for most of them. Now that I have to share you with Steven."

"Ah, yes, Steven. Talk about fortuitous," Chelsea said.

"Yes, we can't forget about him. No matter what your sisters are dealing with, this wedding is more important than they are. Your sisters will work things out, but right now, you need to focus on what makes you happy."

Chelsea nodded, though the worry didn't entirely leave her face.

"I'll try. But you know me, I can't help but worry about them."

"And that's why they're lucky to have you as their sister," Maggie said with a smile. "But let's take it one step at a time. Tomorrow, they'll be here, and as chaotic as things might get around here, we've got to find you a dress."

Chelsea rolled her eyes. "Oh gosh, can you believe I haven't even given that a thought? Where am I going to get something appropriate to wear? I'm not exactly a young bride."

Maggie laughed. "I've been down this road myself not that long ago, so I know what you're talking about. Let's go into Ft.

Myers first thing in the morning. I'm sure we can find something just right.

Chelsea managed a small smile. "Perfect."

Maggie was quiet for a moment, then asked, "I'm curious, do you think your sisters' issues stem from what happened with your parents?"

Chelsea took a deep breath, considering the question.

"I think so, at least partly. Our mother left our father when we were young. She had to. He wasn't physically abusive, but he was controlling, and manipulative. I saw it all—how he would undermine her confidence, how he made her feel like she wasn't worth anything without him. Eventually, she couldn't take it anymore, and she left. But she only took me with her."

Maggie's brow furrowed in concern. "Why only you?"

"Because I was the oldest, and she thought I'd be better off with her. She wanted to protect me, but she didn't have the resources to take all of us. She was barely scraping by as it was, and our father made sure she had nothing when she left. So, Tess, Leah, and Gretchen stayed with him. I think it was the worst thing she could have done. Like I said, they weren't at risk of being physically abused, but a girl growing up with a man like that can only mean one thing."

Maggie shook her head. "They wouldn't develop any confidence at all."

Chelsea nodded. "That's right, at least that's my theory."

"That must have been so hard for you, knowing your sisters were still with him."

"It was," Chelsea admitted, her voice heavy with regret. "I hated leaving them behind. But I was a kid, too, and I didn't have any say in the matter. I stayed with my mom, and she did her best to raise me on her own. She was a strong woman, but I know she always felt guilty for leaving them."

"And how did your sisters handle it?"

Chelsea sighed. "Not well, I think. They were too young to

understand why she left, and my father made sure they resented her for it. He poisoned their minds against her, made her out to be the villain who abandoned them. By the time they were old enough to understand the truth, the damage had already been done."

Maggie's expression softened with sympathy. "It's awful what people do to children with their choices. Sometimes it doesn't matter what kind of upbringing a person has. I know someone who was always strong and confident. Then, she met someone who she believed loved her, but his idea of love was control. I remember thinking that she was abused, but she didn't think she was. Slowly, over time, she came to believe she didn't know how to do anything. He criticized her driving, cooking, even the smallest things most people overlook. He wore her down until she could barely put one foot in front of the other."

"What happened to her?"

"With the help of a good friend, her family, and a good therapist, she eventually left and divorced him. She said the day of the divorce, when she was in the courtroom, she never felt so empowered. The stress, anxiety and pain just fell off her shoulders and she could breathe again. She's thriving now, and when I talked to her the last time, she said she'd never let anyone do that to her again. She's back where she was before marrying him and hasn't looked back on that terrible time since leaving him."

Chelsea smiled. "She was brave."

Maggie nodded. "She was...and is. Your sisters' past doesn't dictate their future. I know it hasn't mine, or yours. They can choose something different."

"You're right," Chelsea said, nodding. "I think that's where the difference comes in. My mother raised me to be strong, to believe in myself. She always told me I deserved the best, and that I should never settle for less than I'm worth. But my sisters... they didn't get that. They grew up with a man who constantly undermined their self-esteem, who made them feel like they weren't good enough on their own. It's no wonder they ended up in relationships where they were treated badly."

Maggie listened quietly, understanding the deep-rooted pain in Chelsea's voice. "So you think that's why you've always had such a good sense of your own worth?"

Chelsea considered this for a moment. "Maybe. I mean, I had a wonderful marriage with Carl. He was my rock, my best friend. Losing him to cancer was the hardest thing I've ever gone through, but I never doubted my worth even then. And now, with Steven... I'm lucky to have found another man who treats me the way I deserve to be treated."

Maggie smiled. "You've been through so much, Chelsea, but you've always come out stronger on the other side. Your sisters might not see their own worth yet, but that doesn't mean they can't get there. And you being in their lives, showing them what's possible—it's more important than you know."

Chelsea's eyes welled with unshed tears, and she quickly blinked them away. "I just wish I could do more for them. I want them to find the happiness I've found, to realize they deserve better than the lives they've accepted."

"I know," Maggie said gently. "But you can't do it for them. All you can do is be there for them, support them, and remind them that they're worth it. They have to take that step themselves."

Chelsea nodded, her heart heavy with the weight of her sisters' struggles. "I'm going to keep trying. I just hope this wedding doesn't end up making things worse between them. I want it to be a happy occasion, something that might bring us all closer together."

"It will be," Maggie assured her. "We'll make sure of it."

The two women sat in silence for a while longer, the gentle sound of the waves their only companion.

Maggie felt Chelsea's pain and understood how deeply her friend felt like an accomplice to her sisters' troubles. Although none of it was her fault, Chelsea had carried the weight of this pain her whole life, never mentioning it to anyone, even Maggie, and that was because she couldn't admit it to herself.

As the first stars began to twinkle in the evening sky, Maggie made a silent promise to herself. She would do everything in her power to help her friend reconcile with her sisters, and together they'd help Tess, Leah and Gretchen find the happiness Chelsea and she had.

Maggie and Paolo were blessed in their relationship, and now Chelsea and Steven had the same happiness. But Maggie knew the truth, that she and Chelsea were strong, independent women who didn't see their worth through the eyes of a man or a relationship.

Perhaps this visit would do more than just celebrate a wedding. With any luck, Maggie and Chelsea would strengthen a bond between women who needed each other more than ever before. And, more than anything, teach them that everything they need to feel capable and strong already lives within them.

# CHAPTER 5

Oliver sat on the edge of his bed, his gaze fixed on the floor as he tried to make sense of the thoughts swirling in his mind. The room around him was dimly lit, shadows stretching across the walls in the soft glow of the single lamp. The quiet hum of the ceiling fan above did little to still the storm of emotions brewing inside him.

Philippe was only a short drive away, waiting for him to make the next move. Waiting for him to decide if he was ready to face the ghosts of his past.

Oliver leaned back, running a hand through his hair as he tried to sort through the tangled mess of emotions that had surfaced with his brother's unexpected arrival. He hadn't seen Philippe in years, not since before the flood that had taken everything from him—his wife, his sons, his entire world. And now Philippe was back, trying to reconnect, trying to drag Oliver into a life he had worked so hard to leave behind.

But why? Why now, after all this time?

Oliver's thoughts kept circling back to the same conclusion: their father. The man who had cast a long, dark shadow over their lives, who had always been a master of control and manipulation. Philippe had been sent to bring Oliver back, to fulfill some dying wish, or perhaps, to secure his own place in their father's empire.

A bitter laugh escaped Oliver's lips. It was just like their father to use his own impending death as leverage, to manipulate his sons into doing his bidding one last time.

But Oliver wasn't the same man he had been before. He had rebuilt his life here on Captiva Island, piece by piece, with the help of Maggie and the community at the Key Lime Garden Inn. He had found a measure of peace, even if the scars of his past would never fully heal.

And now, Philippe threatened to unravel it all.

Oliver closed his eyes, trying to push the thoughts away, but they persisted, gnawing at him with relentless determination. He knew he couldn't ignore Philippe's presence, couldn't pretend that his brother hadn't shown up. But what was he supposed to do? Confront him? Reopen old wounds that had barely begun to scab over?

No. He couldn't let Philippe derail everything he had worked so hard for. Not now, not with Chelsea's wedding just days away. He had commitments here, people who depended on him, and he couldn't let them down.

With a deep breath, he made his decision. He would deal with Philippe—just not now. There were more pressing matters at hand, and Philippe would have to wait. But first, he needed to make that clear.

Oliver stood up, the resolve settling into his bones as he walked over to the phone on his nightstand. He picked up the receiver, hesitating for a moment before dialing the operator at the Marriott Sanibel.

"This is Oliver Laurier," he said when the operator answered. "I need to speak with a guest. Philippe Laurier. I don't know his room number."

There was a brief pause as the operator searched for the

information, and Oliver's heart pounded in his chest, the tension coiling tighter with each passing second.

Finally, the operator returned. "Connecting you now, Mr. Laurier."

Oliver waited, listening to the ringing on the other end. His grip on the phone tightened as he braced himself for the conversation he knew was coming.

"Hello?" Philippe's voice was cautious, as if he wasn't sure who might be calling.

"It's Oliver," he said, keeping his tone steady, controlled.

"Oliver." There was a pause, and Oliver could almost hear the relief in Philippe's voice. "I didn't expect you to call."

"I need to be clear about something," Oliver began, cutting straight to the point. "You've come at a bad time. I've got a wedding to handle. There's a lot going on, and I can't deal with whatever it is you've come here for right now."

Philippe was silent for a moment, as if trying to process Oliver's words.

"I understand," he said finally. "But we need to talk, Oliver. It's important."

"I'm sure it is," Oliver replied, his voice hardening slightly. "But it's going to have to wait. I don't have the time or the energy to deal with this right now. So stay put, enjoy the hotel, and we'll talk when I'm ready. Not before."

There was another pause, and Oliver could feel the tension crackling between them like electricity.

"All right," Philippe said, his voice laced with something that Oliver couldn't quite place—disappointment? Frustration? "I'll wait."

"Good," Oliver said, already reaching to hang up. "I'll be in touch."

He didn't wait for a response before disconnecting the call. The moment the line went dead, he felt a strange mix of relief and guilt wash over him. He had done what he needed to do, had set the boundaries he needed to protect himself. But he knew this wasn't over. Not by a long shot.

As he set the phone back on the nightstand, his thoughts drifted to what lay ahead. The wedding, the preparations, the need to be there for Chelsea and the others. He couldn't let Philippe's arrival disrupt that. Not now.

But in the back of his mind, he knew the confrontation was coming. He had bought himself some time, but eventually, he would have to face his brother. And when that time came, he would need to be ready.

For now, though, he had other priorities. Oliver took a deep breath, letting the tension slowly seep out of his muscles as he turned his thoughts to the task at hand.

But no matter how hard he tried to focus on the present, the shadow of his brother's presence lingered, a constant reminder that the past was never as far behind as he wanted it to be.

Philippe Laurier stared at the phone in his hotel room, the sound of the dial tone echoing in his ears long after Oliver had hung up. He had expected resistance—Oliver was nothing if not stubborn —but the outright dismissal still stung.

He stood and began pacing the length of the room, his mind racing with a mix of frustration and determination. The hotel room was pristine, impeccably decorated, but it felt like a cage. He was here to bring his brother back into the family fold, to fulfill their father's dying wish—or at least, that was the official reason. But the truth was more complicated, more self-serving.

Philippe had spent years in his father's shadow, always the dutiful son, always striving to meet the impossible standards set before him. And now, with their father's health declining, the power that Philippe had been promised seemed more precarious than ever. If he could bring Oliver back, if he could somehow repair the rift between them, their father had promised him more —more money, more influence, more control.

But it wasn't just about the inheritance. It was about finally stepping out of that shadow, finally proving himself as the rightful heir, the one who could hold the family together when it suited him and not before.

Oliver had always been the wild card, the one who defied expectations, who refused to play by the rules. And that had always infuriated him, after spending his life doing exactly what was expected of him. But there was more to it than that, wasn't there? Beneath the resentment, beneath the rivalry, there was something else. A need to be seen, to be valued. A need to control his future. A need that had gone unmet for far too long.

Philippe stopped pacing, his gaze fixed on the window, where the lights of Captiva twinkled in the distance. Oliver had said he didn't have time to deal with this now, that he was preoccupied with some wedding. But Philippe knew better. His brother was buying time, trying to delay the inevitable.

Philippe couldn't wait forever. Their father's condition was worsening by the day, and time was running out. If Oliver didn't come around soon, the whole plan could fall apart.

He turned away from the window, his mind sharpening with resolve. He would give Oliver the time he asked for—just enough to keep up appearances. But then he would push. He would force Oliver to confront the reality of their father's condition, to face the consequences of turning his back on the family.

And if that didn't work, well, Philippe had other ways of getting what he wanted.

He reached for his phone again, this time scrolling through his contacts until he found the number he was looking for. It was time to put his backup plan into motion.

As the phone rang, Philippe's lips curved into a cold smile. He hadn't come all this way to fail. He would bring Oliver back into the fold, one way or another.

❄

The SUV jostled slightly as it navigated the roads toward Fort Myers, laughter filling the air as Maggie, Chelsea, Sarah, Lauren, Beth, and Becca crowded inside. The cramped quarters of Lauren's rental only added to the fun, with elbows bumping and playful nudges exchanged. Brea, Ciara and Maggie's mother stayed back at the inn to watch the children.

"So, what's the plan?" Sarah asked, glancing at Chelsea in the front seat. "Are we going for the classic elegant bride, or do we want to surprise Steven with something completely unexpected?"

Chelsea grinned, her excitement clearly bubbling over. "I'm open to suggestions, but I'm leaning towards something that'll make Steven's jaw drop."

"Steven's jaw drops every time he sees you, Chelsea," Lauren said from the driver's seat, her tone playful. "But I get it. You want that wow factor."

Beth, sitting beside Becca, chuckled softly. "Just remember, it's a beach wedding, so maybe avoid the fifty-pound ball gown."

"Definitely," Maggie agreed, turning in her seat to look back at the group. "But a little sparkle never hurt anyone."

Becca, her five-month-pregnant belly making her shift slightly for comfort, smiled and added, "Just make sure it's something you can dance in. The last thing you want is to be tripping over your dress while you're trying to have fun."

Chelsea glanced at Becca's growing bump, her expression softening.

"How are you feeling, Becca? Are you sure you're up for all this?"

Becca waved her off with a smile. "I'm fine, really. I have more energy these days than I ever have. Besides, I wouldn't miss this for the world."

"But just in case, let's make sure there's a comfy chair in every boutique we go to, so you can take a break when you need to," Sarah added.

As they pulled into the shopping district, the women were buzzing with anticipation. They had made a pact to find the perfect dress, and nothing was going to stand in their way.

The first boutique they entered was a cozy little shop with a charming display of wedding gowns in the window. The moment they walked in, they were greeted by the warm scent of vanilla candles and the soft rustle of silk fabric.

Chelsea's eyes lit up as she scanned the rows of dresses, her fingers itching to start browsing. "Okay, ladies, let's find something amazing."

Maggie and Beth immediately started sifting through the racks, pulling out dresses and holding them up for the group to see. "What about this one?" Beth asked, displaying a sleek, lace-trimmed gown.

Chelsea tilted her head, considering it. "It's beautiful, but maybe a little too formal for the beach."

"Good point," Maggie said, hanging it back up. "Let's find something that says, 'elegant but relaxed.'"

Lauren found a dress with a flowy chiffon skirt and delicate beading along the bodice. "This could be perfect," she said, handing it to Chelsea. "It's light, airy, and still has that wow factor."

Chelsea took the dress, running her fingers over the soft fabric.

"I love it. I'll definitely try this one on."

The saleswoman smiled at Chelsea. "That will look amazing on your figure. Can I ask, when is the wedding?"

"In two days," Maggie said, waiting for the woman's reaction.

"Oh my, well, in that case, there won't be time to alter the dress. You might be forced to take something as is," she said.

"Fine by me," Chelsea said. "That's what I told my fiancé. I'll marry you but don't even think of trying to change me. You get me 'As Is.'"

Everyone laughed.

"I doubt there's a person on this planet who could change you, Chelsea Marsden," Maggie teased.

The group settled into the fitting area, Becca shifting in her seat to find the best view. Chelsea emerged from the dressing room a few minutes later, wearing the first dress—the chiffon gown Lauren had picked out.

The room fell silent for a moment as everyone took in the sight. The dress was a perfect fit, the soft fabric flowing gracefully around Chelsea's figure.

"Well?" Chelsea asked, turning slightly to see herself from different angles.

"It's beautiful," Maggie said, her voice full of emotion. "You look stunning, Chelsea."

"Steven's definitely going to lose his mind when he sees you in that," Lauren added, her tone teasing but sincere.

"Maybe we should keep looking," Beth suggested with a grin. "I mean, if this is the first dress you try, what if there's something even better out there?"

Chelsea laughed. "I wouldn't be opposed to finding something that makes him a little weak in the knees."

The next dress Chelsea tried on was a sequined number Sarah had found. It hugged her curves in all the right places, with just the right amount of sparkle to catch the light without overwhelming the design.

"Okay, now this one is something special," Chelsea said as she stepped out of the fitting room.

The collective "wow" from the group said it all. The dress was a showstopper, but still elegant enough for a beach wedding.

"Now, this is a dress that says, 'I'm the star of the show,'" Sarah said with a grin. "You're going to outshine the sun in that one, Chelsea."

Chelsea beamed. "I think this might be the one."

Becca leaned back in her chair, her hand resting on her belly. "You're going to look amazing, Chelsea. Steven's a lucky man."

Chelsea's smile softened. "I'm the lucky one. I've found someone who makes me feel like I'm the only person in the world."

Maggie's eyes glistened as she watched her friend. "That's how it should be, Chelsea. You deserve nothing less."

After a few more twirls in front of the mirror, Chelsea made her decision. "This is it. This is the dress."

The group erupted in cheers, their excitement filling the small boutique.

"Would you like to take a picture with this sign?" the saleswoman asked, holding up a "She said Yes to the Dress" sign.

Chelsea shook her head.

"Thank you, but no. That's for the young kids."

Beth stepped up and grabbed the sign. She smiled at Chelsea and said, "You're only as young as you feel. Come on, let's do this."

Chelsea laughed and held the sign next to her as all the women took photos with their phones.

Maggie smiled and tried not to cry. Every step toward Chelsea's wedding day made her teary eyed. She was over the moon with happiness for her best friend and could only imagine how excited Chelsea must feel.

"Looking good, honey," Maggie added with a thumbs up.

As they finalized the purchase and prepared to head back to Captiva, there was a sense of accomplishment and joy that made the trip feel even more special.

Piled back into Lauren's SUV, the women chatted and laughed, the energy high as they made their way home.

"This wedding is going to be perfect," Maggie said, glancing at Chelsea with a knowing smile. "And so are you, Chelsea."

"Thanks to all of you," Chelsea replied. "How lucky am I to

have found something off the rack? I couldn't have done this on my own."

As the SUV sped down the highway, filled with the sound of laughter and the promise of what was to come, Maggie smiled at her friend. She couldn't help but feel that everything was finally falling into place for Chelsea.

The dress, the wedding, the life she was building with Steven —it was all coming together, and she had her friends and family by her side every step of the way. Nothing was better than that.

# CHAPTER 6

*C*hristopher stood in his room, one hand resting on the desk, his body slightly tense. Only a few years earlier the room had been a place of healing and solitude for months, and now it felt almost too quiet. He shifted slightly, the weight of his prosthetic leg grounding him in the present. It was a reminder of how far he'd come, but also how much he'd left behind.

Maggie leaned against the doorway.

"Hey, Chris," she said. "I've been thinking about when you first came back to us. You spent a lot of time in this room."

Christopher didn't turn around immediately. He glanced down at the polished floorboards, then at the familiar bed and the chair near the window where he'd spent so many days trying to make sense of his new reality.

"Feels like a different lifetime," he muttered.

Maggie came closer, the concern she always carried for her children reflected in her eyes.

"It does, doesn't it? You've come a long way from those days."

"Have I?" He finally turned to face her, his face serious but calm. "I guess it doesn't feel like that sometimes. I mean... it's all still in here."

He tapped his head lightly, trying to express the internal weight he still carried.

Maggie nodded, understanding exactly what he meant. She had watched her son go through the darkest period of his life, not just physically but mentally and emotionally.

She sat down on the edge of the bed, the same spot where she had sat so many times when he first returned.

"You know, Chris," she said gently, "when you first got here, I wasn't sure you'd ever leave this room. There were days when I didn't know how to help you."

"I didn't want help."

He crossed the room and sat down on the chair by the window. He stared at his prosthetic leg for a moment, his fingers tracing the metal joint.

"I wanted to be left alone. I thought I could deal with it on my own."

Maggie folded her hands in her lap, watching him carefully.

"You shut us all out. But that's not how healing works, Chris. You needed to let people in, even if you didn't want to admit it."

Christopher's gaze didn't leave the leg.

"You were there for me, though. I know that now. Back then... I don't think I could see anything but the pain. The anger."

He leaned back in the chair, as if trying to put some distance between himself and those memories.

"I was angry at everything. At myself, at the world... at you."

Maggie blinked, her heart aching at the honesty in his words.

"I know," she said softly. "I could feel it, but I never took it personally. You were going through something no one else could truly understand. All I wanted was for you to know that you weren't alone, no matter how far away you felt."

Christopher looked out the window. The garden outside, meticulously tended by his stepfather Paolo, was thriving, vibrant and full of life—such a contrast to how he had felt during those early days.

"I didn't feel like I deserved to be here. I'd lost... so much." He paused, swallowing hard. "The guys. Nick. I kept thinking it should have been me."

Maggie's heart broke for her son's memory.

"I know you blame yourself, Chris. But those kinds of things... they're not in our control. You know that."

He sighed heavily, his shoulders slumping slightly.

"That's what everyone says, right? But when you're in it, when you've lived it, that doesn't matter. I was supposed to be there for them. I wasn't."

Maggie stood up and walked to him. She rested a hand on his shoulder.

"You were there. You survived. And that's what matters now. You've done so much since then."

He glanced up at her, his eyes clouded with memories.

"Like what? I came back here and hid away in this room for months. It was all I could do to get up some days."

"You learned to walk again," Maggie reminded him, her voice firm but kind. "You took steps—literally and figuratively—that I wasn't sure you'd ever take. Do you remember how scared I was the first time you went out of the room on your own? You were so determined to prove you didn't need anyone's help, but I knew how much effort it took for you to even want to try."

Christopher managed a small smile and nodded.

"Yeah, I remember that. I was so stubborn. Didn't want anyone seeing me struggle. Didn't want you to pity me."

Maggie chuckled softly. "I wasn't pitying you. I was proud of you. Every step you took was a victory, even if you didn't see it that way."

He leaned back, staring at the ceiling.

"It just felt like failure after failure back then. But now... now it's different." He looked down at his leg again. "This thing... it's become a part of me. I don't even think about it like I used to."

"That's because you've accepted it," Maggie said, squeezing his shoulder gently. "And that's one of the hardest parts of healing. It takes time."

Christopher was silent for a moment, then nodded. "I guess I have. I don't know when it happened exactly, but... yeah, I'm not angry about it anymore. I don't hate it."

Maggie smiled, her heart swelling with pride. "I knew you'd get there, eventually."

He let out a breath, a mixture of relief and resignation. "I don't think I could have without you, Mom. You and Paolo, and even Becca. You all kept me grounded, even when I didn't want to be, and Beth...she's something, that sister of mine."

Maggie stood up, patting his shoulder and laughed.

"Your sister is the smallest of all of us but I swear she's the most formidable. She refused to let you wallow in your sadness. I remember how tough she was during that time."

Christopher smiled. "I guess that's what family's for. We don't give up on each other."

Maggie leaned down and kissed the top of his head. "Don't you forget it."

As Maggie moved toward the door, she paused, turning back to Christopher with a gentle smile.

"You know, with all this reflection, I almost forgot—you're going to be a daddy. How are you feeling about that?"

Christopher's expression softened, and a smile crept across his face, this time filled with warmth and a different kind of emotion.

"I've been thinking about it a lot lately. It feels surreal. One minute I'm struggling to find my footing again, and the next, I'm about to become a dad. In time, it'll be me teaching a little one to walk. I guess I've got a lot of practice, so who better than me to teach him?"

Maggie smiled. "I hadn't thought of it like that, but you're right. You're going to teach that little baby so many wonderful things. I can't wait to see it. Life has a way of throwing those surprises at us, doesn't it? But this—this is the best kind. A new life to care for, to love." She walked back to him, leaned down and hugged him. "It's a reminder, Chris. Life is for the living."

Christopher nodded, the weight of those words settling comfortably this time. "Yeah, I get that now. I spent so much time stuck in the past, but now, with the baby coming... I want to focus on what's ahead."

Maggie chuckled. "Good. Because I have a feeling that little one will make sure you don't have much time to think about anything else."

Smiling as she pulled away. "Life keeps moving forward, Chris. And now, you get to help guide that new life. How beautiful is that?"

Christopher couldn't agree more.

Becca rocked gently on the back porch swing, her hands resting on her belly as she glanced over at Beth, who sat cross-legged, sipping iced tea.

"You know," Becca said, shaking her head with a soft smile, "I've been meaning to tell you—none of this would've happened if it weren't for you. You pretty much shoved me right into Christopher's arms."

Beth raised an eyebrow, a grin forming.

"Well, someone had to do it. You were dragging your feet like you were stuck in quicksand. You're lucky I didn't physically throw you into his lap."

Becca laughed. "I wouldn't put it past you."

Beth winked, taking another sip.

"Oh, you shouldn't. I mean, you two were dancing around each other like a couple of teenagers who couldn't decide if they were going to kiss or run away. It was painful to watch."

"I was nervous," Becca admitted, rubbing her belly absentmindedly. "He had been through so much. I didn't want to rush anything."

Beth set her glass down with a playful huff. "Please. You've known him since forever. What were you afraid of? That he'd forgotten how much he loved you? That man looked at you like you hung the moon—always did, always will."

Becca smiled, the memory of those early days coming back. "I wasn't sure... I thought maybe he wouldn't want me in his life after everything. I mean, he's been through hell."

"Yeah, he has," Beth agreed, her expression softening for a moment. "But you know what? You didn't give him nearly enough credit. That guy? He needed you. Probably more than he even realized. And you—" she pointed her iced tea glass at Becca — "needed to stop playing coy and just get in there."

Becca smirked, shaking her head. "You make it sound so simple."

"That's because it is." Beth leaned forward, her eyes twinkling with mischief. "You're the one who was overcomplicating things. I mean, come on, you love the guy. He loves you. Done deal."

Becca chuckled. "I guess you're right. All I know is that you seem to know exactly the right thing to say at just the right time."

Beth leaned back with a triumphant smile. "Of course I do. It's my job as your witty, charming, and obviously brilliant sister-in-law to break things down for you. You were stuck in your head, Becca. Someone had to pull you out of that fog."

"You did more than that," Becca said, her tone growing more serious. "You saved Chris' life. I mean it. He wouldn't have gotten out of that bed if not for you. You pushed me, and then you pushed Chris. You were a force of nature."

Beth tilted her head, her eyes narrowing playfully.

"Pushed? I prefer 'gently encouraged with the force of a hurricane.'"

Becca laughed. "That's one way to put it."

Beth took a deep breath, letting the teasing fall away for a moment.

"Listen, Becca, the truth is, Christopher needed you more than you realized. He was lost, but you—you were his anchor. You reminded him of who he was before everything happened, and that's not something just anyone can do."

Becca's eyes softened. "I wanted to be there for him, but I was scared. Scared that he'd changed too much, that he wouldn't want me to see him like that."

Beth rolled her eyes dramatically. "Puh-lease. You were the one person he wanted to see. And honestly, if you'd let it go on much longer, I would've dragged him over to your house myself and made you two talk."

"Knowing you, I believe it," Becca said with a grin.

"You're darn right," Beth shot back, her voice full of sass. "But I didn't have to. Because you, my dear, finally saw sense. And look at you now—happily married, about to pop out a baby, and living your best life."

Becca rubbed her belly with a smile.

"Yeah, it's kind of amazing how everything worked out."

Beth raised her glass, her voice full of mock seriousness.

"To my undeniable genius and match-making prowess. You'll be naming the baby after me, right?"

Becca clinked her glass against Beth's with a laugh.

"We'll have to talk about that. But, I toast to your undeniable genius. I'll give you that one."

Beth's grin widened. "That's all I needed to hear. Now, when the baby arrives, don't be surprised if she takes after me. Spunky, smart, sharp wit. You're welcome in advance."

Becca shook her head, smiling as she rested her hand on her belly again.

"Heaven help us if this baby takes after you."

"Hey," Beth said with mock offense, "this kid is going to have the best of both worlds—your heart and Christopher's strength.

51

And just a touch of my personality. Perfect combo, if you ask me. But, I have to admit, I love the name Eloise. She's going to be a very special baby."

The two women fell into an easy silence, the kind that comes from years of shared moments, both big and small.

Becca glanced over at Beth, feeling a deep sense of gratitude for her.

"Seriously, Beth," Becca said quietly. "You've always been there for us, and I don't think I ever properly thanked you."

Beth waved a hand dismissively.

"Oh, stop. I'm just here to keep you on your toes. Besides, what are sisters-in-law for if not for a little tough love and the occasional kick in the pants?"

Becca chuckled softly. "Well, you're good at both."

Beth winked. "You bet I am."

# CHAPTER 7

*T*he delivery truck rumbled down the sandy road toward the beach, its trailer packed to the brim with the wedding tent that was supposed to "pop up in minutes." Gabriel, Paolo, Trevor, Jeff, Steven, and Maggie's son, Michael, stood in a semi-circle, watching it approach. Michael, tall and broad-shouldered, crossed his arms and glanced at the others.

"This is the tent?" Michael asked, his deep voice full of skepticism.

Gabriel squinted at the truck. "Looks like it's bigger than my garage."

Steven let out a nervous chuckle. "Just a little thing for my wedding, huh?"

Paolo, the eternal optimist, clapped his hands.

"Come on, guys, we'll get it done in no time. It's just a tent."

Michael raised an eyebrow. "A tent that size? You're sure about that?"

Trevor patted Michael on the shoulder. "Hey, you're here now. We'll just have you lift the whole thing yourself."

Michael laughed. "Yeah, right. But seriously, how hard can it be?"

As if on cue, the delivery guy hopped out of the truck, slamming the door shut with a grin.

"Here's your tent, fellas! You'll love it—'pops up in minutes,' they say." He winked and started unloading the mountain of pieces onto the sand.

Paolo beamed. "See? Easy peasy."

Michael eyed the pile of poles and connectors skeptically. "Easy, huh?"

Gabriel scratched his head, already suspicious. "Hold on. Don't most tent rental places set this thing up for you?"

The delivery guy gave Paolo a look. "Oh, we don't do that. You ordered the 'self-setup special.' You boys are on your own."

A collective groan rippled through the group, and everyone turned to Paolo.

"You did what?" Steven asked, his eyes wide with disbelief.

Paolo looked sheepish, rubbing the back of his neck.

"Uh, yeah... turns out I ordered from the wrong place. I thought it was one of those setups where they do everything. Apparently not."

Maggie, who had just walked down to check on the progress, overheard the conversation and immediately zeroed in on her husband.

"Wait a minute—you mean to tell me you ordered a tent we have to set up ourselves?"

Paolo grinned weakly. "I may have... misread the fine print."

Maggie rolled her eyes, but there was a smile tugging at the corner of her lips. "Leave it to you to find the one place that makes you do all the work. What I don't understand is why you got this one. We've had several functions here and have ordered tents the vendors put up for us. Why not this time?"

"Because it's a last minute request. Everyone was booked. I couldn't get the usual people, so this is what we've got. I say we make the best of it."

Maggie shook her head, laughing. "Great. Now I've got to

watch all of you try to put this thing up without killing each other."

Jeff held up the instruction manual, flipping through the pages with a frown. "Well, it says here it should only take... three to five hours."

Michael groaned. "Three to five hours? For a tent?"

Gabriel nudged Michael's arm. "Don't worry, big guy. With you here, we'll get it done in two."

Michael smirked. "If I lift the whole thing by myself, maybe."

Paolo clapped his hands again, trying to rally the troops. "All right, come on! Let's get it done before Chelsea shows up and sees us standing around like idiots."

Steven rubbed his temples, already sweating. "Yeah, let's do this... I guess."

The men got to work, spreading out the poles, connectors, and canvas on the sand. It didn't take long for them to realize they were in over their heads.

Michael lifted one of the heaviest poles with ease, holding it up like a spear. "Okay, where does this one go?"

Gabriel squinted at the pile of connectors. "Uh, I think... over there? Maybe?"

Trevor, on the other side, was trying to figure out which poles connected to the central frame. "No, no, that's wrong. This one's supposed to go in the middle, right?"

Jeff, still glued to the instruction manual, muttered, "Step one: Lay out all poles and connectors." He looked up. "Well, we did that. Step two... 'Assemble central frame.' What's the central frame?"

Paolo picked up two poles and tried to fit them together. "I think it's this part... or maybe this part?"

Steven watched the chaos unfold, his eyes wide. "Guys, this is a disaster."

Michael grinned, lifting another pole. "It's fine. We've got muscle, we've got instructions. What could go wrong?"

Gabriel snorted. "Famous last words."

As they fumbled with the poles and connectors, Maggie stood off to the side, arms crossed, watching the scene unfold with a bemused expression. "This is what happens when you leave the men in charge."

Paolo grinned at her. "We've got it under control."

Maggie raised an eyebrow. "Sure you do. Just remember, if that tent collapses during the wedding, it's on you."

Paolo gave her a thumbs up. "No worries. This tent will be a masterpiece."

Michael, who was holding up one side of the tent frame by himself, grinned. "Yeah, a masterpiece of chaos."

After another hour of mishaps, incorrect pole placements, and a few accidental trips over the canvas, the tent finally started to take shape—albeit in a slightly lopsided fashion.

Gabriel stepped back, wiping sweat from his brow. "It's standing... sort of."

Trevor nodded, still holding one of the support poles. "Is it supposed to lean like that?"

Steven squinted. "It's got... character."

Jeff folded his arms, nodding. "Yeah, character. That's what every wedding tent needs."

Maggie, now standing beside Paolo, smirked. "You know, Paolo, if this thing falls down halfway through the ceremony, Chelsea's going to have your head."

Paolo chuckled nervously. "It's fine. It's stable. Right, guys?"

Gabriel waved his hand dismissively. "Yeah, stable enough. What's a little tilt? Adds personality."

Michael crossed his arms, surveying their handiwork. "If by 'personality,' you mean 'structural risk,' then sure."

Steven, finally laughing at the absurdity of it all, shook his head.

"Well, it's up. That's all that matters. Let's just hope it stays that way."

Paolo, ever the optimist, threw an arm around Steven's shoulders. "It'll be perfect. And if it does fall down, we'll just... blame the wind."

Maggie rolled her eyes, smiling as she watched the group stand in front of their wobbly, but mostly functional, tent. "Boys and their toys."

As the guys stepped back to admire their questionable work of art, Michael turned to Paolo. "Next time, maybe read the fine print before ordering the 'self-setup special,' huh?"

Paolo laughed, throwing his hands up. "Lesson learned."

Maggie chuckled, shaking her head. "Good. Because next time, we're hiring professionals."

The small bell above the gallery door chimed as Chelsea stepped inside, her footsteps muffled by the sleek wooden floors. The gallery was perfectly lit—soft, carefully positioned lighting accentuated the artwork on the walls without casting harsh shadows.

Chelsea admired the clean lines, the way the space was arranged to draw the eye naturally from one piece to the next. It was understated but elegant, just like Jacqui had always envisioned.

Chelsea paused, taking it all in. The transformation of the space was incredible—it was professional, yet full of Jacqui's personality, a far cry from the uncertain artist Chelsea had first met.

Jacqui emerged from behind a partition, wiping her hands on her apron, her eyes lighting up when she saw Chelsea.

"Well, look who decided to come for a visit!" she called, her voice carrying across the room with its usual spark of humor. "I thought you were too busy for little ol' me now that you're planning this big, fancy wedding."

Chelsea smirked and walked toward her, arms crossed.

"Fancy? Who told you that? It's just a little beach wedding—no big deal."

Jacqui gave her a mock eye-roll. "Uh-huh, sure. That's not what I heard."

Chelsea chuckled and then turned her attention to the walls.

"This place... it's incredible, Jacqui. Really. You've done a hell of a job with it."

Jacqui glanced around, her pride tempered by her usual humility.

"Yeah? I think it's coming along."

"No, it's more than that," Chelsea said, her voice softening. "I remember when we first started painting together. You were all over the place, no direction... but this," she gestured to the room, "this is who you are. And it's beautiful."

For a moment, Jacqui looked like she was going to brush off the compliment, as she often did, but then she caught the sincerity in Chelsea's gaze and smiled.

"Thanks, Chelsea. That means a lot coming from you."

Chelsea nodded, looking around again, her hands resting on her hips.

"I mean it. You've grown so much. Back when we first met, I wasn't sure you'd stick with anything. But look at you now. Running your own gallery, people buying your work... you've come a long way."

Jacqui laughed, leaning against a nearby counter.

"Yeah, well, I had a good teacher. You didn't let me give up, even when I wanted to."

Chelsea met her eyes and shrugged, a teasing smile on her lips.

"I have to admit, you were difficult. But I wasn't about to let you quit on yourself."

Jacqui rolled her eyes, and her grin widened.

"Yeah, I remember. You weren't exactly subtle about it."

They both laughed, the memory of their tough beginnings hanging in the air between them. It had taken a while for Jacqui to trust Chelsea, and for Chelsea to figure out how to break through Jacqui's walls. But now, they stood on the other side of that struggle, stronger for it.

Chelsea's laughter faded, replaced by a warm, affectionate look.

"You know, Jacqui, I came here for more than just admiring your work."

"Oh?" Jacqui leaned in, her eyebrow raised. "What, did you finally come to buy a piece or offer to display a few of your paintings?"

Chelsea shook her head. "Not this time. No, I came here because I wanted to invite you to the wedding."

Jacqui's face softened into a smile.

"Of course I'll be there, Chelsea. You didn't think you had to invite me, did you? I planned to crash it if you didn't."

Chelsea laughed and shook her head, but there was a vulnerability in her eyes now, something rare for her.

"What I'm trying to say is that I want you there. Not just as a guest. I want you there because you've become like family to me, Jacqui. Like a daughter."

Jacqui's eyes widened, and for a moment, she was speechless, which was an unusual state for her. She blinked, her usual composure faltering. "Chelsea…"

Chelsea shrugged, trying to play it off, but the emotion was still there, lingering between them. She'd never had children, a pain that sometimes pulled at her heart.

"Look, I know we didn't have the easiest start. But you've become important to me. I've watched you grow, and… I'm proud of you. I'm proud of the woman you've become. And I just wanted you to know that."

Jacqui's tough exterior cracked, just for a second, as she stood there, processing Chelsea's words. "I… I don't know what to say."

"You don't have to say anything," Chelsea said, stepping forward and placing a hand on Jacqui's arm. "Just know that I mean it. And that I'm so damn happy to have you in my life."

Jacqui swallowed, her voice quieter now. "You've been like a mom to me, Chelsea. I didn't even realize it until now, but... I don't know where I'd be without you. My mother never gave me the support I needed for my art. You came into my life at such a crucial time. You saw something in me that I didn't see in myself. Without you pushing me, I don't know where I'd be right now."

Chelsea, always the one to keep things light, smirked.

"Probably still out partying, wasting your potential."

Jacqui chuckled, wiping at her eyes. "Yeah, probably. But seriously... thank you. For everything."

Chelsea waved her hand, as if brushing off the emotion.

"You don't have to thank me. Just show up to the wedding, and we'll call it even."

Jacqui shook her head, smiling softly. "I wouldn't miss it for the world."

They stood there for a moment, the weight of their words hanging in the air, both of them trying not to get too sentimental. After all, they were both tough women, and too much emotion was almost unbearable.

But beneath the teasing and the sarcasm, there was a deep, unspoken bond that had formed between them. And as Chelsea turned to leave, she glanced over her shoulder, her voice soft.

"Keep up the good work," Chelsea said.

Afraid her emotions would get the better of her, Chelsea tried to leave, but Jacqui wouldn't let her.

Suddenly running to Chelsea, Jacqui threw her arms around her. Chelsea felt her eyes watering and tried not to cry. Instead, she held the young woman and whispered, "I love you, kid."

# CHAPTER 8

*M*aggie walked through the soft sands of Captiva Island's beach, enjoying the stillness of the early morning before the day's bustle took over.

She made her way to the porch of the cottage where Michael and his family were staying for the holidays. It had been a long year for all of them, but seeing Michael alive, well, and gradually returning to his usual self was a blessing she didn't take for granted.

She paused for a moment before entering, letting the sight of the sun rising over the water calm her. Then, she knocked lightly and opened the door.

Inside, Michael was sitting at the small kitchen table, cradling a cup of coffee. His expression was peaceful, but Maggie, being his mother, could always sense the deeper currents of thought beneath the surface. He looked up as she stepped inside, offering a small smile.

"Morning, Mom," he greeted.

"Morning, honey," she replied, crossing the room to join him at the table. "How'd you sleep?"

"Pretty well, actually," Michael said. "The island air helps. And the quiet. Boston's been... loud lately."

Maggie sat down beside him, folding her hands on the table. "I imagine it has been. How are things going? You and Brea seem... good, but I know it hasn't been easy, especially since you went back to work."

Michael sighed, running a hand through his hair. "Yeah, it's been a transition. Sitting behind a desk for months wasn't great, but at least Brea wasn't so worried all the time. Since I went back on the street, she's been on edge. I know she trusts me to be careful, but... you know how it is."

Maggie nodded thoughtfully. She knew all too well the fear and worry that came with having a loved one in such a dangerous job. "She's scared, Michael. And that's natural. After everything you've been through... it's hard for her to let go of that fear."

Michael leaned back in his chair, his eyes drifting to the window where the sun glinted off the water. "I get it. I do. I mean, I still have nightmares sometimes. It's not easy going back, but I didn't want to stay stuck behind that desk forever. It just didn't feel like me."

"You've always loved the work you do," Maggie said gently. "But have you and Brea talked about how it's affecting her? Really talked?"

Michael was quiet for a moment before shaking his head. "Not as much as we should have. We've been kind of... avoiding it. We've got the kids, and she's busy, and I guess I didn't want to bring it up. I don't want to make her more nervous than she already is."

Maggie placed a hand on her son's arm, squeezing it gently. "You two have always been good about working through things together. But you can't avoid this forever. If she's scared and you're not talking about it, that's just going to build up."

Michael sighed again, clearly thinking about her words.

"Yeah, you're right. I don't want to ignore it. I just don't know how to start that conversation without making her more upset."

Maggie smiled softly, knowing that even after all these years, Michael still worried about saying the right thing. "Sometimes the hardest part is just starting. But once you do, it'll get easier. Why don't you and Brea take some time for yourselves while you're here? Have a date night—just the two of you."

Michael looked at her, surprised. "A date night? With the kids here?"

Maggie chuckled. "Yes, with the kids here. Paolo and I will watch them. You and Brea need some time away from everything —no work, no kids, no stress. Just the two of you, like when you first got together."

Michael's expression softened as he thought about it. "You think she'd go for that?"

"I know she would," Maggie said. "She loves you, Michael. And she wants to feel like the two of you are in this together. Give her that space to reconnect. And don't worry about the kids. Paolo and I will handle them. It'll be good for all of you."

Michael nodded, a slow smile creeping across his face. "I think you're right. We could both use a break. A real break."

"Then do it," Maggie encouraged. "Go out, have dinner, take a walk on the beach. You don't even have to plan something fancy. Just be together."

Michael leaned forward, resting his elbows on the table. "Thanks, Mom. I didn't even realize how much we needed that until you said it. I've been so focused on work, on making sure I'm okay, that I kind of forgot Brea's been carrying this, too."

"That's what marriage is, sweetheart," Maggie said with a knowing smile. "It's carrying the weight together. But every now and then, you need to stop and take a breath. Remind yourselves why you fell in love in the first place."

Michael took a deep breath, the weight of the past few months visibly lifting from his shoulders. "You know, I don't think I've really told Brea how much I appreciate her for sticking by me through all of this. I've been so focused on getting back to work that I haven't been as present as I should have been."

"Then this is your chance," Maggie said. "Tell her. Show her. Sometimes we get so caught up in life that we forget the simple things—like telling the people we love how much they mean to us."

Michael gave his mother a grateful smile. "I'll do that. Tonight, I'll ask her if she's up for a date night. I think it'll be good for both of us."

Maggie patted his hand. "I'm sure it will be. And if you need anything—anything at all—you know where to find me."

Later that evening, after the kids were settled in with Paolo and Maggie, Michael approached Brea with a hesitant smile. She was sitting on the porch, gazing out at the sunset, her face illuminated by the warm glow of the fading light.

"Hey," he said, sliding into the seat next to her.

"Hey," Brea replied, her tone soft but tired. "How are the kids?"

"Fast asleep," Michael said with a grin. "Mom and Paolo are on duty now. Which means we have the evening to ourselves."

Brea raised an eyebrow, curious. "We do?"

Michael reached for her hand, his touch gentle but firm. "Yeah. I was thinking... we haven't really had time to ourselves in a while. Between the kids, your classes and my job, it feels like we've been running on autopilot."

Brea's expression softened, and she leaned into his touch. "You're right. It's been... a lot."

"I know," Michael said, his voice filled with sincerity. "And I've been thinking... maybe we should take a break tonight. Just the two of us. No work, no kids. A real date night."

Brea looked at him, surprised. "A date night? Here? On the island?"

Michael nodded. "Yeah. Just us. We can go out for dinner, take a walk, whatever you want. I saw a small seafood restaurant about a block from here. I think it's called Sunshine and Seafood, or something like that. I think it would be great to take a little time for ourselves. My mother and Paolo can watch the kids. I miss spending time with you like we used to." Brea's eyes softened, and a small smile tugged at her lips.

"I'd like that. I miss that too."

Michael squeezed her hand. "Good. Then it's settled. Let's go out, have some fun, and forget about everything else for a little while."

As they stood to leave, Michael pulled her into a gentle embrace. "I know I haven't been the easiest person to be around lately, and I know you've been worried about me going back to work. I just want you to know that I appreciate you. More than I can say. You've stuck by me through everything, and I don't take that for granted."

Brea rested her head against his chest, her arms wrapped around him. "I love you, Michael. And I worry because I can't imagine life without you. But I know you love what you do, and I want you to be happy."

Michael kissed the top of her head. "We're going to be okay, Brea. We'll figure it out, together."

Brea pulled back slightly to look up at him. "Together."

They shared a quiet moment, the weight of the past few months seeming to ease as they stood there holding each other. For the first time in a long time, it felt like they were both on the same page again—ready to face whatever came next, as long as they were together.

"Now," Michael said with a grin, "how about we go grab that dinner?"

Brea laughed, nodding. "Let's do it."

✳

As Michael and Brea strolled down the sandy path leading from the cottage to a cozy restaurant by the beach, the air was filled with the sound of the gentle waves lapping at the shore. The night was cool, and the stars were beginning to emerge, twinkling against the darkening sky. It felt peaceful—far removed from the rush of their lives in Boston.

They arrived at a charming little restaurant tucked into the dunes, its soft lighting and flickering candles casting a warm glow over the outdoor seating area. A hostess greeted them with a smile, guiding them to a private table by the water. The sound of the ocean created a soothing backdrop as they settled into their seats.

Michael glanced across the table at Brea, who seemed to relax for the first time in weeks. He reached for her hand, their fingers intertwining naturally. "This is nice," he said softly. "Just us, no distractions."

Brea smiled, though there was still a hint of tension behind her eyes. "It is," she agreed. "I didn't realize how much I missed this—us—until now."

As the waiter approached and took their orders, they fell into an easy rhythm, sharing small stories about the kids, their time on the island so far, and the little things that had gotten lost in the chaos of their everyday lives. For the first time in a long while, the conversation felt light and unburdened.

Halfway through the meal, Michael leaned back in his chair, watching Brea as she laughed at a funny story he had shared from work. He smiled, feeling a sense of contentment he hadn't felt in months. But beneath that contentment, he knew there was still something they needed to talk about—something they both had been avoiding.

"Brea," Michael said gently, his voice soft but serious, "I know

I haven't really talked to you about how you've been feeling... about me going back to work."

Her smile faded slightly, and she looked down at her plate, pushing her food around with her fork. "You don't have to worry about that right now," she said, trying to dismiss it. "We're supposed to be relaxing tonight."

"I know," Michael said, reaching across the table to touch her hand again. "But it's important. I don't want us to keep avoiding it. I can tell you've been scared... and I get it, Brea. I do. I'm scared sometimes too."

Brea looked up, her eyes meeting his, and for the first time that night, the wall she had been holding up seemed to crack. "Michael... I don't know how to stop being scared," she admitted, her voice trembling slightly. "Every time you leave the house, I'm terrified something is going to happen. I know you're good at what you do, but I can't help thinking about what almost happened last time."

Michael squeezed her hand, his thumb brushing over her skin in a soothing motion. "I know," he said quietly. "I think about it too. But I want you to know that I'm doing everything I can to stay safe. I'm not reckless, and I promise I won't take unnecessary risks. I want to be here, with you and the kids. That's what matters most to me."

Brea's eyes welled up with tears, and she blinked them back, trying to keep her emotions in check. "I just... I don't know if I can go through that again, Michael. When you were in the hospital, when we didn't know if you were going to make it... it was the worst thing I've ever been through. And now, every time you put on that uniform, I'm reminded of how fragile everything is."

Michael leaned forward, his voice filled with conviction. "Brea, I can't promise that nothing will ever happen. But I can promise that I'm going to do everything in my power to come home to you. And I need you to trust that. I need you to trust me."

Brea nodded, her lips pressed into a thin line as she absorbed his words. "I do trust you, Michael. I've always trusted you. It's just... hard sometimes."

"I know," Michael said softly. "And I don't want you to carry that burden alone. We're in this together, remember? You don't have to keep pretending you're okay when you're not. I want to be there for you, just like you've always been there for me."

Brea let out a shaky breath, her shoulders relaxing a little. "I've missed this," she admitted. "I've missed feeling like we're on the same page."

Michael smiled, his eyes warm and full of love. "Me too," he said. "And I want to make sure we stay on the same page. No more avoiding the tough stuff, okay? We talk about it, we face it together."

Brea squeezed his hand, a small smile finally breaking through. "Okay," she agreed. "Together."

As they finished their meal, the mood between them had shifted—lighter, more open, as if the weight of their unspoken fears had finally been lifted. Michael suggested they take a walk along the beach before heading back, and Brea agreed.

The night air was cool as they strolled down the shoreline, the moon casting a silver glow over the water. The sound of the waves crashing softly against the sand provided a peaceful rhythm as they walked hand in hand, their footsteps leaving a trail behind them.

For the first time in months, Michael felt a sense of calm wash over him. He had been so focused on getting back to work, on proving to himself that he could still do the job, that he hadn't realized how much he had been neglecting the most important part of his life—his relationship with Brea. But tonight, walking beside her, he felt more connected to her than he had in a long time.

"You know," Michael said after a while, breaking the comfortable silence, "I think we should do this more often."

Brea looked up at him, raising an eyebrow. "What, take walks on the beach?"

Michael chuckled. "Well, that too. But I mean spending time together. Real time, without distractions. Just the two of us."

Brea smiled softly, leaning into him as they walked. "I'd like that," she said. "I think we need that."

They continued walking until they reached a small outcropping of rocks, where Michael pulled Brea close and wrapped his arms around her. "I love you," he said, his voice low and filled with emotion. "I know I don't say it enough, but I do. More than anything."

Brea looked up at him, her eyes shining in the moonlight. "I love you too," she whispered. "And I'm so glad we're here. Together."

As they stood there, wrapped in each other's arms, the world around them seemed to fade away. For the first time in what felt like forever, they weren't thinking about work, or the kids, or the worries that usually filled their minds. All that mattered was the love they shared and the promise that, no matter what life threw at them, they would face it together.

Eventually, they made their way back to the cottage, where Maggie and Paolo were waiting with stories about how the children had kept her and Paolo on their toes but finally fell asleep and were carried to their rooms.

Michael and Brea exchanged a glance, knowing that their night together had been exactly what they needed—time to reconnect, to talk, and to remember that through it all, they still had each other.

As they settled in for the night, Michael pulled Brea close, whispering in her ear, "We'll be okay. I know we will."

And for the first time in a long while, Brea believed it.

# CHAPTER 9

*M*aggie stood at the kitchen counter, her hands busy with the last of the dinner prep, but her mind was far away.

She'd noticed Oliver had been more withdrawn than usual these past few days, something tugging at him beneath the surface. It wasn't like him to be so quiet, so distant in the one place he usually thrived. The kitchen had always been his sanctuary—yet now, he seemed distracted, lost in thought.

As she arranged the last of the dishes, she glanced over at him. Oliver stood near the window, staring out at the sunset, but clearly not seeing it. His shoulders were tense, his brow furrowed. Maggie wiped her hands on a towel, watching him for a moment before deciding it was time to ask.

"Oliver," she called gently, moving toward him, "something on your mind?"

He turned to face her, his expression softening slightly, though the weight of whatever was bothering him still lingered in his eyes. "Yeah," he said, his voice quieter than usual. "Actually, I wanted to talk to you about something."

Maggie nodded, motioning toward the table. "Why don't you sit? I've got some tea brewing."

Oliver hesitated, but then sat down at the kitchen table, rubbing his hands together as if trying to figure out how to start. Maggie poured the tea and joined him, settling across from him as she waited for him to speak.

"I've been thinking," he began slowly, "that after Chelsea's wedding, I'm going to go see my father."

Maggie's eyebrows lifted in surprise. She hadn't expected this. Oliver rarely talked about his family, let alone his father, who she knew had been a source of pain for him for years. "Your father?" she repeated softly, trying to gauge his mood. "I didn't realize you were considering that."

Oliver let out a short, humorless laugh. "Neither did I. But my brother's arrival has me reconsidering. He says our dad's sick. Maybe even dying. It feels like... I should go. I've been avoiding returning home long enough."

Maggie didn't say anything right away, letting the weight of his words hang in the air. She could see the tension in his posture, the unease in his voice. It wasn't just about his father—it was about everything that had happened between them, everything that had kept Oliver away for so long.

"You think this is something you're ready to face?" she asked gently.

Oliver shrugged, staring down at his hands. "I don't know. But if he is dying, I can't ignore it. I've always found a reason not to visit. Now... I don't have an excuse."

Maggie watched him closely, sensing Oliver's internal conflict. She knew that a lot of his struggles were due to losing his family, and from what little he had shared, she knew he was still grieving. But she also knew how strong Oliver was, even if he didn't always give himself credit for it.

"How do you feel about your brother?" she asked, careful to tread lightly.

71

Oliver sighed, shaking his head. "That's the thing—I don't know if I trust his motives. He's always been the one trying to keep the family together, but there's always been something... I don't know. He's good at making you feel like it's your responsibility to fix things, even if it's not."

Maggie understood the kind of sibling dynamics that could exist. There was so much about this situation she didn't understand.

"You're not responsible for fixing anything," Maggie said, her voice steady but soft. "You go for you. If you feel like it's something you need to do—for closure, for peace of mind—then that's what matters. But don't let anyone pressure you into doing something you're not ready for."

Oliver nodded slowly, though the tension in his shoulders didn't ease. "I know. I just... I don't want to go and end up regretting it. Or worse, go and realize nothing's changed. I don't want to get sucked back into all that."

Maggie reached across the table, resting a hand on his arm. "You've come a long way, Oliver. Whatever happens, you've built a life for yourself here. A life you're proud of. Nothing your brother or your father says can take that away."

He looked up at her, a faint smile tugging at the corner of his mouth. "Thanks, Maggie. That means a lot."

She smiled back, giving his arm a gentle squeeze before pulling away. "How long do you think you'll be gone?"

"Just a few days," Oliver said quickly. "I don't want to stay longer than necessary. I'll go, see what's going on, and then come back. I'll make sure everything's squared away here before I leave."

Maggie nodded. "Don't worry about the inn. Iris should be back soon from her holiday with Alex, so she'll be around to help out while you're gone."

She noticed the way Oliver's face softened at the mention of Iris. There was something there, something quiet and unspoken. Maggie didn't press, though. She had a feeling Oliver wasn't ready to acknowledge it—maybe even to himself. But there was no denying that Iris had become a steady presence in his life, one that seemed to ground him in a way that few others could.

Still, Maggie kept her thoughts to herself. She wasn't one to push when it came to matters of the heart. People had their own journeys to make, and Oliver had been through enough to know what he needed—or at least, to figure it out in his own time.

"Take your time with this," Maggie said after a moment. "You've got people here who care about you, no matter how long you're gone."

Oliver nodded again, his expression more thoughtful than before. "Thanks. I'll let you know before I leave. And I appreciate the support, Maggie. It helps, knowing I've got a place to come back to."

Maggie smiled warmly, her eyes soft with understanding. "You'll always have a place here, Oliver. Don't ever doubt that."

As the conversation wound down, Maggie couldn't help but think about what the future held for Oliver. His decision to see his father was a big step—one that could bring healing, or at least some form of closure. But part of her wondered if Oliver would finally open up in other areas of his life. Maybe, just maybe, that friendship with Iris could become something more in time. But for now, she let the thought pass, content to know that Oliver was finding his way—one step at a time.

Chelsea sat back in her chair, enjoying the sound of the ocean waves in the background as she sipped on her iced tea. The wedding was just around the corner, but today, she and Steven were focused entirely on something else—their honeymoon. She smiled, letting the weight of wedding planning slip away for a moment as she imagined herself and Steven somewhere far from here, just the two of them.

Steven leaned forward, resting his elbows on the small table they had set up on the veranda. He had that look in his eyes—the one that told her he was already a step ahead, thinking through all the details.

"We've been through a lot lately," he said, his voice gentle. "We deserve a proper honeymoon, somewhere where we can completely unwind."

Chelsea smiled at that. "You're absolutely right. But I can't decide where. We've thrown around so many ideas—Italy, Greece, even the South of France."

"True," Steven agreed, "but I've been thinking about something a little different. Something more... relaxing but still luxurious."

Chelsea arched an eyebrow. "Oh? What did you have in mind?"

Steven pulled out his phone, tapping a few times, before looking up at her with a grin.

"What do you think about Hawaii? I know we haven't talked about it, but I was reading up on some of the best resorts there, and I think it could be perfect for us."

"Hawaii?" Chelsea asked, surprised. She hadn't considered it before, but the more she thought about it, the more it made sense. "Tell me more."

"Well," Steven started, "I was thinking we could split our time between two islands. We could start in Oahu and stay at the Four Seasons Resort Oahu at Ko Olina. It's one of the most luxurious resorts on the island, secluded but still close enough to explore some of the island's natural beauty. It has everything—private beaches, infinity pools, world-class spa treatments. We could spend our days lounging by the ocean, but also do a bit of exploring."

Chelsea's interest piqued as he described it. "That does sound amazing. What else?"

"Then," Steven continued, "after a couple of weeks in Oahu, we could fly to Maui. I was thinking we'd stay at the Fairmont Kea Lani. It's one of the top resorts in Wailea, with beautiful private suites, amazing dining options, and a stunning beach-front. It's all about relaxation, but if we feel like it, there's snorkeling, whale watching, or even helicopter tours of the island. How does one whole month sound to you?"

Chelsea smiled, already envisioning it in her mind. The idea of spending a month in such luxurious surroundings, with a perfect blend of adventure and relaxation, sounded like a dream come true.

"I love it," she said, leaning back in her chair. "It sounds like the perfect mix. We get to explore, but we also get to completely unplug. I'm not so sure about the helicopter thing, but why not? You only live once, right?"

Steven grinned, clearly pleased that she liked the idea.

"Absolutely. I'm glad to see we're on the same page. I know how much you've been craving some time away, just the two of us. I think this is the perfect place for us."

Chelsea nodded, her thoughts drifting to the months leading up to this moment. Wedding planning had been stressful, no doubt, but it wasn't just that. Life had felt so hectic lately— between their respective responsibilities, there had been little time to simply be together. The honeymoon felt like more than just a vacation; it was a much-needed escape.

"Everything is moving so fast, I completely forgot about a honeymoon. I've been so focused on the wedding," Chelsea said, her voice softening, "that I almost forgot we get to have this time together afterward. I'm so glad you brought up Hawaii. It feels... right."

Steven reached across the table, taking her hand. "We deserve this, Chels. After everything. And I want to make sure we do it right."

She squeezed his hand, appreciating his thoughtfulness. Steven always had a way of grounding her, of reminding her what really mattered. The wedding was important, of course, but this honeymoon felt like the start of something deeper.

"So," Steven said after a moment, leaning back in his chair with a satisfied smile, "are we settled on Hawaii?"

Chelsea grinned, feeling a sense of peace wash over her.

"Yes. Let's do it. Oahu and Maui, the most luxurious places we can find. I'm all in."

"Great," Steven said, clearly pleased. "I'll take care of the reservations."

Chelsea watched as he began typing on his phone again, no doubt already making notes on their plans. She laughed softly to herself—Steven was always one step ahead, making sure everything was perfect. It was one of the things she loved about him. He knew how to plan, how to make sure everything ran smoothly, and yet he always left room for spontaneity when it mattered.

"You know what I'd love to do in Hawaii?"

"Tell me," he said.

"Paint. I'd love to find a spot to paint. The tropical landscape has to be beautiful. Nothing would thrill me more than to capture that beauty on canvas."

Steven smiled. "Then that's what we'll do. I'll make sure to find perfect spots for you."

"Tell me more about Oahu," Chelsea said after a moment, her curiosity piqued. "What should we do while we're there?"

"Well," Steven said, looking up from his phone, "the resort is in Ko Olina, which is a quieter part of the island, but it's close enough to explore some of the major sights. I was thinking we could visit Pearl Harbor, maybe take a hike up Diamond Head if you're feeling adventurous."

"Hike? Did you say hike?" she asked. "I'm more of a sit by the pool with a drink in my hand kind of girl."

Steven laughed. "You don't know that you'll hate it until you try it. Trust me, nothing is more exhilarating than hiking in Hawaii. I promise you'll love it."

Chelsea smiled. "I'm not so sure about that, but I've always wanted to see Pearl Harbor."

"And then," Steven continued, "we can spend our afternoons by the pool or at the spa. The resort has this beautiful beachfront, too, so we could just relax there, watch the sunset..."

"Now you're talking," she said.

She closed her eyes for a moment, picturing it. The sound of the waves, the warm sun on her skin, the peace that came with being far away from everything else. It felt like exactly what they needed.

"And in Maui?" she asked, opening her eyes.

"Maui is all about luxury," Steven said with a grin. "The Fairmont Kea Lani is right on Wailea Beach, and we'll have a private suite with an ocean view. We can snorkel if we feel like it, or just relax by the pool. There's also a spa, of course, so we can get a massage or two."

Chelsea laughed. "I think I'm going to need a week at the spa after all this wedding planning."

Steven laughed. "Whatever you want, my love. Your wish is my command."

They spent the next hour discussing their plans in more detail —what to pack, what excursions they might want to take, and how they would balance relaxation with adventure. Chelsea loved the way Steven's eyes lit up when he talked about their trip, and she could feel her own excitement building as they worked through the details.

By the time they had finished, Chelsea felt lighter than she had in months. The stress of the wedding seemed to fade into the background, replaced by the excitement of what was to come.

She knew their honeymoon wouldn't solve everything—life would still be waiting for them when they got back—but it felt like a fresh start, a chance to truly connect and enjoy each other's company without the distractions of the outside world.

As they wrapped up their conversation, Chelsea looked out at the ocean again, feeling a deep sense of gratitude for the life they were building together.

"I can't wait to start this next chapter with you," she said softly, turning to Steven.

He smiled, reaching out to take her hand. "Me too."

They sat in comfortable silence for a while, both of them lost in their thoughts about the future. For Chelsea, the wedding had been a whirlwind of planning and details, but now, with the honeymoon set and the promise of four blissful weeks in Hawaii on the horizon, she felt like she could finally breathe again.

The road ahead was unknown, but as long as Chelsea had Steven by her side, she knew they could face anything together.

And Hawaii, well, it was just the beginning.

# CHAPTER 10

*C*helsea stood by the front window of her home, nervously twisting the engagement ring on her finger as she waited for her sisters to arrive.

Though she'd been relaxed leading up to the wedding, her sisters' arrival was the one thing making her anxious. There had been something off in their last phone call, something she couldn't quite put her finger on, but enough to make her wonder if things weren't as perfect as they were pretending.

It had been months since she'd last seen Tess, Leah, and Gretchen, and while she was excited to have them here for her wedding, a small voice in the back of her mind reminded her of the complicated history they shared.

The last time they'd all been together in Key West, her sisters had been thrilled about their new venture. Ideas about the CoiffeeShop were thrown about like it was a sure thing...only it wasn't. They had been so full of hope, and although Chelsea had doubted their plans at first, she eventually got on board and even helped them financially. But now, as they were coming for her wedding, she couldn't shake the feeling that something had changed.

She glanced at the clock again. They were supposed to be here half an hour ago. Tess and Leah were always late, but Gretchen? Punctuality was her thing. The fact that they were late made Chelsea's stomach churn with unease.

Finally, a car pulled up in front of her house. Chelsea let out a slow breath, smoothing down the front of her dress before stepping outside to greet them. Her heart raced, but she told herself it was just pre-wedding jitters. Surely everything was fine.

The car door opened, and as soon as Tess and Leah stepped out, Chelsea could feel it—the tension between them. Tess had her oversized sunglasses on, and while her smile was wide, it felt more like a mask than anything else. Leah's smile was there too, but it didn't reach her eyes, which flickered with an edge Chelsea couldn't quite place.

And then there was Gretchen. Always the rock. Yet today, even Gretchen seemed subdued, her usual steady composure giving way to a softer, more distant expression. Chelsea's heart sank.

"Hey!" Chelsea called out, waving as she walked toward them. "I've missed you guys!"

Tess was the first to come forward, wrapping Chelsea in a tight hug that lasted just a little too long.

"We've missed you too!" she said, her voice full of enthusiasm. But when Chelsea pulled back, she could see the faint lines of tension in Tess's face, like she was trying too hard to keep things light. The truth was that Chelsea didn't grow up with her sisters and had little understanding of what made them tick. But she could recognize cracks in her sister's façade.

Leah was next, pulling Chelsea into a looser hug.

"You look amazing, Chels," Leah said, stepping back to take in Chelsea's appearance. "I can't believe you're getting married."

"Thanks," Chelsea said with a light laugh, though her gaze quickly shifted to Gretchen, who had lingered near the car, quieter than usual. Chelsea approached her sister, pulling her into a warm embrace.

"It's so good to see you, Gretch."

"You too," Gretchen replied softly, though her voice lacked its usual warmth. She gave Chelsea a quick smile before glancing over at Tess and Leah, an unreadable look in her eyes.

The tension between the sisters was undeniable now, heavy and lingering in the air like a thick fog.

Chelsea could feel her instincts kicking in, that gut feeling she always had when something wasn't right. Whatever was going on now, they were clearly hiding it from her.

"How was the drive?" Chelsea asked, trying to keep the conversation light as she gestured toward the house. "You guys must be exhausted after that long trip."

Leah let out a small laugh, but it sounded forced.

"It was... fine," she said, waving her hand. "You know how traffic from Key West can be. But we're here now, and that's all that matters."

"Yeah," Tess chimed in, her voice a little too chipper. "We're just happy to be here. It's your weekend, Chelsea! This is all about celebrating you!"

Chelsea forced a smile, her eyes scanning their faces for any clue about what was really going on. Tess was always the one to deflect, to keep things upbeat even when there was something bubbling beneath the surface. Leah was the peacekeeper, and Chelsea could already tell she was working overtime to smooth things over. But Gretchen? She was an anchor, and her silence spoke louder than any words.

"Are you guys okay?" Chelsea asked, trying to sound casual even though the knot in her stomach was tightening. "You seem... I don't know, a little off."

Tess laughed quickly, brushing off the question.

"Of course, we're okay! We're just a little tired, that's all. But don't worry about us—this is your wedding weekend! Nothing else matters."

Chelsea wasn't buying it. Tess's smile was too wide, too fake. Leah was avoiding eye contact, and Gretchen? Gretchen was staring off into the distance, lost in thought. Something was definitely wrong, and it was clear they weren't telling her the truth.

"Everything's great, Chels," Leah added, her tone equally forced. "We're here to celebrate you. That's what matters, right?"

Chelsea narrowed her eyes slightly, watching as Tess and Leah exchanged a quick glance, one they clearly hoped she wouldn't notice. Whatever was going on, they were doing their best to hide it from her. But why? Was it about the CoiffeeShop? Had something gone wrong in Key West? Or was it something else entirely?

Gretchen, who had been unusually quiet throughout the conversation, finally stepped forward and placed a hand on Chelsea's arm.

"We'll talk later, Chels," she said softly, her eyes meeting Chelsea's with a sincerity that made Chelsea's heart ache. "Let's just enjoy being here for now."

Chelsea nodded slowly, sensing that whatever was going on, Gretchen would tell her in time.

"Okay," she said, though the unease still sat heavy in her chest. "I'll hold you to that."

The four of them stood in silence for a moment, the tension still hanging in the air despite their best attempts to push it aside. Chelsea forced a smile, deciding to let it go for now. This weekend was supposed to be about her wedding, after all. The last thing she needed was to get caught up in whatever drama was brewing between her sisters. But she couldn't shake the feeling that the truth would come out eventually—whether they wanted it to or not.

"Come on," Chelsea said, motioning toward the house. "Let's

get you guys settled in. I've got drinks ready, and I'm dying to hear more about Key West."

As they walked toward the house, Chelsea couldn't help but notice the way Tess and Leah exchanged another glance, their expressions tight and unreadable. Gretchen, walking behind them, seemed lost in thought, her brow furrowed.

Whatever was going on, Chelsea knew she'd find out eventually. But for now, she'd focus on what mattered—her wedding, her soon-to-be husband, and the new chapter of her life that was about to begin.

Just as Chelsea ushered her sisters into the house, there was a knock at the door. Before she could turn to open it, the door swung open, and Maggie walked in with her usual bright smile, holding a basket of fresh pastries.

"Hello, ladies!" Maggie chimed, stepping into the room with a warm energy. "I thought I'd drop by to say hello and welcome the bridesmaids to the island. I also brought some of my favorite croissants from the bakery in town."

Chelsea grinned, grateful for the interruption.

"Maggie, you're a lifesaver. Come in, sit down in the kitchen with us."

Everyone pulled out a chair at the table and Maggie set the basket down on the counter.

"Maggie, it's so good to see you again," Gretchen said.

"You look as beautiful as ever," Tess added.

"Absolutely," Leah joined in. "Thank you for the pastries. We haven't eaten since breakfast, and I'm starving."

"I've made coffee, too if you'd rather," Chelsea said, getting coffee mugs from the kitchen cabinet.

"So," Maggie said, her eyes lighting up as she turned toward Tess, Leah, and Gretchen, "how are things going in Key West?"

Tess shifted in her seat, exchanging a quick glance with Leah. Gretchen, ever the composed one, smiled politely but said nothing at first. Chelsea immediately noticed the tension, but before she could ask anything, the front door opened again. This time, it was Steven walking in, looking as casual and handsome as ever in his button-down shirt and khakis.

"Oh, Steven! Come say hi," Chelsea said, her voice bright but already feeling the heat of embarrassment creeping up her neck. Her sisters hadn't met him yet, and for some reason, she felt a little nervous about their first impressions.

Steven smiled, walking into the living room and offering a friendly wave. "Hey, everyone. Nice to finally meet you."

Tess and Leah both sat up straighter at the sight of him. Leah's eyes widened slightly, and Tess elbowed her in the ribs, barely hiding a grin. Chelsea knew that look—they were about to make things awkward, and there was no stopping them.

"Well, well, well," Tess said with a mischievous grin, eyeing Steven from head to toe. "Now I see why you've been keeping this one a secret, Chels. He's a looker!"

Leah giggled, giving Chelsea an exaggerated wink.

"Yeah, I totally get it now. No wonder you're head over heels."

Chelsea groaned internally, feeling her face flush.

"Guys, please," she muttered, trying to hide her mortification as Steven stood there, his smile turning more awkward by the second.

"I mean, seriously," Tess continued, completely ignoring Chelsea's discomfort. "You didn't mention how handsome he is. You were really underselling him."

Leah leaned forward, resting her chin on her hand, her eyes sparkling with amusement. "I'd have a ring on my finger too if I had someone like him around."

Steven chuckled nervously, running a hand through his hair as he looked to Chelsea for help. "Uh, thanks? I guess?" he said, his voice laced with awkwardness.

Chelsea couldn't take it anymore.

"Okay, okay, that's enough," she said, waving her hands in front of her face. "Steven's great, yes, but can we please not embarrass me in front of my fiancé?"

Maggie, who had been quietly watching the exchange with a glint of amusement in her eyes, let out a laugh.

"Come on, Chelsea. They're only teasing."

"That's what you think." Chelsea mumbled, giving her sisters a playful glare.

Steven, ever the gentleman, stepped closer and wrapped an arm around Chelsea's shoulders.

"I think I'll survive. But it's nice to know I have the approval of your sisters already," he said, winking at Chelsea.

Tess grinned, clearly enjoying the lighthearted teasing.

"Oh, you definitely have our approval. Now we just need to make sure you're not stealing our sister away from us completely."

"Don't worry," Steven replied, trying to play along despite the awkwardness. "I'll make sure she still gets her sister time. I guess that means an annual trip to Key West, which sounds like fun to me."

"Have you ever been?" Gretchen asked.

Steven nodded. "I have, several times, especially when I was younger. I've made lots of good memories there, some I won't repeat and will leave to my youth."

"Good answer," Leah said with a nod, still chuckling under her breath.

Once the teasing subsided, and the awkwardness faded into comfortable laughter, Chelsea noticed Maggie's eyes twinkle with amusement as she turned her attention back to the original topic.

"Now, where were we? Ah, yes—the CoiffeeShop. How's the business going, ladies?"

The atmosphere shifted slightly. Tess's grin faded, and she

glanced at Leah, who immediately busied herself with adjusting her bracelets. Gretchen sat quietly, her hands resting in her lap. Chelsea knew her sisters too well to let this slide.

"It's been... an experience," Leah finally said, her tone careful.

"Who are we kidding?" Tess responded. "There is no Coiffee-Shop. We're still trying to figure out how to make a living down there. It's not easy."

Chelsea narrowed her eyes, noticing the way her sisters exchanged looks again. That nagging feeling in her gut resurfaced, stronger this time.

"I don't understand. What happened to the money I gave you to get started?"

Leah sighed softly, leaning back in her chair. "Let's just say it's been harder than we expected. We ran into some bumps along the way."

"Bumps? What kind of bumps?" Chelsea asked.

Steven got in the middle to calm tensions.

"How about we save this discussion for another day? We've got lots of happy memories to create."

Tess, never one to let things stay too serious for long, quickly added, "Right, there's nothing to worry about. We've been dealing with a few roadblocks here and there."

Maggie's brow furrowed slightly, but she didn't push too hard. "That's understandable. Starting something new always has its challenges."

Chelsea wasn't buying it. She could tell there was more to the story. The forced smiles, the quick answers—it wasn't adding up.

"Are you guys sure everything's okay?" she asked, her concern growing. "You don't seem... yourselves."

Gretchen, the most reserved of the three, was the one who spoke up again. "It's not just the business, Chels. We've had some disagreements. Living together, working together—it's been a lot."

Tess shrugged, waving it off. "Yeah, you know, the usual sister stuff. We argue, we get over it."

Chelsea's heart sank a little. She had hoped this business would bring her sisters closer, but now it seemed like it was driving them apart.

"Why didn't you say anything?"

Leah offered a weak smile. "We didn't want to bother you. You've got the wedding to think about."

Maggie, ever the perceptive one, gave Chelsea a reassuring glance before turning back to the sisters.

"Well, sometimes it's okay to admit when things aren't perfect. You're allowed to struggle, and you're allowed to ask for help. No one expects you to have it all together all the time."

Chelsea nodded, her heart heavy with concern for her sisters. She glanced at Gretchen again, sensing there was something more going on with her sister. Gretchen had been unusually quiet since they arrived, and Chelsea could see the weight she was carrying in her expression.

"Gretchen?" Chelsea asked softly, her voice full of gentle concern. "Are you okay?"

Gretchen looked up, meeting Chelsea's eyes for a moment before glancing away. "I'm fine," she said, her voice quiet but firm. "Steven's right, we should talk about this later. I don't want to get into it now, not before the wedding."

Chelsea didn't push. Not now. But she knew there was more to Gretchen's story than she was letting on. Whatever was going on, it was big enough that Gretchen wasn't ready to share it— not yet.

For now, though, she would let it go. This was supposed to be a happy time, a time to celebrate. She would deal with the rest later.

# CHAPTER 11

*C*helsea hesitated outside Gretchen's bedroom door. She could hear the faint sound of movement but wasn't sure if she should knock or just open the door a crack.

Taking a deep breath, Chelsea knocked lightly on the door before peeking in. "Hey, are you busy?"

Gretchen, seated in the corner chair, glanced up from her phone. "Not too busy for you. Come in."

Chelsea stepped into the room, noting how quiet and still it felt compared to the lively chaos happening downstairs. Gretchen's phone rested in her hand, but her attention was fully on her now.

Chelsea felt a twinge of guilt for not checking in with her earlier, but there had been so much to do with the wedding preparations. Finding Gretchen alone was the perfect opportunity to get to the bottom of what was going on between her sisters.

"I was just thinking," Chelsea began, lingering by the door, "I haven't shown you my wedding dress yet. Want to see it?"

Gretchen's face lit up, the slight tension around her eyes easing.

"Of course! I'd love to see it."

Chelsea's heart warmed at her sister's genuine excitement. She led the way to her bedroom, where the dress was hanging on a special rack by the window, the soft white fabric catching the fading daylight. It was simple but elegant, with lace details and a subtle shimmer that made Chelsea feel like a bride every time she looked at it.

As they entered her room, Chelsea carefully pulled the dress out from its protective clear cover, holding it up for Gretchen to see. "What do you think?"

Gretchen stood there for a moment, taking in the sight of the dress. Her eyes softened, and for the first time that day, she seemed to relax fully. "It's beautiful, Chels. You'll look amazing in it. It's so... you."

Chelsea smiled, gently laying the dress across her bed.

"I hope so. I wanted something that felt true to who I am, you know? Not too over-the-top but still special."

Gretchen nodded, running her fingers lightly along the lace. "You made the right choice. It's perfect."

After a beat of silence, Chelsea looked at her sister, feeling a small knot of nervousness form in her chest.

"There's something I need to talk to you about," she began slowly, sitting on the edge of the bed. "It's about the wedding."

Gretchen raised an eyebrow but remained silent, waiting for Chelsea to continue.

"I didn't know how to choose just one of you to be my maid of honor," Chelsea admitted, her voice soft. "I love all of you, and I didn't want anyone to feel left out or hurt. So... I asked Maggie instead. She's my best friend, and it felt right to ask her. I hope that's okay."

Gretchen's face relaxed into a smile, her eyes warm and understanding.

"Of course it's okay. You didn't want to choose between your sisters, and Maggie's practically family. None of us will be upset, Chelsea. Don't worry about it."

Chelsea felt relieved by Gretchen's response. "I'm glad you understand. I've been stressing over it for days."

"You don't need to stress about us," Gretchen assured her. "This is your day. We're just happy to be here and to support you."

There was a moment of silence as Chelsea looked at her sister, grateful for the support but knowing there was something more beneath the surface. She had noticed Gretchen's quietness, the way she'd seemed distracted ever since she arrived.

Chelsea bit her lip, unsure of how to approach it, but finally, she decided to just ask. "Now that we're alone... why not tell me what's really going on?"

Gretchen's smile faltered slightly, and she glanced down at her phone, her fingers idly fidgeting with the case.

"What do you mean?"

"I can tell something's bothering you," Chelsea said gently, sitting beside her on the bed. "You've been quieter than usual, and I know it's not just the business in Key West. You don't have to pretend with me."

For a moment, Gretchen didn't respond, her eyes focused on her phone. But then, with a heavy sigh, she set it aside and turned to face Chelsea.

"You're right. There is something going on."

Chelsea's heart tightened, but she waited, giving Gretchen the space to speak.

"I'm not going back to Key West," Gretchen said, her voice soft but steady. "At least, not to live."

Chelsea blinked, surprised. "What? You're not?"

Gretchen shook her head, her expression a mix of resignation and relief.

"I haven't told Tess and Leah yet. I'm waiting until after the wedding to bring it up. But I can't stay in Key West anymore. It's not for me."

Chelsea sat back, processing her sister's words. "Why? I thought you were all excited about starting the CoiffeeShop."

"I was," Gretchen admitted, her voice tinged with sadness. "But when that fell through, I felt a weight lifted. Right away I thought it was a sign. The truth is, Tess and Leah are perfect for that place. They love the nightlife, the energy, the constant activity. They thrive there, and I'm happy for them. But I don't belong in Key West. I feel out of place. It's too much for me. I need something quieter, slower."

Chelsea nodded slowly, understanding beginning to dawn. "So, you're going to move, but where will you go?"

"Yes," Gretchen said, meeting Chelsea's eyes with a small, hopeful smile. "I've decided to move here, either Fort Myers, Sanibel or Captiva. I've looked at real estate in Sanibel and Captiva and I was shocked at the prices. I'm not sure I can afford anything here. I can manage a mortgage in Fort Myers and it's as close to you as I can get. I'll keep looking though. I'd love to live on the island."

Chelsea didn't say anything, taking it all in.

"Did you hear me? I said I want to be closer to you. I've been thinking about it for a while, but I didn't want to say anything until I was sure."

Chelsea's heart swelled with emotion.

"You're moving to be near me?"

Gretchen nodded, her smile growing.

"Yeah. I've realized that I need a change, but more importantly, I need family. Being near you, having a more peaceful life... it's what I want now. Plus, Kaitlyn can have a place to visit without the craziness of Tess and Leah. My daughter is an adult, but I still feel I've got wisdom to share with her. A home of our own is important. You don't mind, do you?"

Chelsea couldn't help but smile, her earlier tension melting away.

"I think it's a wonderful idea. I'm thrilled you and Kaitlyn will

91

be close. I've missed you so much."

"Me too," Gretchen said, the relief evident in her voice. "But I haven't figured out how to tell Tess and Leah yet. And, I don't want to ruin the wedding by dropping this bombshell on them."

Chelsea placed a hand on her sister's arm, squeezing gently.

"Don't be silly. You won't ruin anything. I do think it's a good idea to wait until after the wedding because you and I both know that Tess and Leah could elevate the drama. You know how they can be. After the wedding, we can figure out the best way to tell them. But for now, let's keep it between us—and Maggie, if that's okay."

Gretchen smiled, nodding. "I agree. I don't want to overwhelm them right now. And Maggie... well, she'll understand."

Chelsea leaned back, a sense of peace settling over her.

"This is going to be great. We'll find you a perfect home somewhere around here. You'll love it."

Gretchen chuckled softly. "I hope so. I'm ready for something new, something that feels more like home."

"Fort Myers is perfect," Chelsea said, excitement bubbling in her chest. "And when Steven and I go on our honeymoon, you can stay here and watch Stella. She'll love the company, and when we get back, we'll start house hunting. How does that sound?"

Gretchen's eyes softened with gratitude. "That sounds perfect. I'd love to stay here while you're away. And Stella and I have always gotten along."

"Then it's settled," Chelsea said with a wide smile. "We'll make this work."

Chelsea suddenly realized it might not be that easy.

"Wait! Don't you have to get back to Key West and pack?"

Gretchen laughed. "Nope. Everything I need I've got right over there," she said, pointing to her two suitcases. "Tess and Leah complained I had too much luggage. It was hard to keep the truth to myself when they said that."

Chelsea laughed. "Leave it to you to be a step ahead of everyone else."

After Chelsea's conversation with her sister, she walked down to the beach to join Maggie's family. Trevor's laughter echoed across the beach as he raced up and down the shore, pulling a makeshift sled with jingle bells chiming behind him.

The children took turns hopping on, giggling as they skidded along the sand, their shouts of delight filling the warm afternoon air.

Sarah stood nearby, arms crossed and grinning as she called out, "It's not snow, but it's just as much fun!"

The whole family watched from just beyond the wedding tent. The kids ran in and out of the water, with Trevor pulling from left to right and then back again.

Occasionally, Jeff and Gabriel took turns to give Trevor a break, and the other adults sat nearby in their lounge chairs sipping wine and enjoying the last hours of daylight before the wedding the next day.

Chelsea made her way over to Maggie who was sitting next to Paolo.

"Maggie," Chelsea said, touching her shoulder gently. "Can we talk for a minute?"

Maggie looked up, her expression brightening when she saw Chelsea.

"Of course. Let's head up to the porch."

The two walked together toward the inn, the beach fading behind them as they stepped onto the porch where a familiar swing awaited.

It was a quiet place, one where they had shared many heart-to-heart conversations over the years. The swing creaked as they sat down, the gentle breeze swaying them.

"What's on your mind?" Maggie asked, her perceptive eyes locking onto Chelsea's.

Chelsea smiled, glancing out at the horizon for a moment before speaking. "I thought I'd update you on my sisters' latest news."

Maggie leaned in, curiosity piqued. "Oh?"

Chelsea nodded. "Gretchen told me earlier today that she's not going back to Key West. She hasn't told Tess and Leah yet, but she's decided it's not the right place for her. She's moving to Fort Myers... to be closer to me."

Maggie's face lit up with excitement.

"Oh, Chelsea, that's wonderful news! I had a feeling she wasn't quite settled in Key West, but I didn't know she was planning to move."

"I know," Chelsea said, her own excitement bubbling up. "She's going to stay at my place and watch Stella while Steven and I are in Hawaii. When we get back, we'll start looking for houses for her."

Maggie gave Chelsea's hand a little squeeze, her eyes twinkling. "And you're going to Hawaii! When did you decide this?"

Chelsea laughed, feeling a rush of joy at the thought of their upcoming honeymoon. "We just finalized the plans. We're spending four weeks there—Oahu and Maui. It's going to be amazing."

Maggie's smile grew wider. "You deserve it. You and Steven both. A beautiful wedding and then four weeks in paradise? Sounds perfect."

Chelsea nodded, her mind wandering briefly to all the things she and Steven would do together—sunsets on the beach, exploring the islands, finally getting time to just be.

"I can't wait," she said softly. "It's going to be the perfect way to start our life together."

Maggie leaned back on the swing, her gaze thoughtful.

"You've come so far, Chelsea. I think back to the day you and Carl bought your house on Andy Rosse Lane. It seems like it was just yesterday. It's hard to believe how much has changed since then."

Chelsea glanced at her, feeling the weight of their shared history.

"I know what you mean. Sometimes I look around this island, and it feels like it's always been home. Even when I didn't realize it."

Maggie nodded, her eyes distant for a moment.

"This place has a way of becoming home for people who need it, doesn't it? Captiva has seen us through so much—joy, loss, and everything in between."

Chelsea smiled, thinking of all the places on the island that had become special to her. The inn itself was filled with memories, from the first time she'd stayed here to the countless moments spent laughing with Maggie, Sarah, and the rest of the crew.

The beach, with its endless sunsets, had been a place of healing for her after Carl's passing. And The Thistle Lodge on Sanibel, where they had shared countless family gatherings, had become a symbol of love and togetherness.

In true Chelsea form, she found a memory to laugh about.

"Do you remember the time we were sitting at Jensen's Marina looking up at the stars and you said the Big Dipper seemed upside down?"

Maggie laughed. "I can't be held responsible for something I said after one glass of wine. You know I don't really drink."

Chelsea chuckled. "Do you remember my answer?"

Maggie nodded. "I most certainly do. You said it was because we were in Florida instead of Massachusetts and being so much further south, the stars will look different."

"You believed me. I almost spit out my wine when you didn't dispute my observation. It was priceless."

"We've had some fun times on this island, haven't we?" Maggie asked.

"You make it sound as if it's the end of something. Please don't think that. We've got many more years of mischief on this island. Don't wimp out on me now."

Maggie laughed and put her hand on Chelsea's shoulder.

"I'm sorry, I didn't mean to sound that way. I'm ready for whatever you want to do, my friend."

Chelsea touched Maggie's hand.

"I know you are. You've been the best friend anyone could ever have. I'm so glad we met when we did."

"Speaking of book clubs..." Maggie added.

"I finished the book. How about you?" Chelsea said.

Maggie nodded. "Me too. I read it in an afternoon. I hope the next book is much longer. I need a story I can sink my teeth into."

Chelsea nodded. "By the way, I told Gretchen about you being Matron of Honor. I don't expect any of my sisters to fuss about it. I know they're family, but...well, the Wheeler and Moretti clan is my family too."

Maggie smiled. "That's because family isn't just the people you're related to by blood. It's the people who stand by you, who love you no matter what. You've always been family to us, Chelsea. From the very beginning."

Chelsea felt a lump rise in her throat. "I don't think I'd be who I am today without all of you."

Maggie's eyes glistened with emotion as she squeezed Chelsea's hand.

"And we wouldn't be the same without you. Look at how much our family has grown over the years. The people we've added, the memories we've made... it's incredible to think about."

Chelsea nodded, her heart swelling with gratitude.

"You're right. Our families have grown in ways I never could have imagined. And I feel like Carl's been with me through it all, watching over us."

Maggie smiled softly, her voice gentle. "He's proud of you, Chelsea. I know he is. He's smiling down on you, happy that you've found love and joy again."

Chelsea blinked back tears, a wave of warmth spreading through her.

"I feel him with me sometimes, especially now, with everything happening. I know he'd want me to be happy."

Maggie nodded, her eyes full of understanding. "He would. And you deserve all the happiness that's coming your way."

They sat in comfortable silence for a few moments, the gentle sway of the swing and the sound of distant laughter from the beach filling the air. Chelsea felt at peace—more at peace than she had in a long time.

Maggie's voice broke the quiet. "So, tomorrow's the big day. Are you ready?"

Chelsea let out a small laugh, her excitement bubbling up again.

"Yes. I'm more than ready. I can't wait to marry Steven."

Maggie grinned, her joy for Chelsea clear in every line of her face.

"It's going to be a beautiful day, Chelsea. And you've got all of us—your family—right here with you."

Chelsea smiled, her heart full of love and gratitude. "I know. And that's what makes everything feel right."

As they sat there on the porch swing, watching the sun dip lower in the sky, Chelsea knew without a doubt that this was where she was meant to be—surrounded by love, by family, and by the island that had given her a new life.

# CHAPTER 12

*P*hilippe sat alone at a small table in the corner of the hotel restaurant, absently swirling the melting ice cubes in his drink. The muted hum of conversation filled the air, but it barely registered with him.

Outside, through the large windows, he could see the distant lights of Sanibel Island flickering on as dusk settled over the horizon. Captiva was just beyond that, close enough that it felt like an extension of his thoughts, yet far enough that he could pretend it didn't matter.

He shouldn't be here. That much was obvious, and yet here he was, sitting in this restaurant just before the Sanibel Island Bridge, brooding over everything he had spent years trying to control. His chest tightened, the familiar unease creeping up again as the waitress approached, offering a polite smile.

"Would you like to order something else, sir?"

He glanced down at the half-eaten plate of food before him, then shook his head. "No, I'm fine. Just the check, please."

The waitress nodded, retreating with the same forced cheeriness that Philippe had come to expect from these vacation spots. This place—so calm, so inviting—wasn't for him. He preferred

New York, the tension, the energy of the city, where things moved fast, and distractions were easy to find. Here, everything moved at a slow, agonizing pace. It gave him too much time to think.

His phone buzzed on the table, and he glanced down. A message from Sabrina. He let out a slow breath before opening it.

*Any luck with Oliver? Did you find him?*

The knot in his chest tightened as he stared at the message. It had been like this for weeks now—Sabrina's growing interest in Oliver, the endless questions about where he was, what he was doing, how he was coping. Her curiosity had started subtly, a passing remark here or there about Oliver's life after the flood that had taken his family. At first, Philippe hadn't worried. Oliver was grieving, broken, and so far removed from their world that he posed no threat.

But then the questions became more frequent, more insistent. Sabrina was no longer satisfied with vague answers. She wanted details. She wanted to know where Oliver was and, worse, why Philippe wasn't doing more to reach out to him. It was as if the distance between Oliver and the family had only made Sabrina's feelings for him grow stronger.

Philippe clenched his fist under the table, his knuckles whitening. Oliver. Always Oliver. The golden boy who had walked away from everything—the family, the money, the life Philippe had built—and still managed to hold Sabrina's heart. No matter what Philippe did, no matter how much he tried to win her over, it was never enough.

The memory came flooding back. Years ago, when they were both younger, Sabrina had been Oliver's girlfriend. Philippe, always the ambitious one, had been drawn to her, not just because she was beautiful, but because he had seen something in her—a spark, a vitality that he admired. He had convinced

99

himself that he deserved her more than Oliver ever could. He was the one who could give her a life, a future, security. So, he'd pursued her.

And it had worked—at least on the surface. Sabrina had married him, but deep down, Philippe knew that part of her had never stopped caring for Oliver. Even though Oliver had quietly stepped aside when Sabrina chose him, Philippe had never shaken the feeling that their marriage was built on something fragile, something incomplete.

The sound of the waitress returning with the check pulled him from his thoughts. He paid quickly, his hands shaking slightly as he signed the bill. He needed to clear his head, to focus. This wasn't about Sabrina, not right now. It was about Oliver. He had to get ahead of this before it spiraled out of control.

Pushing his chair back, Philippe grabbed his phone and stood, making his way out of the restaurant. The evening air hit him as he stepped onto the terrace, the salty breeze from the Gulf bringing no comfort. He walked to the edge of the patio, staring out at the darkening horizon. Captiva was just a short drive away, but that might as well have been another world. Oliver was there, living in some rundown house, isolated from the rest of them, exactly as he wanted it.

Philippe unlocked his phone, staring at Sabrina's message for a long moment before switching to his father's contact info. So far, he'd gone through the motions of appearing that he wanted his brother to return to New York with him, but the truth was something far less altruistic. What Philippe wanted most was to control the narrative and he couldn't do that by phone. With no other choice than to track Oliver down and then arrive on Captiva Island, Philippe was ready for the next phase in his plan. He had to make the call. He had to keep Oliver away.

The phone rang twice before his father's frail voice came through, each word laced with the exhaustion of a man nearing the end.

"Philippe," his father rasped. "Have you... have you spoken to your brother?"

Philippe swallowed, steeling himself. "I have, Dad. But he's not coming home."

A long silence followed, and Philippe could hear his father's labored breathing on the other end. He knew what was coming next. The disappointment, the regret.

"I see," his father finally said, his voice soft, broken. "I was hoping... I was hoping I could see him again. Before... before it's too late."

Philippe clenched his jaw, willing himself to stay calm. "Dad, you know Oliver. He's always been... different. He's not like us. He doesn't care about the family, or about what's important."

His father's sigh crackled through the line. "I know. But I thought, after losing his family... I thought he might want to come back. Be with us. With me."

Philippe closed his eyes, frustration boiling beneath the surface. Of course, Oliver didn't want to come back. That wasn't who he was. Oliver was always the one to leave, to abandon everything, even when their father had wanted him to stay.

"Oliver's made his decision," Philippe said, his voice firmer now. "He's cut ties. He won't be coming back, not now, not ever."

The weight of those words settled between them, heavy and final. Philippe could almost hear his father's heart breaking, and for a brief moment, guilt tugged at him. But he couldn't afford to let that guilt take root. This was about survival. His survival.

"I understand," his father said after a long pause. "I just... I had hoped."

"I know," Philippe murmured. "But it's better this way. You don't need the stress, Dad. Focus on resting. I'll be home soon to take care of you."

His father's voice grew fainter. "Thank you, Philippe. I appreciate everything you're doing. It was worth a try."

Philippe hung up the phone, staring at the screen as his

father's final words echoed in his ears. He had lied to his father. Again. He had told him what he needed to hear to keep Oliver away, to keep everything in place. But it didn't feel like a victory.

He glanced down at Sabrina's message once more, the knot in his chest tightening even more.

*Any luck with Oliver? Did you find him?*

He hesitated, his thumb hovering over the keyboard before finally typing a response.

*I'm handling it. Don't worry.*

But he was worried. He was worried that Sabrina's patience was wearing thin, that her questions would soon become actions, and that she would go looking for Oliver herself. And once that happened, everything he had built, everything he had fought for, would fall apart.

He slipped his phone back into his pocket, his thoughts swirling. He needed to act quickly. As soon as Oliver finished catering the wedding, he'd be ready to go back to New York. He couldn't let that happen. At least now the will wouldn't be updated, nor would there be any provision for Oliver going forward. Unless his brother was desperate for cash, no funds were required.

Taking a deep breath, Philippe started walking back toward the hotel. Tomorrow, he would figure out his next move. Tomorrow, he would confront Oliver. And tomorrow, he would make sure that the brother who had always walked away stayed gone for good.

Iris stood on the familiar doorstep of the Key Lime Garden Inn, the soft sounds of the island carrying on the breeze. It was a world away from the cold, bustling streets of New York City, where she had just spent the last couple of days with Alex, her now ex-boyfriend. She hadn't expected to return so soon—her original plan had been to stay through the New Year, but after everything with Alex, she needed to be back where she felt grounded. And this place, with its warm, welcoming energy, was home.

She hesitated for a moment before opening the door and stepping inside. The familiar scent of citrus and tropical flowers greeted her, instantly calming her nerves. As she set her bags down, she saw Maggie approaching from the hallway, her expression lighting up when she spotted Iris.

"Iris! You're back already!" Maggie exclaimed, hurrying over to pull her into a warm hug.

Iris smiled, though there was a slight weariness in her eyes. "Yeah, I decided to cut the trip short."

Maggie pulled back, her brow furrowing slightly. "What happened? I thought you were staying in New York through the holidays."

Iris sighed, running a hand through her hair. "That was the plan, but... things with Alex didn't exactly go the way I expected."

Maggie's expression softened with understanding as she gestured for Iris to follow her into the kitchen. "Come on, sit down. You need to tell me everything."

Iris followed, grateful for the familiarity of the inn. She took a seat at the kitchen table as Maggie poured them both a cup of tea. The warm steam curled up from the cups as Iris gathered her thoughts.

"It wasn't that we had a big fight or anything," Iris began, tracing the edge of her cup with her finger. "It's just... it became clear that we didn't really know each other all that well. We'd built up this idea of what it would be like, but the reality didn't match."

Maggie nodded, her eyes filled with compassion. "Sometimes that happens. You and Alex reconnected after so many years, and it's easy to get caught up in the past."

"Exactly," Iris said, grateful for Maggie's understanding. "We had this connection from when we were kids, but that was years ago. We've changed. And after spending a few days together in New York, it just felt... forced. Like we were trying too hard to make something work that wasn't there."

Maggie reached out and placed a comforting hand on Iris's arm. "I'm sorry it didn't work out, but it sounds like you made the right decision."

Iris nodded, feeling the weight lift slightly as she spoke. "Yeah, I think so. I just didn't want to stay there and keep pretending. So I decided to come back early. It's not like I'm heartbroken or anything—we barely knew each other, really. It was more of a... realization."

Maggie smiled gently. "Well, I'm glad you're back. We missed you around here. Oliver will be thrilled. Chelsea's wedding is tomorrow and I know he could use the help. That is, if you're up to it."

Iris chuckled, the sound light but still a bit subdued. "Are you kidding? I'd love to get back to work. I need to get back to my life and what's most important to me. I missed this place. It feels good to be home."

Maggie gave her a warm smile before standing. "Sounds good. Why don't you relax and have some eggnog or hot chocolate. The kids were having a blast on the beach earlier and came back wanting to keep Christmas alive. There are still tons of Christmas cookies too."

Iris laughed, feeling a wave of gratitude wash over her. "Thanks, Maggie. I'll do that."

As Maggie bustled out of the kitchen, Iris leaned back in her chair, letting out a long breath. The breakup with Alex wasn't the hardest thing she'd ever gone through, but it had been a reminder that sometimes the past didn't align with the present. It was freeing in a way, but still, there was that lingering sense of what could have been.

She shook the thought away and stood, deciding to take Maggie's advice and give herself a moment to relax. But first, she wanted to unpack and get into something lighter than her New York attire.

As she made her way down the hallway toward her room, she nearly bumped into Oliver, who had just come in from the garden. His usual calm demeanor seemed to have an extra layer of care today, and Iris could see him taking in her expression with quiet concern.

"Iris," Oliver said, his voice gentle. "You're back earlier than I thought."

Iris smiled. "Yeah, change of plans. I decided to come back sooner than expected."

Oliver's gaze lingered on her, understanding flickering behind his eyes. "Did something happen?"

Iris hesitated for a moment before shrugging. "Not really. Alex and I... we broke up."

There was no pity in Oliver's expression, only quiet empathy. "Do you want to talk about it?"

Iris blinked, surprised at the offer. Oliver wasn't one to pry, but the sincerity in his voice made her feel like maybe she could open up a little more. She nodded and gestured toward the inn's small lounge area just off the main hallway.

They sat down in the comfortable chairs, and for a moment, Iris wasn't sure where to begin. But Oliver put the garden basket down and waited patiently, his calm presence making it easier to speak.

"It's not that I'm heartbroken," Iris began, fiddling with the hem of her shirt. "We were never that serious, honestly. It was more of a... a chance we took. You know, we knew each other as kids, and when we reconnected, it felt like maybe it was something we should explore. But once we actually spent time together, it just didn't feel right. To be honest, I feel silly and a bit embarrassed about it."

Oliver nodded, his expression thoughtful. "No, you mustn't. Situations like that can happen sometimes. What seems right in memory doesn't always translate to reality."

"Exactly," Iris said, feeling a little lighter with each word. "We had this idea of each other, but it wasn't real. And when we were together, it just felt... forced. Like we were holding on to a version of ourselves that didn't exist anymore."

Oliver leaned forward slightly, his voice steady. "It's good that you recognized that now, before it went further."

Iris nodded, feeling reassured. "Yeah, I think so too. It's just... I don't know. Disappointing, I guess. I thought maybe it would work out. That maybe we'd recapture some of that magic from when we were kids. But it wasn't there."

Oliver smiled gently. "It's hard when the past doesn't live up to our expectations. But it sounds like you made the right choice for yourself."

Iris sighed, leaning back in her chair. "Thanks, Oliver. I guess I just needed to say it out loud to make it real."

He nodded, his eyes soft with understanding. "Anytime you need to talk, I'm here."

They sat in comfortable silence for a moment, and Iris couldn't help but feel grateful for Oliver's presence. He was always steady, always calm, and though they weren't more than friends right now, there was a closeness between them that made her feel safe.

Iris felt a sense of peace settling over her. It wasn't the kind of peace that came from having everything figured out, but the kind that came from knowing she didn't have to figure it all out alone.

And for now, that was enough.

# CHAPTER 13

*C*arrying a cup of tea, Maggie stood in the doorway of the living room, her eyes softening as she watched her daughter, Beth, curled up on the sofa with a mug of hot chocolate.

The remnants of Christmas lingered all around—the faint twinkle of lights on the tree, gift wrap strewn across the floor, and the soft hum of Christmas music still playing in the background.

For a moment, Maggie hesitated, taking in the peaceful scene. Beth had always been strong, but Maggie sensed that underneath the calm exterior, there was something on her mind.

"Hey there," Maggie said softly as she walked into the room, the warmth of her voice cutting through the quiet. "Mind if I join you?"

Beth glanced up, a small smile tugging at her lips.

"Of course, Mom. There's plenty of room."

Maggie settled into the armchair beside the sofa, tucking her feet under her. She wrapped her hands around the cup of tea she had been nursing all afternoon and gave Beth a sideways glance.

"Everything all right?" Maggie asked, her voice gentle but

probing. "You've been a bit quieter than usual today. Or did you not get enough fun on the beach? Did you see how excited the kids were to be pulled up and down on that sled?"

Beth laughed. "It reminded me of when Dad used to do that in the snow when we were little."

Maggie smiled. "I think you had the most fun of all the kids."

"That's because I thought it was more fun to intentionally fall off the sled than the ride itself."

Maggie nodded. "Of all my children you always were the one to do something different than everyone else."

Beth sat up and put her mug on the coffee table.

"That was me all right. Look at me now. I'm still doing everything different than the rest."

"What? How so?"

Beth shrugged. "I'm the only one not in a hurry to have children. Now with Chris about to be a father, I'm the last one standing."

"Is that such a bad thing?" Maggie asked.

Beth glanced at the Christmas tree, her gaze distant for a moment before she spoke.

"It's just... I don't know. Christmas is wonderful, but sometimes it brings up all these feelings, you know? It makes me think about everything that's changed."

Maggie nodded, understanding immediately. "It does that, doesn't it? The holidays always seem to bring the past and the present crashing together."

Beth leaned back into the cushions. "I've been thinking about the orchard, and everything I need to do to make it flourish again. But it's more than that. Every time we're all together, I'm reminded of all the things I've been avoiding."

Maggie didn't rush to fill the silence, giving Beth the space to gather her thoughts. She knew from years of experience that her daughter would open up when she was ready.

"I know I haven't always handled things the best way. With

Dad... and everything that happened back then." Beth's voice was soft, almost hesitant. "But now, with the family all here, I feel this weight. Like I'm supposed to have everything figured out, and I don't."

Maggie set her tea down and leaned forward slightly, her eyes never leaving Beth's. "Beth, no one expects you to have it all figured out. Least of all me. Life is messy and complicated, and the truth is, none of us ever really figure it all out."

Beth looked down, a slight frown creasing her forehead.

"But you've always seemed like you have, Mom. You've always known what to do, how to handle things."

Maggie chuckled softly. "Oh, honey. If only you knew how much of this," she gestured around them, "has been me figuring it out as I go. I'm just as much a work in progress as anyone else."

Beth smiled faintly but didn't respond right away.

Maggie leaned closer, her voice softening even more. "Is this about the orchard, or is it about something else?"

Grabbing her hot chocolate, Beth hesitated, her thumb rubbing absently along the edge of her mug. "I guess it's a bit of everything. The orchard, the family, even Dad... I just feel like I need to prove something. Like I'm supposed to make things right for everyone."

Maggie sighed softly, giving Beth's knee a reassuring squeeze. "Sweetheart, you don't have to carry all of that by yourself. What happened with your dad wasn't your burden to bear. And you don't have to fix everything for the rest of us. I hate that you were so young when you first understood what was happening with your Dad. It was a burden you carried alone, and that will haunt me for the rest of my life."

Beth blinked. Maggie could tell her daughter was surprised by the gentle firmness in her voice.

"No, Mom, you shouldn't feel that way. I think because of what happened I lost my footing for a while. I couldn't commit to work, I struggled to find my place in the world. Mostly, I hated not being in control of things, even though I was a child. Now, it feels like I'm the only one in this family who insists on moving forward at a fast pace. I know I can be difficult. Gabriel is always reminding me that not everyone deals with things the way I do. Am I that much of a bully?"

"Oh, honey, you are hardly a bully, bossy maybe, but never a bully. It's true that the rest of us move at a slower pace than you, but there's nothing wrong with you."

"What you mean is that I jump quickly before thinking things through. Is that what I did when I quit my job?"

Maggie shook her head. "No, you took time off and thought hard on what was best for you. I think you did the right thing. I think you are being too hard on yourself. You must stay true to who you are, and you're doing that."

Maggie's heart ached as she reached out and placed a hand on Beth's knee. "As far as the orchard goes, I think it's an exciting thing that you and your sister-in-law are planning, and with your father-in-law's help, I think it will be a great success."

Beth swallowed hard, her grip tightening on the mug.

"Thanks, Mom. I guess I just needed to hear that."

Maggie smiled warmly, her heart swelling with pride and love for her daughter. "That's what I'm here for. We're all in this together, Beth. You're not alone."

Beth nodded, a tear slipping down her cheek as she gave her mother a soft smile. "I love you, Mom."

Maggie leaned over and wrapped her daughter in a tight hug, her voice soft in Beth's ear. "I love you too, sweetheart. Always."

For a moment, they sat in silence, the warmth of their embrace lingering as the fire crackled softly in the background. Maggie pulled back gently, studying Beth's face as if sensing there was more to the conversation.

"Is there something else on your mind?" Maggie asked, her voice softer now, her intuition kicking in.

Beth hesitated, biting her lip before setting her mug back

down on the coffee table. She exhaled slowly. "Gabriel wants to start a family."

Maggie's eyebrows lifted slightly, but she remained silent, waiting for Beth to continue.

"And I know he's been patient with me, but I've told him that I wanted to focus on the orchard first. I didn't think I could handle both... and honestly, I wasn't sure I even wanted children. Not right away."

Maggie leaned back slightly, giving Beth space to explore her thoughts. "You sound as if that was in the past. How do you feel about it now?"

Beth stared at the Christmas tree, her hands fidgeting in her lap. "I don't know. I guess... something's changed. Watching everyone with their kids during Christmas celebration—it made me realize that maybe I do want that. The idea of having a baby... it doesn't seem as impossible as it used to."

Maggie smiled gently, understanding the internal conflict her daughter was wrestling with. "It sounds like your heart is starting to open up to the possibility."

Beth nodded slowly. "Yeah, but it's scary. I've spent so much time focused on the orchard planning and researching, and now with Gabriel's father coming back east to live with us and help us run the place... it feels like I'm finally getting things in order. I don't want to lose that momentum. But then, when I see the way Gabriel looks at me when we talk about having a baby... I don't know, Mom. I'm torn."

Maggie reached over and took Beth's hand, squeezing it gently. "You don't have to choose one over the other, you know. You're allowed to want both. The orchard will still be there, and it sounds like you'll have help. If your heart is telling you that it's time, you don't have to be afraid of following that."

Beth looked at her mother, her eyes softening with gratitude. "But what if I can't balance it all? What if I'm not cut out for motherhood and the orchard?"

Maggie laughed. "Let's see, I'm pretty sure I've heard this before. Your sister, Sarah blatantly told all of us there was no way she wanted children. She didn't even think she wanted marriage. Now, look at her, happily married to Trevor and mother to three children. Lauren is always worried she's not a good mother. Becca is scared that she won't be able to handle a new baby and also be a good doctor. There isn't a woman in this family who feels they've got it all together. I'd say you're in good company."

Beth laughed.

"You're more than capable, Bethy. You've always been strong and determined. And you won't be doing this alone. You'll have Gabriel by your side, and you've got the family here. There's no perfect formula for this, but if anyone can find the balance, it's you."

Beth let out a small, nervous laugh. "Gabriel would love to hear you say that. He's been so ready for this."

Maggie laughed softly. "Of course he has. He's going to make a wonderful father, and you, my sweet girl, will be an incredible mother. Never worry about how much a heart can hold. Women carry love, compassion, empathy, and understanding at the same time they're working and running things at home. We're strong, and you are one of the strongest. It doesn't mean you have to figure everything out right now. Take it one step at a time."

Beth's eyes filled with a mix of emotion—excitement, fear, and a touch of relief. "Maybe it's time. Maybe I'm ready for both. The orchard... and a baby."

Maggie leaned forward, wrapping her daughter in another warm hug.

"My sweet Bethy. Whatever you decide, just like the rest of us, you've got lots of women to love and support you. Just don't forget to laugh and have fun. Life always seems better when you can find humor in it."

❄

The evening air was warm and gentle, carrying the faint scent of jasmine from just outside the screened in lanai. Chelsea and Steven sat across from each other, the glow of candlelight flickering between them.

"It's hard to believe tomorrow is the big day," she said, her voice soft but filled with excitement. "It feels like we've been planning forever even though it's been only a week."

Steven reached across the table, taking her hand in his. His thumb traced slow circles on her skin. "I can't wait to marry you," he said, his eyes full of affection.

Chelsea grinned, squeezing his hand. "Me too. It feels surreal. But... there's something we haven't really talked about yet, and I suppose now's as good a time as any."

Steven raised an eyebrow, intrigued but relaxed. "Oh? What haven't we covered?"

She gave him a playful smile, though there was a hint of seriousness beneath it. "Where we're going to live. I know, I know," she added with a chuckle, "it's probably late to be bringing this up the night before the wedding, but better late than never, right?"

Steven laughed softly, his eyes twinkling. "You're right, it is a little late. But you know I'm always happy to talk about anything with you."

Chelsea's smile softened, and she glanced around the lanai, her gaze lingering on the house that had been her home for years.

"I love this place, Steven. I always imagined I'd live here forever. It's not just a house to me—it's where I feel at peace, where everything in my life just... fits." She paused, meeting his gaze. "I don't want to give it up."

Steven's expression softened as he listened, understanding immediately what she was getting at. He had always admired how rooted Chelsea was, how much she loved her home and her island life.

"I get it," he said, his voice gentle but certain. "This is your home, Chelsea. I wouldn't dream of asking you to leave it."

Chelsea's eyes brightened with relief, though a part of her still felt the need to clarify. "Are you sure? I mean, I know you have your condo, and I don't want you to feel like you're giving up something important. I just... I need to know we're on the same page."

Steven leaned forward, his fingers still tracing her hand. "I'm more than sure. That condo—well, it's convenient, but it's never felt like home the way this place does for you. I'll gladly give it up and move in with you."

For a moment, Chelsea could only stare at him, her heart swelling with happiness. "Really?" she asked, her voice filled with a mix of joy and disbelief. "You'll move in here with me?"

Steven smiled, his gaze full of warmth. "Of course. I've always loved it here. And being with you in this home—that's all I want. This place already feels like home because you're in it."

Chelsea's face lit up, and she let out a little laugh, over-whelmed with emotion. "I can't tell you how happy that makes me, Steven. I've been holding onto this house for so long, and I never imagined I'd share it with anyone. But now... I can't wait to start this new chapter with you here."

Steven stood, walking around the table to pull her into a hug. He pressed a kiss to her forehead, holding her close. "It'll be our home now," he whispered. "And I wouldn't want it any other way."

Chelsea leaned into his embrace, feeling a sense of peace settle over her. The excitement for their wedding tomorrow was bubbling just beneath the surface, but for now, this moment was perfect—just the two of them, together, in the place she loved most.

After a few moments, she pulled back slightly, a playful glint in her eye. "There is one more thing I've been thinking about..."

Steven raised an eyebrow. "Oh? Another surprise?"

Chelsea laughed. "Not really. It's just... I've been thinking about what name I'm going to go by after tomorrow."

Steven leaned against the railing, watching her closely. "I figured you might be thinking about that," he said gently. "Do you want to keep Marsden?"

Chelsea's expression softened as she thought about it. "Marsden was my late husband's name, and I've held on to it for a long time. But now... I think I'm ready to let it go. I'm ready to be Chelsea Thompson."

Steven's eyes brightened, but he remained calm. "That makes me really happy, but I want you to do what feels right for you. If you want to keep Marsden, or even go back to your maiden name, I'd be okay with that too."

Chelsea smiled at him, appreciating his understanding. "Thank you, but no. I'm ready for a new chapter, with you."

Steven grinned, his eyes sparkling with humor. "Well, that's a relief because with my business, I don't think I could handle changing my last name to Marsden," he teased.

Chelsea burst out laughing, swatting him playfully. "You're right. Thompson has a nice ring to it, and I think we'll keep it that way."

Steven chuckled, pulling her closer. "I think you're going to make the perfect Chelsea Thompson."

She smiled up at him, her heart full. "I'm ready for it, Steven. I'm ready to be your wife."

Steven kissed her softly, a lingering kiss that held the promise of all the tomorrows they were about to share. When he pulled back, he looked into her eyes with a mixture of love and excitement. "And I'm ready to be your husband. Tomorrow can't come fast enough."

# CHAPTER 14

*M*aggie's mother arrived before anyone else, and as usual, had opinions about everything. She swept into the inn like a small but determined hurricane, her sharp eyes scanning every detail of the preparations.

"Well, well," she said, eyeing the flower arrangements in the foyer. "These are nice, but you know, a touch more color wouldn't hurt. Brighten the place up a bit." Her voice carried through the room, a note of critique but also of care, even if she didn't mean it to sound that way.

Maggie, who had been arranging some last-minute details, gave her mother a quick smile. "Mom, we went for subtle elegance. No neon flowers today. I think Sanibellia did a wonderful job."

Her mother sniffed but let it pass.

"Subtle's good, I suppose. Just don't let it get boring." She turned her attention to the candles. "Well, at least you didn't forget those. A wedding without candles is like soup without salt."

Maggie chuckled to herself. "Right. Soup without salt."

Her mother pushed a bit of hair behind Maggie's ear. "You

look lovely, dear. That dress makes you look slim. I'd keep that one for future occasions."

Maggie thanked her for the compliment, but as always, it somehow still felt like a criticism.

Sarah, Trevor, and their children arrived, and the children couldn't wait to join their cousins.

Noah, almost nine, looked determined to be helpful, though his eyes kept wandering toward the big tent outside where the men were gathering. Sophia, her four-year-old daughter, was already spinning in her Christmas dress, her tiny feet tapping on the floor as she twirled. Little Maggie, the baby at just over a year old, was perched on Trevor's hip, observing everything with wide eyes.

"We made it!" Sarah called, greeting Maggie with a hug. "How's everything going?"

"So far, so good," Maggie replied, then glanced meaningfully toward her mother. "We've had our quality control inspection."

Sarah laughed, catching her grandmother's eye. "Is she giving you a hard time?" she asked Maggie.

"Oh, not at all. Just a few helpful pointers," Maggie said, dripping with sarcasm.

Maggie's mother, now standing by the window, looked over her shoulder.

"I'm just saying what everyone's thinking. Better to hear it now than after."

The women exchanged amused glances but said nothing more.

"I think we all better get upstairs in the carriage house. Chelsea is already getting dressed," Maggie added. "Lauren, Jacqui and Beth are with her."

Sarah looked at Trevor. "Why don't you take the kids down to the beach. I think the rest of the kids are there already. I want to help Mom."

Sarah and Grandma Sarah followed Maggie to the carriage

house where the mood was chaotic but fun. Despite the growing crowd in the room, the laughter and warmth between the women made it feel cozy rather than cramped. Chelsea stood in front of the mirror, her wedding gown a soft shimmer in the afternoon light. She took a deep breath, trying to let the joy of the day sink in and calm her nerves.

"I can't believe it's finally here," she whispered to Maggie, who was helping her adjust the flower in her hair.

"Just breathe," Maggie said, her hands gentle as she fixed the last few strands of Chelsea's hair into place. "Everything's perfect."

Around them, the room was alive with chatter. Her sisters Gretchen, Tess and Leah were putting the finishing touches on their own makeup. Becca, Lauren, Jacqui, Brea, Ciara, and Beth flitted about, adjusting their dresses, offering Chelsea bits of encouragement, and making sure everything was in place.

"Did you see the flowers Paolo's company brought in?" Jacqui asked as she handed Chelsea her bouquet. The soft whites and greens, with touches of lavender, were a perfect match for Chelsea's understated elegance.

"They're beautiful," Chelsea said, her voice soft. "Remind me to thank him later."

Maggie accepted her own bouquet from one of the nursery workers. It was vibrant, full of life and color. She held it up, grinning.

"Well, if nothing else, we've got some fantastic flowers to look at if the tent collapses."

The women burst into laughter, Maggie's comment pulling them out of their pre-wedding jitters. Sarah glanced over at Chelsea. "You're going to be stunning out there. Not even a tilted tent could ruin this day."

"Oh, don't remind me about the tent," Chelsea said with a small groan. "Steven and the guys have probably spent half the morning worrying about it."

Maggie's mother, from her spot by the window, chimed in. "Well, maybe if they'd measured it right the first time, we wouldn't have a tilted tent, now would we?"

The room filled with laughter again. Chelsea couldn't help but smile. Even on her wedding day, Maggie's mother managed to keep everyone entertained with her blunt observations. But she held a comment or two back, instead, offering kind words to Chelsea.

"I've come to think of you like a daughter, Chelsea Marsden, so don't you forget how much we all love you...even me. I know I can be a bit snarky sometimes, but that doesn't mean I don't love my family, and you're very much an important member. I'm very happy for you."

Chelsea smiled and hugged Grandma Sarah.

"Thank you so much. I feel very much the same."

Maggie looked on and tried not to cry.

"I've got these false eyelashes on, so I can't cry today. These things will probably fall off if I do," she said.

Beth laughed. "Mom, we're all wearing them. Can you imagine if a little crying knocked these things off our eyes? They'd be all over the place."

"Speaking of family," Jacqui said. "I thought you might want something blue."

Jacqui handed Chelsea a small stone, painted blue with the word *family* written in the center. She shrugged. "You know, something old, something new, something borrowed, something blue. This is the blue part."

Chelsea smiled and hugged Jacqui. "Thank you sweetie."

"Hey, I've got something old," Grandma Sarah announced and kissed Chelsea on the cheek. "How's that? You got a kiss from an old lady. I think that counts."

Everyone laughed, and Chelsea nodded. "I'll take it even though you're not old. I don't think I need something new. Everything I'm wearing fills that requirement," she said.

Maggie stepped up and handed Chelsea a small box. "I've got the something borrowed covered."

Chelsea opened the box and inside was a bracelet with letters spelling the word *Loved* written on the chain.

"A very wise woman gave this to me a long time ago. I was only eighteen years old."

Maggie looked over at her mother. "On the days when I forget where I came from and *who* I came from, I remember this bracelet."

"Thank you, Maggie," Chelsea said. "Help me put it on."

Maggie took the bracelet, wrapped it around Chelsea's wrist and fastened the clasp.

With tears in her eyes Grandma Sarah said, "I don't have false eyelashes on, but that doesn't mean I want to cry. Let's get this show on the road."

Meanwhile, outside, the men had gathered around the infamous tent. The slight tilt from the day before hadn't worsened overnight, but it was still... well, tilted.

Paolo, who was the best man, stood with his arms crossed, examining the structure like a man who had built many things and wasn't entirely sure this one would hold up.

"It's not leaning more than it was yesterday," he said, more to reassure himself than anyone else.

Gabriel shook the nearest pole, which swayed slightly but remained upright. "It's definitely still leaning."

"Yeah, but no more than it was," Jeff added, bouncing baby Daniel in his arms. The infant was fast asleep despite the men's ongoing discussion about structural integrity.

Trevor, with little Maggie perched on his hip, eyed the far side of the tent. "I don't know. That corner looks a little more... diagonal than I remember."

Paolo sighed. "We decided yesterday that trying to fix it would probably make it worse. Remember? We're living with it."

The groom looked over the tent with a half-smile. "I'm just saying, if the tent collapses halfway through the ceremony, I'm blaming Paolo."

"Blame the wind," Paolo shot back. "I'm just the guy who handed you the hammer."

"Pretty sure I did the hammering," Crawford said dryly, crossing his arms as he surveyed the tent. "But sure, let's blame Paolo. Always easier to blame the best man."

Gabriel walked to the far corner of the tent and gave the rope a tug. "If it was a little more tilted, we could just call it 'rustic chic.' It's almost a trend at this point."

Steven chuckled, glancing looking around the group. "So what you're all saying is… this is fine. Everything's fine."

"Oh, it's fine," Trevor agreed, a grin spreading across his face. "And if it collapses, we'll just move everything inside and tell everyone the tent was for decoration."

Paolo clapped Steven on the back. "Look at it this way: If the tent holds, your marriage will last forever."

"And if it doesn't?" Steven asked, eyebrow raised.

"Then you'll have a hell of a story for the grandkids."

Jeff adjusted baby Daniel in his arms, joining in the banter. "We could start a new business. 'The Tilted Tent Company: Events with a Twist.'"

"I like it," Gabriel said with a laugh. "We'll add a tagline: 'Our tents are always a little off, but your wedding won't be.'"

The group erupted in laughter. Even Steven, despite the mild anxiety of the day, couldn't help but laugh along. The tent might have been less than perfect, but in that moment, surrounded by his closest friends and family, it felt like a perfect symbol for the day. Slightly off-kilter, but full of love and laughter.

His friend Sebastian wheeled up to join them, his wife Isabelle behind, pushing the wheelchair.

"Did you all realize the tent is a little tilted?" Sebastian asked.

"Really?" Steven answered, amusing the group. "I hadn't noticed."

As the musicians continued setting up near the tent, the breeze caught the edge of the fabric, causing a collective pause among the men. The tent swayed ever so slightly, but it stayed upright.

"See?" Paolo said, nodding to the group. "Nothing to worry about."

"Yet," Crawford muttered, but even he couldn't keep a straight face.

Back in the carriage house, the mood was equally lighthearted. The women had finished helping Chelsea into her dress, and the final touches were being made on hair and makeup. Maggie's mother, still standing by the window, surveyed the scene with a critical eye.

"Well, I suppose it'll do," she said, and though the words were gruff, there was a twinkle in her eye that showed just how much she cared. "Just make sure you don't trip in those heels."

"Thanks, Mom," Maggie replied, rolling her eyes but smiling all the same.

"Do you think they've fixed the tent yet?" Chelsea asked, smoothing her hands over her gown one last time.

"Nope," Maggie said, chuckling. "But don't worry. If it falls, we'll just move everything inside and blame Paolo."

Chelsea laughed, her nerves finally settling. No matter what happened with the tent—or anything else—the day was already perfect in its own, imperfect way.

She took a deep breath and looked around at the women who surrounded her. These were the most important women in her life, the ones who would be with her through life's celebrations and challenges. She captured the moment in her mind and knew she'd treasure it for the rest of her life.

With one last smile, she turned toward the door. It was time.

# CHAPTER 15

*P*aolo made sure potted hibiscus and jasmine plants were placed along the path leading through the garden toward the beach.

As soon as Chelsea and Maggie stepped out of the carriage house and into the lush garden surrounding the Key Lime Garden Inn, the breeze carried the floral scent.

"Can you smell that?" Chelsea asked Maggie.

"Paolo thought of everything. I just love that man," Maggie said.

"Listen to the rustling of the palm trees. Am I crazy or is this the most perfect day?" Chelsea asked through tears that threatened to fall.

Maggie grabbed Chelsea's hand. "You're not crazy," she answered.

Maggie could feel the excitement humming in the air as they made their way down the winding path that led to the beach.

Beside her, Chelsea took a deep breath. "I can't believe it's really happening," she whispered, her voice filled with a mix of nerves and joy.

Maggie smiled, squeezing her best friend's hand gently. "You've got this. It's going to be perfect."

Chelsea, who looked every bit the radiant bride, smiled at Maggie.

"He's here."

"Who?"

"Carl. I feel his presence. I don't know what it is, it just feels with every breeze he's smiling and watching this whole thing."

Maggie swallowed, a lump forming in her throat. Her best friend had gone through so much these last several years, and Maggie couldn't be happier for Chelsea. She nodded and squeezed Chelsea's hand.

"I believe you're right, honey."

As they reached the path that led from the garden to the beach, Maggie could see the guests already seated, their faces turned toward the aisle that had been marked by a simple line of seashells and soft, white sand.

The ocean stretched beyond, its rhythmic waves providing the perfect soundtrack for the moment. The musicians, set up to the side, were playing something soft and melodic—Maggie couldn't quite place the song, but it was beautiful and calming.

Maggie's sisters, Gretchen, Tess, and Leah were seated in the front row, their smiles warm and supportive.

Leah gave Maggie a little wave, and Maggie couldn't help but smile back. This was the kind of day they had all dreamed of one filled with love, laughter, and just a little bit of that chaos they always seemed to thrive on.

Paolo, standing beside Steven at the altar, caught Maggie's eye and gave her a wink. The tent behind him—the one everyone had joked about for the past few days—was still standing, albeit with its charming tilt. Maggie stifled a laugh. They weren't getting married under it, thank goodness, but she could already imagine the jokes that would be made at the reception.

Everyone's eyes were on them, and Maggie smiled and waved

to her family. Her grandchildren wanted desperately to be in the wedding even though they had no idea what it was all about. But Maggie put her foot down and said there would be no children in the wedding. More than anything, she wanted them well-behaved and the only way to accomplish that was to keep them close to their parents and out of trouble.

"Ready?" Maggie asked Chelsea, her voice soft.

Chelsea nodded, her eyes shining with emotion. "More than ever."

Maggie took her cue, stepping onto the sandy aisle first. She could feel the soft grains beneath her feet as she made her way toward the altar, where Steven stood, waiting. His face lit up the moment he saw Chelsea, and Maggie could feel her own heart swell. This was what love looked like—simple, true, and steady, even in the midst of everything.

Once Maggie reached her spot beside Paolo, she turned to watch Chelsea begin her walk. The world seemed to hold its breath as she moved gracefully down the aisle, her smile growing with each step. Every face in the crowd was focused on her, but Chelsea's eyes were locked on Steven. Maggie tried not to cry and was glad for the tissue she held in her hand. How many times had they dreamed about this day? And now, here it was.

The ceremony itself was simple, just like Chelsea and Steven wanted it. No over-the-top decorations or grand speeches—just two people, ready to start their life together.

As Chelsea reached the altar, she handed Maggie her bouquet and then turned to Steven who took Chelsea's hands in his, his smile soft but full of love.

Paolo and Maggie stood close by, silent witnesses to the moment. The officiant began with a few words about love and commitment, but Maggie's attention was more on the couple in front of her. She knew what this day meant for Chelsea—not just a wedding, but the beginning of something new after so much heartbreak and doubt.

Steven took the ring from Paolo and then held Chelsea's hand as he slid the wedding ring on her finger.

"Chelsea, from the moment I met you, I knew there was something different about you. You're unlike anyone I've ever known. You're full of life and have so much love to give. I've watched you be the best friend to Maggie and are dearly loved by so many who are here with us today. You've brought light into my life in ways I never expected, and today, I promise to always be your partner, your support, and your greatest cheerleader. I promise to laugh with you, to cry with you, and to build a life together full of love, adventure, and growth. You are my everything, and I am so incredibly lucky to be standing here with you today."

Maggie handed Chelsea Steven's ring.

Chelsea put the ring on Steven's finger and began reciting her vows.

"Steven, you've been my rock, my best friend, and the person I didn't know I needed until you came into my life. I promise to stand by you, to love you through the highs and the lows, and to always cherish the life we build together. I can promise you that your life will never be dull with me as your wife."

Everyone laughed. Chelsea turned to look at her friends.

"See? They all agree. But seriously, you've given me more than I ever dreamed of."

Chelsea hesitated, trying not to cry. When she composed herself she continued.

"I'm incredibly blessed to be loved by you, but I want to thank you for letting me love you in return. I never thought I'd find someone who I could give my whole heart to. Loving you has been the greatest gift of my life and I can't wait to spend the rest of it with you."

There was a soft murmur from the crowd, a collective sigh of joy and contentment. Maggie could feel the emotion radiating through the guests—everyone was so invested in this moment. It wasn't lost on her that several were wiping tears from their faces.

The officiant smiled and took a deep breath before speaking.

"Love is not just a feeling, but a choice you make every day. It's in the small moments, the laughter, the shared dreams, and even in the challenges that strengthen your bond. It's the glue that binds two souls together, even when life tries to pull you apart."

He paused, allowing the words to settle over the gathering.

"Steven and Chelsea, today you are choosing to stand side by side as partners, as teammates, and as best friends for the rest of your lives. May you continue to grow together in love, supporting one another, and finding joy in the journey ahead. By the power vested in me, and in front of all your friends and family, I now pronounce you husband and wife. Steven, you may kiss your bride."

With a gleam in his eyes, Steven stepped forward, gently cupping Chelsea's face, and kissed her to the cheers and applause of the crowd.

Maggie wiped a tear from her cheek, laughing at herself.

As the couple turned to face their guests, hands clasped together, Maggie caught Chelsea's eye and winked. "You did it."

Chelsea grinned back. "We did it."

The guests rose to their feet, and Steven and Chelsea raised their joined hands in the air.

The path to the reception was set up along the beach, where the now-famous tilted tent stood proudly in the background. As everyone made their way toward it, Maggie couldn't help but laugh at the sight. Despite the jokes, despite the nerves, it had all turned out perfectly.

Gretchen, Tess, and Leah caught up to Maggie as the crowd began to mingle, all of them laughing and exchanging opinions on the event.

"That tent," Tess said, shaking her head. "If it holds for the reception, I'll be amazed."

"Well, Paolo's confident," Maggie replied, glancing at her husband, who was already checking the stakes one last time. "And if it doesn't, we'll just dance on the beach."

Leah grinned. "I'd like to see that."

As the sun began to set, casting golden hues over the water, Maggie looked out at the scene before her. Chelsea and Steven, now mingling with their guests, looked so at ease, so right together. The music, the laughter, the soft hum of conversations —it was all exactly as it should be.

Paolo appeared at her side, his hand resting on her shoulder. "You okay?"

Maggie smiled up at him, leaning into his familiar warmth.

"Better than okay. It's been a perfect day."

"Even with the tent?"

"Especially with the tent."

They both laughed, and Maggie glanced once more at Chelsea, who caught her eye from across the beach. For a moment, time seemed to slow, and all Maggie could feel was gratitude—gratitude for this day, for these people, and for the love that had brought them all together.

She looked up at the sky and smiled. Chelsea was right, Maggie could feel Carl's smile. Her heart swelled with the understanding that her best friend was truly blessed to be loved by two wonderful men. It was, in fact, the blessing she had always prayed for, and she felt immense gratitude that she was here to witness it all.

# CHAPTER 16

*a*s the sun dipped lower over the horizon, casting warm hues of pink and orange across the sky, the guests began making their way under the infamous tilted tent.

The jokes about its precarious lean were already making the rounds, but it stood firm, much to everyone's relief. It didn't stop the men from looking at each other every time the wind blew.

The soft strains of music floated through the air as Iris and Oliver, the culinary masterminds behind the evening's food, wheeled out trays of dishes that immediately set stomachs rumbling.

Maggie smiled as she watched her family gather around the tables set up along the perimeter of the tent. There were only a handful of people here, really—just family and close friends—but the intimate nature of the gathering made it all the more special.

Iris directed Millie, who was bustling around in her usual efficient manner, her arms loaded with plates and silverware.

"Millie, can you make sure the bartender has everything he needs?"

Millie gave a quick nod, already on her way to check in with the bartender. Maggie smiled at how seamlessly everyone had fallen into their roles, even at an event like this. Iris and Oliver were a well-oiled machine in the kitchen, and Millie, though normally on housekeeper duties, seemed perfectly content to lend a hand in serving tonight.

The buffet spread was nothing short of magnificent. Tropical salads with avocado and mango, fresh seafood from the surrounding waters, grilled vegetables, and an assortment of freshly baked bread and desserts—everything was as bright and vibrant as the setting itself. Oliver had outdone himself, as usual, and Iris's touches made it all feel so personal.

"Looks amazing, doesn't it?" Sarah said, coming to stand beside her mother as they surveyed the buffet. "Iris really knows how to make things beautiful."

Maggie nodded. "She does. And Oliver's food—well, I'm just glad I skipped lunch." She laughed, already eyeing the dishes with anticipation.

As more guests began to line up at the buffet, Maggie spotted Steven and Chelsea at the front, both laughing and talking with their guests as they filled their plates. They looked so happy, so at ease, that Maggie couldn't help but feel a surge of joy herself. This was their day, and it had gone off without a hitch—even if the tent was still a little tilted.

"Think the tent's going to make it?" Trevor asked as he walked by, balancing two plates—one for him and another for Sophia, who was trailing after him, dressed in her twirly Christmas dress and eyeing the dessert table.

Maggie laughed. "I think we're safe for now. But keep an eye on that pole just in case."

Trevor grinned. "I'll keep my eye on it. Maybe if it does fall, we'll have an even better story to tell."

Paolo wandered over next, his plate already stacked with food.

"The tent's not going anywhere," he said confidently. "I double-checked the stakes before everyone came in."

Maggie raised an eyebrow. "You? Mr. 'It'll Hold, Don't Worry About It' actually double-checked?"

Paolo shrugged, his grin giving him away. "I like to be thorough."

As the evening wore on, the tent became a hub of lively conversation, laughter, and clinking glasses. The playlist that had started with soft background music slowly transitioned to more upbeat tunes as the night progressed. The first notes of a 1970s dance song floated through the air, and a collective ripple of excitement passed through the guests.

"Oh, this is my song!" Leah called out, grabbing Tess and Gretchen by the hands. "Come on!"

Without hesitation, the three of them made their way to the small makeshift dancefloor that had been set up away from the buffet area. Chelsea's sisters had always been the first to get up and dance at any family gathering, and tonight was no exception. Their laughter was contagious, and within minutes, more people were joining them.

"I'll be right back," Maggie said to Paolo, who was still seated and happily munching on dessert. "I think I need to join the ladies."

Paolo waved her off with a grin. "Have fun."

Maggie made her way to the dancefloor, where Leah, Tess, and Gretchen were already busting out moves that could only be described as 1970s-inspired. The music thumped through the speakers, the beat infectious, and soon Maggie found herself lost in the rhythm of the night. Chelsea joined in moments later, her arms in the air as she twirled to the music, her face radiating pure joy.

"I love these old songs!" Chelsea declared.

"I knew the 70s playlist would get you all up on the dance-floor," Maggie said.

"You know me too well."

As the song continued, even the kids joined in, twirling

around the edges of the dancefloor with their own playful spins. Sophia giggled as Noah tried to show her how to dance, and their cousins Olivia, Lilly, Quinn and Cora joined them.

The reception was a perfect blend of celebration and relaxed enjoyment. Everyone was mingling, dancing, and savoring the food, which Iris and Oliver had artfully arranged in a way that felt both elegant and inviting. Millie, ever the multitasker, was darting between tables, refilling water and making sure everyone had everything they needed.

As the evening continued, Maggie found herself standing off to the side for a moment, just watching it all unfold. She could see Paolo, now talking with Steven, both men looking relaxed and content as they sipped their drinks. Iris was laughing with Becca near the buffet, and Oliver had finally stepped out from behind the scenes, enjoying a plate of his own food.

Even the guests who had been more reserved at the start of the evening were now fully immersed in the celebration, swaying to the music or chatting animatedly at their tables.

Everything was perfect, even if Isabelle Barlowe kept reminding everyone that it was she and her husband, Sebastian, who introduced the newlyweds. Taking credit once was acceptable, but by the fifth time, Maggie tried not to roll her eyes every time Isabelle cornered a guest with her story.

Chelsea, catching Maggie's eye from across the dancefloor, broke away from the group and made her way over.

"How are you holding up, Matron of Honor?" she asked, her smile as radiant as ever.

Maggie laughed. "I'm great, except my feet are killing me. It's possible I made a bad choice with these shoes, but I couldn't resist these beauties. How about you? Feeling like a married woman yet?"

Chelsea grinned. "Still sinking in, but it feels pretty good so far."

They both stood for a moment, watching the party swirl

around them. Maggie couldn't help but feel a deep sense of satisfaction. Everything had come together exactly as it was meant to, and despite the small quirks—like the tent—it all felt right.

"I have to say," Chelsea began, glancing toward the now-tilted-but-still-standing tent, "that tent's become a bit of a character at this wedding."

Maggie laughed. "It's definitely memorable. But hey, at least it didn't collapse."

"Yet," Chelsea teased.

"Let's not jinx it."

Paolo joined them, looking in the direction of his sister Ciara and her husband Crawford. "Did you see who just showed up?"

"Who?"

"Crawford's son, Finn and his girlfriend, Jillian."

"Oh, I've got to go say hello. I didn't know they were coming. We should make sure to have a place setting for them. I'll talk to Millie," Maggie said.

Maggie waved to them as she and Paolo made their way to the group.

"Finn! I'm so glad to see you. Hello, Jillian, it's so good to see you both."

"Hello, Maggie," Finn said, hugging her. "No, please don't bother. I was looking for my dad and when I couldn't find him, thought I'd check here. I had no idea you were hosting a wedding."

"I can't believe my eyes. Chelsea got married?" Jillian asked.

Maggie laughed. "I don't think she can believe it either."

"That's wonderful," Finn added.

"Join us," Maggie said. "There's plenty of food. I'm sure Chelsea would love to see you."

"Yes, I'll get a couple of extra chairs," Paolo said. "I'll be right back."

"Are you sure?" Finn asked.

"Absolutely. Spend some time with your father. It's been too long," Maggie answered.

"Thanks, Maggie," Jillian added.

Once Paolo got them settled, Maggie walked back to Chelsea. "Do you see what I see?" she asked.

"Yes, Finn and Jillian came. I'll go say hello," Chelsea responded.

Maggie grabbed her arm. "No, wait. Not yet. Look at Jillian and Finn's left hands."

Chelsea's face lit up. "They're married?"

Maggie smiled and nodded. "In about five minutes, something tells me Crawford is about to get the shock of his life."

When he returned, Maggie whispered to Paolo about her observation. "I wonder how Crawford will take it," Maggie said.

Paolo smiled. "Wonder no more. Take a look."

Crawford and Ciara hugged Finn and Jillian and then Crawford called Luke, Joshua, and Becca over to congratulate their brother. Everyone was looking at Jillian's ring.

"By the looks of things, everyone is happy about it," Chelsea added.

"I should let Sarah know. Jillian's sister Emma is her best friend. I'm sure she'll want to know." Maggie turned to Chelsea. "Do you need anything?"

Chelsea smiled. "Only my husband. I think it's time I get him on the dancefloor."

As the night drew on, the energy of the reception only grew. More 70s hits played, each one drawing more people to the dancefloor. Even the older guests, who had initially stayed seated, were now clapping along or tapping their feet, unable to resist the infectious beat.

Finally, as one particularly lively song ended, Maggie found herself back at her table, catching her breath. Paolo was sitting beside her, looking thoroughly entertained. "You're quite the dancer," he said, handing her a glass of water.

"I learned from the best," Maggie replied. "Can I convince you to get up there with me?"

Paolo chuckled. "I'm not sure these knees are what they used to be, but I'll give it a shot."

As they reached the dancefloor, the tempo shifted, and a soft, slow melody began to fill the room. The crowd seemed to sense the change, couples pairing off, swaying gently to the rhythm. Maggie smiled up at Paolo, her hand resting on his shoulder as his arm wrapped around her waist.

"You planned this, didn't you?" Paolo teased, his voice low, but full of affection.

Maggie laughed softly. "I might've had a word with the DJ to slow it down. I know you're getting better all the time, but technically, you're still recuperating from the surgery."

"Great. I can use that excuse for why I can only slow dance," he teased.

They swayed together in comfortable silence, the music wrapping around them like a warm embrace.

As the song played on, they moved slowly, lost in their own world. Paolo pressed a gentle kiss to the top of her head, and Maggie closed her eyes, feeling utterly at peace in his arms.

When she lifted her head she looked into the crowd and found Chelsea and Steven staring into each other's eyes. Content that she'd pulled off a magical wedding for her best friend, Maggie rested her head on Paolo's shoulder again and smiled.

# CHAPTER 17

*O*liver stood at the door of the inn, his hand resting on the door knob, hesitating as the evening breeze brushed against his skin. The island had quieted down after Chelsea's wedding, and the stillness of the night only magnified the noise in his head. Philippe's arrival had stirred something inside him that he hadn't wanted to face, not now, not ever. But there it was, nagging at him, a shadow from the past he had worked so hard to escape.

Behind him, the faint clatter of dishes and the hum of kitchen activity broke the silence. He glanced back, catching sight of Iris as she wiped down the counters, her focus intent on cleaning up the remnants of the evening. The wedding had been beautiful, but for Oliver, it had been a reminder of what he had lost.

He turned his attention to the ring on his finger, the simple gold band he still wore even after all this time. He slipped it off, holding it between his thumb and forefinger, twirling it absently as memories of his wife flooded back. The weight of it felt heavier tonight.

Iris noticed him standing in the doorway, her brow furrowing in concern as she wiped her hands on a towel and approached.

"You're leaving tomorrow?" she asked softly, sensing the heaviness in his posture.

Oliver nodded, slipping the ring back onto his finger. "Yeah, I've got to meet Philippe at the Marriott, and then I assume I'll fly to New York."

Her eyes dropped briefly to his hand, where the ring rested, before looking at his face. She smiled, but it was tinged with a quiet curiosity.

"You've been... different tonight. I can tell something's bothering you."

Oliver sighed, running a hand through his hair. He wasn't ready to dive into all that, not with Iris, not with anyone. But Chelsea's wedding had brought it all to the surface—the love, the loss, the reminder of what he no longer had. He shifted slightly, his fingers grazing the ring again. "I've just got a lot on my mind."

Iris nodded and crossed her arms, leaning against the counter, her tone soft but probing. "Does it have to do with your brother?"

He looked away, his jaw tightening as he thought of Philippe, of their father, of all the years that had been lost. But it wasn't just Philippe weighing on him tonight. The wedding had cracked open a wound he thought had started to heal.

"It's more than that," he admitted quietly, his voice barely above a whisper.

Iris tilted her head, waiting, her patience a quiet invitation for him to speak. She had a way of listening, not pushing, just being there. And for some reason, it made it harder for him to keep it all bottled up.

"You know the story of my wife and sons?" he said after a long pause, his fingers twirling the ring again.

Iris nodded slowly. She knew bits and pieces of his story, the tragedy that had driven him to Captiva Island, but he rarely talked about it. She didn't push him then, and she wasn't going to push him now. She just waited, letting the moment unfold.

Oliver took a deep breath, staring at the ring on his finger.

"It was a little more than a year ago now but it feels like it was just yesterday." His voice wavered, and he clenched his hand into a fist, the weight of the ring pressing into his skin.

"I wear this ring because I feel like I'm still married to her. She's still my wife."

Iris didn't say anything at first, just stepped closer, her presence a steadying force in the room. She glanced at his hand, understanding now why he always wore the ring, why he seemed so distant tonight. The wedding had stirred up memories he wasn't ready to confront.

"It's perfectly understandable. You loved her very much," Iris said softly, her tone not a question but a simple truth. "You always will, and that's a good thing."

He didn't say anything but nodded.

Iris could hear the guilt in his voice, the weight of a grief that he carried with him every day. She wanted to reach out, to comfort him, but something in his posture told her he wasn't ready for that. So, instead, she spoke gently, her voice filled with quiet compassion. "There's no time limit with grief. The pain never truly leaves you."

He nodded, swallowing hard as he slipped the ring back on his finger. "Sometimes I think I should take it off, you know? Move on. But... it doesn't feel right."

Iris smiled softly, her eyes kind as they met his.

"It's not about the ring, Oliver. It's about what's in your heart. You'll know when you're ready."

Oliver's gaze met hers, and for a moment, the weight of everything he'd been holding on to seemed to lift, just a little. She didn't pity him. She didn't try to tell him how to feel. She just stood there, offering him her presence, and it was enough.

"I'm sorry," he said, shaking his head slightly. "I didn't mean to unload all of this on you."

"Don't apologize," Iris replied, her voice firm but gentle. "I'm here for you whenever you want to talk and...even if you don't."

Oliver hesitated, feeling the pull of those words. He wasn't used to letting people in, not since the accident. But Iris... she was different. She wasn't trying to fix him, just offering a space where he could be vulnerable, where he didn't have to pretend that everything was okay.

"Will you be okay for the next few days while I'm away?"

"Yes, of course. I can handle whatever is needed. I think we've got a couple of guests arriving. They'll be here for the island's New Year's Eve festivities."

The thought of facing his brother, of rehashing the past with him, felt like too much right now. But he also knew that he couldn't keep avoiding it indefinitely.

"I should get to bed," he said, his voice low, though he didn't make a move to leave just yet.

Iris nodded, understanding in her gaze. "If you ever want to talk... about anything, I'm here."

Oliver's lips twitched in a small, grateful smile. "Thanks, Iris. I really appreciate it."

For a brief moment, they stood there in comfortable silence, the connection between them deepening in the quiet. There was no need for more words; the unspoken understanding was enough. Oliver didn't know what the future held for him, but tonight, in this moment, he felt a little less alone.

As he finally turned to go, he felt the weight of the ring on his finger, a reminder of the past he couldn't quite let go of yet. But maybe, just maybe, he didn't have to carry it all by himself anymore.

As Maggie shifted in her chair, she watched as Iris and Oliver lingered by the large oak tree in the distance, and then made their way back to the inn's kitchen.

Maggie smiled as Iris and Oliver's heads were bent toward each other, locked in conversation. Oliver said something that made Iris laugh—a soft, genuine sound that floated across the garden to where Maggie sat.

As the two chefs carried platters inside, Maggie followed their movements and was startled when Paolo sat next to her.

"Oh, you scared me!" Maggie said.

Paolo placed his hand on his wife's shoulder and laughed.

"Were you expecting someone else?" he teased.

Catching the look on his wife's face. He raised an eyebrow, his curiosity piqued. "What's that smile for?"

Maggie turned her head slightly, making sure Oliver and Iris were still far enough away not to hear. She lowered her voice to a whisper. "I think there's something going on between those two."

Paolo followed her gaze to where Oliver and Iris stood. He leaned back in his chair, considering them for a moment. "You think so? Oliver's been pretty closed off since... well, you know. And Iris—she's always been so focused on her work here. Besides, I think she's still upset about Alex."

Maggie shook her head, keeping her voice hushed. "I know that, but she and Oliver have become pretty close lately. I think he feels he can confide in her. I know they're friends but lately, I've noticed a shift. There's a softness to how Oliver looks at her. And Iris... she's always finding an excuse to be around him. The way she smiles when he's nearby, it's different."

Paolo chuckled, folding his arms. "What am I going to do with you? You see romance and love in everyone. Maybe you're seeing something you want to see...nothing more."

"Not love," Maggie replied quickly, "but something's brewing. Something gentle, like the start of a fire that just needs a little kindling. They've both been through so much, and maybe they're finding comfort in each other."

Paolo tilted his head, taking in his wife's words. He glanced at Iris again, watching the way she stood next to Oliver, her body language relaxed but attentive. "Iris has always been strong. She doesn't seem like the type to let her guard down easily."

"That's exactly why this is interesting," Maggie said, her excitement tempered by a sense of protectiveness. "Oliver's been carrying the weight of his grief for so long. Losing his wife and boys... I don't think he's let himself even imagine moving on. But maybe Iris is helping him see that there's more to life than his pain."

Paolo nodded, sensing the gravity in Maggie's voice. "She's good for him, then."

"I think so," Maggie whispered, her eyes never leaving the pair. "But it's delicate. Oliver still wears his wedding ring. I've seen him twirling it in his hand when he thinks no one's looking. And Iris... well, she's been through her own heartaches. It's like they're both standing on the edge of something but are too afraid to take the leap."

Paolo leaned in closer, his voice matching Maggie's quiet tone. "How about my wife and I go upstairs to bed and leave this snooping for another day? Everyone has gone home or gone to bed. I say we do the same. If I leave you here, before midnight you'll be nudging them into a relationship before they're ready."

Maggie smiled, shaking her head gently. "No nudging. Not yet, at least. I think they need to figure this out on their own. Pushing too hard might scare them both away from something good. Besides, they're already finding reasons to be around each other. We'll just stay out of it for now."

Paolo smirked. "I'll believe that when I see it. That's not your usual style. You love a good matchmaking scheme."

Maggie laughed softly. "I do, but this is different. It's more fragile. They've both had enough pain in their lives. If this is going to happen, it needs to be on their terms, in their time."

They sat in silence for a moment, the evening breeze rustling through the garden. The sounds of the twinkling windchimes blowing in the distance.

Maggie reached for Paolo's hand, giving it a gentle squeeze. "I just hope Oliver can let go of the past, you know? He deserves happiness, even if he doesn't believe it yet."

Paolo's thumb brushed over her knuckles, his gaze thoughtful. "He does. And maybe Iris will be the one to help him see that."

Maggie smiled at her husband's words, her heart warming at the thought. She had always believed in the power of love, even in the most unexpected places. And perhaps, Oliver and Iris were beginning to discover that for themselves.

As the garden grew quieter, Maggie felt a sense of peace settle over her. The future was uncertain, as it always was, but sitting here with Paolo, watching two people slowly find their way to each other, made her hopeful for what was to come.

She got up from her chair and let Paolo wrap his arm around her waist.

"I think you're right, though. Whatever will happen will happen. I'm ready for bed. It was a wonderful wedding, wasn't it?"

Paolo smiled and nodded. "Honey, it was the best, and I know Chelsea and Steven appreciate it."

Before they reached the carriage house, a loud noise came from the beach. They ran toward the sound and Gabriel and Jeff came running outside to join them.

When they reached the beach, they found the tent had completely imploded and was lying flat on the sand.

Maggie put her hand over her mouth to suppress a chuckle, but when they all stood looking at the mess in front of them, not one could hold back their laughter.

"I can't believe this thing finally came down," Jeff said.

"Well, no harm done. Everyone is gone," Paolo said. "I'll call the place and have them come remove it in the morning."

Exasperated with Paolo, Maggie put her hands on her hips.

She was about to voice her frustration, but the look on Paolo's face stopped her.

She knew he'd felt bad that he'd made a huge mistake ordering the tent from the wrong company. No amount of admonishing him now would help the situation. Instead, she put her arm around his waist and kissed his cheek.

# CHAPTER 18

Oliver pulled into the parking lot of the Sanibel Marriott, his stomach twisting in a familiar knot of tension. Philippe had texted him the room number, and Oliver hesitated for a moment. His fingers gripped the steering wheel as he debated turning around and driving back to the inn. But he knew he couldn't avoid this, not if he wanted to lay the past to rest.

The breeze carried the scent of the nearby ocean as he locked the car and walked inside. The hotel lobby's muted light cast a warmth that felt oddly comforting. Yet, as he stepped into the elevator and pressed the button for the fourth floor, his chest tightened. This wasn't a casual visit. There would be no easy conversation with Philippe, and he knew his brother hadn't come to Captiva with an olive branch.

Outside Philippe's room, Oliver took a steadying breath and knocked. The door swung open almost immediately, revealing his brother's figure framed in the warm light from inside. Philippe's expression was unreadable, a mixture of surprise and something colder, like he'd been preparing himself for this moment as well.

"Oliver," Philippe greeted, voice crisp, as he gestured for him to come in.

Inside, the room was dimly lit, the quiet hum of the air conditioning the only sound until the door clicked shut behind them. Oliver took a seat on the arm of a chair near the window, and Philippe settled across from him, leaning back with his arms crossed, his gaze calculating.

"How was the wedding? Did you get everything done that you wanted?" he asked.

Oliver nodded. "It was fine. I'd rather skip the small talk, if you don't mind. You wanted to talk, so let's talk."

Philippe's lips twisted into a half-smile. "I thought you might want to know what's going on with Father."

Oliver nodded, trying to keep his expression neutral. "I have to assume it's not good or you wouldn't be here. Is he dying?"

A flicker of something passed through Philippe's eyes, something Oliver couldn't quite read, though he was accustomed to his brother's guarded expressions.

"He's not himself. Hasn't been for a while," Philippe said, his tone almost too casual. "The doctors say it's his mind... he hardly recognizes anyone. I thought you should know what you're walking in to if you choose to come home."

Oliver absorbed this, the familiar sting of resentment creeping into his chest. Philippe's tone was deliberately matter-of-fact, the underlying message clear. It would be pointless, perhaps even humiliating, to go back. Philippe had always known how to twist words to cast doubt in the subtlest of ways, and Oliver wasn't about to let him win this round.

"I can handle it," Oliver replied evenly, his gaze steady. "Now that you told me, you can return home. I'll fly up in the next day or two. That was your intention, am I right? I am allowed to say a final goodbye to my father, don't you agree?"

Philippe's smile tightened. "Of course. I wouldn't be surprised if he was more alert at the sight of his favorite son returning to the fold. I'm sure our father would love to see you give up that little chef job you're so attached to and return to the family business. He's said as much."

Oliver's jaw clenched at the insinuation. "I doubt Father said anything like that. He was never particularly invested in what I did."

Philippe's eyebrows rose slightly, as if amused. "You'd be surprised. Father was... disappointed when you left. Said it was a waste of talent. Of course, he thought you'd come back eventually, but here you are."

Oliver's gaze hardened. "Maybe that's for the best. I didn't exactly fit in with the family's... values."

Philippe let out a short, cold laugh. "Family values, Oliver? Is that what you think kept you away? I'd say it had more to do with... certain other distractions." He paused, his gaze flickering with an unmistakable glint of malice. "We both know you've always had a habit of getting... sidetracked."

The implication was as clear as if Philippe had spelled it out. Oliver felt a surge of anger but kept his tone controlled. "If you're talking about Sabrina, you've already won that round. Or have you forgotten?"

Philippe's smile faded, replaced by a hint of something darker. "Don't kid yourself. Sabrina didn't leave you because of me. She left because she knew you'd never make anything of yourself outside of Father's control."

Oliver's eyes flashed. He fought to keep his composure. "Sabrina chose to be with you because you manipulated her, just like you've manipulated Father and the entire family. It's how you work, Philippe—always pulling the strings and stepping over people to get what you want."

Philippe leaned forward, his voice cold. "Let's not play the victim here, Oliver. You left. You threw everything away, and that was your choice."

Oliver leaned back, crossing his arms. "I didn't leave the

family. I left the toxicity that comes with it—the scheming, the controlling, the constant manipulation." He let his gaze drop to the polished floor, then back to Philippe, the bitterness still there but tempered by years of restraint. "Maybe that's why I'm better off out of it."

Philippe studied him for a moment, the calculating gleam in his eyes returning. "Funny, I'd think you'd be grateful to have a chance to come back, even if Father doesn't quite remember who you are these days."

He shrugged, as if the thought amused him. "He's at least given me the responsibility to look after family matters. And I'll tell you this—he doesn't need a 'chef' wandering in and taking advantage of his decline."

"Is that why you're here?" Oliver asked, his voice low. "To remind me how little I matter to this family, or is it something else? Are you afraid of what might happen to your inheritance if I return?"

Philippe's smile returned, colder now. "Actually, I'm here to make sure you know exactly where you stand. Father may not remember you, but he certainly hasn't left you in his will. That position belongs to me—and my wife. He cut you out years ago and I haven't seen him change the will since."

The mention of Sabrina made Oliver's stomach churn. He'd long ago let her go, moved on, fallen in love again, and built something real...a family.

Sabrina had come from a wealthy family herself, raised with all the trappings of privilege that made her feel at ease among people like his father. As a young man, Oliver had been swept up in her charm and beauty. Sabrina had set her sights on him, undeterred by the fact that he was indifferent to the wealth and status that defined her world. But as he'd distanced himself from the family business, focused more on cooking than the boardroom, he sensed Sabrina pulling away.

Eventually, her resolve crumbled, her ambitions threatening

to leave her behind. When Philippe's flirtations began, she hadn't seemed to resist. By then, Oliver had lost the will to fight to keep her, and as he withdrew further, she drifted into Philippe's orbit. This transition felt like betrayal only later, when it was too late to do anything about it.

The wedding had been lavish, everything she likely dreamed of, complete with a high-society guest list and Philippe beside her. To Oliver's horror, he'd been forced to act as best man, giving a hollow toast as he watched his brother marry the woman he'd once considered the love of his life. Though he'd masked his hurt, it was more his pride that was wounded than his heart. What had stung wasn't the loss of Sabrina, but the confirmation that Philippe always took what he wanted, never caring what or who was destroyed in his wake.

And yet, from what he'd heard, Philippe's marriage had been a lonely one, devoid of the warmth and closeness that Sabrina once claimed she wanted. If she'd believed wealth and power would fill that void, she'd been mistaken. But knowing this, Oliver felt no satisfaction, only a quiet reminder of how little he still had in common with Philippe and the life Sabrina had chosen.

Philippe smirked, as if reading his thoughts. "Oh, yes," he continued, catching the change in Oliver's expression. "Sabrina sends her regards. She was... concerned you might come back with grand ideas of family reconciliation. Yes," Philippe said, his smile predatory. "She remembers you fondly, I'm sure. She's worried, you know, about the inheritance." He leaned forward voice dropping to a conspiratorial whisper. "She's been urging me to... keep an eye on you. Make sure you don't interfere."

Oliver felt his jaw tighten, the anger simmering just below the surface. "You can tell Sabrina she has nothing to worry about. I'm not interested in your money or your games. I'm going to see Father, not to deal with your or your wife's petty insecurities."

Philippe leaned back, a hint of satisfaction in his eyes. "Good. Because the family doesn't need another reminder of why you left. Father's legacy is better served by those who understand its... value."

The words stung, but Oliver kept his face impassive. He could see the game Philippe was playing, twisting the narrative to make Oliver seem like an outsider—a reminder that no matter what he did, he would never be one of them. But this was precisely why he had left. The manipulations, the endless jockeying for approval—he wanted no part of it.

As he stood, Oliver's mind drifted to a time when family had meant something warmer. His mother had been the heart of their home, her laughter filling every corner as she taught him to pick tomatoes and stir sauces in the family kitchen. She had been the one to encourage him to find pride in the little things, to savor the moment instead of rushing toward the next achievement. Her presence had been a quiet strength, a calm voice guiding him to be his own person, and he had clung to those memories when everything else fell apart.

After her death, he became a stranger in his own family. His father's indifference and Philippe's disdain cast him as an outsider in the life he once knew. School was no better. Without his mother's guidance, he found himself lost and often ridiculed, his anxiety giving way to a stutter that made him the target of cruelty he hadn't known existed. But in the kitchen, in the garden, he found peace. Cooking and growing things brought him back to her, to the part of himself that she had nurtured.

Now, as he walked toward the door, he felt that familiar resolve settle over him. Philippe's words might have stung, but they only reminded him of how far he had come and how much he had built on his own. He turned to look at his brother again.

"You didn't have to come all the way to Captiva Island to tell me about Father. Why did you?"

Philippe smirked and then shrugged. "I needed to see your face when I told you about him. I need to know that you won't stay long when you visit him." He nodded slightly. "I'm satisfied your visit will be brief."

Oliver chuckled. "You can't control everything. What you see in front of you is a man who has moved on and far away from the very thing you covet...money. You don't have to worry about me, but I can't say as much for Father. What he does with his money is his choice...not yours."

Oliver opened the door to leave as Philippe called out. "We'll see about that," he said.

Leaving Philippe and his schemes behind, Oliver stepped out into the night, the cool air a balm against the tension of the evening. He might never have the family's approval, but he knew he didn't need it. For the first time, he was ready to face his father, not as the son who left, but as the man he had become.

# CHAPTER 19

Chelsea leaned back in her chair on the porch, the soft clink of plates and cups nearby reminding her of the delicious late breakfast she and Steven had just enjoyed together. The table was still dotted with remnants of fresh fruit, flaky pastries, and an empty coffee pot—a breakfast they'd lingered over, savoring each other's company and the quiet of the day after their wedding.

Steven leaned back beside her, stretching his arms with a contented sigh. "Now that," he said, a playful glint in his eye, "was a breakfast worth waiting for. I don't think I've eaten that much in ages."

Chelsea laughed, taking a sip of water and setting her glass down. "Well, we've earned it after yesterday. And now we can just relax... at least for a little while."

Steven smiled, reaching across the table to take her hand in his. He traced gentle circles over her knuckles, his expression softening. "The wedding was wonderful, wasn't it?"

"It really was," Chelsea murmured, a warmth filling her heart at the memory of it all. "Everything turned out perfectly. Even the tent held up, despite that wind."

Steven laughed, shaking his head. "I still can't believe that thing didn't blow away. For a moment there, I thought we'd all be chasing it down the beach."

Chelsea grinned, recalling the scene—Steven, Gabriel, Paolo, Trevor, and Jeff holding down the tent poles like they were wrestling a beast. "You all did a fantastic job. Watching you and the guys scramble to keep it from taking flight was... well, unforgettable."

Steven chuckled, a hint of pride in his voice. "That was teamwork at its finest. I don't think any of us were willing to let that tent get the better of us." He paused, a playful smirk crossing his face. "But watching you walk down the aisle, Chelsea—that was the real highlight. You were absolutely stunning."

Chelsea felt warmth creep into her cheeks, and she squeezed his hand. "Thank you, Steven. And you were... well, let's just say I felt like the luckiest woman in the world." She looked down at her wedding ring, marveling at how right it felt to be here, beside him, as his wife.

They sat in contented silence for a few moments, each of them savoring the memories of the day before. Finally, Chelsea let out a small sigh, glancing at the packed breakfast dishes and the bags by the door.

"We should probably get packing soon," she said, glancing at him with a smile. "Our honeymoon won't wait for us forever."

Steven raised an eyebrow, a teasing smile playing at his lips. "Oh, I don't know. I was rather hoping we'd just stay here forever, lounging around and forgetting about all our plans."

Chelsea laughed. "Tempting, but I think Hawaii is calling our names. Still, there's one little bit of business I need to take care of before we go."

Steven tilted his head, curious. "Oh?"

She nodded, a hint of seriousness entering her gaze. "It's about my sisters. Well, specifically Gretchen."

Steven sat up a little straighter, his expression attentive. "What's going on with Gretchen?"

Chelsea sighed, glancing away for a moment before looking back at him. "Gretchen's planning to tell Leah and Tess that she's not going back to Key West. She wants to stay here, closer to all of us, but she's worried about how they'll react. They've already made a few comments that... haven't exactly been supportive."

Steven let out a low whistle, nodding thoughtfully. "I see. I can understand why she'd be anxious. Tess and Leah don't exactly hold back on their opinions."

Chelsea smiled wryly. "Exactly. So I invited them over this afternoon for some iced tea and lemonade. I want to be there for her, just in case things get... heated. Gretchen asked for me to help keep things calm, and well, I know how our sisterly 'discussions' can sometimes turn out."

Steven chuckled, squeezing her hand in understanding. "You're a good sister, Chelsea. Gretchen's lucky to have you backing her up."

Chelsea leaned against him, resting her head on his shoulder. "I hope it helps. I just want her to feel like she's making the right choice. Staying here, being with family—it makes sense to me, but I know she's looking for their acceptance, too."

Steven placed a gentle kiss on the top of her head. "They'll come around. And with you there to keep things grounded, it'll go smoother. You're like the glue holding everyone together."

They stayed like that for a few moments, Chelsea finding comfort in the quiet rhythm of his breathing. After a while, she lifted her head with a soft smile, glancing over at the bags waiting by the door.

"Well," she said, straightening, "I know we leave day after tomorrow, but I think we should get to packing. Hawaii awaits, and if we don't get started soon, we'll end up forgetting something important."

Steven stood and stretched, his face lighting up. "I'm ready.

Besides, I made a detailed packing list, so we're all set. I've accounted for everything we'll need—socks, sandals, sunscreen. You name it, it's on the list."

Chelsea laughed, following him inside. "Of course you have. I'd expect nothing less from my very prepared husband."

They walked into the bedroom, where Steven started organizing the clothing and essentials already laid out. Chelsea watched him, a soft smile playing at her lips. It felt so natural to have him here, sharing her space, preparing for their first big adventure as a married couple.

As she folded a shirt and added it to her suitcase, her thoughts drifted back to her sisters. She'd seen the flicker of resentment in Tess's eyes and the uncertainty in Leah's whenever Gretchen had mentioned wanting to stay on the island. She knew Gretchen's choice was about more than just where she wanted to live; it was about the family they'd all missed and the closeness they were slowly rebuilding.

She reached over, touching Steven's arm gently. "Thank you, Steven," she said softly, looking up at him. "Thank you for understanding and letting me handle this before we go."

Steven looked at her, his expression tender. "Chelsea, I wouldn't have it any other way. Family is everything to you. And you're everything to me." He covered her hand with his, giving it a gentle squeeze. "Besides, I can't wait to see you in action, keeping those sisters of yours in line."

Chelsea laughed, rolling her eyes. "Oh, don't expect miracles. But I'll do my best."

They shared a smile, then turned back to packing, their quiet companionship filling Chelsea with a deep sense of peace. As she zipped her suitcase shut, she felt ready to face the conversation with her sisters that afternoon, knowing Steven was by her side in every way that mattered.

※

There was little time to get caught up with her sisters before leaving on her honeymoon, but Chelsea needed more time with them to get to the bottom of their family troubles. She had been walking on clouds all morning, and although she knew there was no avoiding this sibling drama, she wanted everything resolved before leaving for Hawaii.

Then the front door opened, and all three of her sisters came walking into the house as if they owned the place.

"Most normal people would knock or ring the bell the morning after my wedding," Chelsea said. "What if we weren't decent?"

"Hey, most people don't invite their sisters over the next day either, so there's that," Leah added.

Chelsea couldn't disagree and said so. "Trust me, you wouldn't be here if it wasn't absolutely necessary."

"Huh?" Tess asked.

"Come into the living room. I've got trays of iced tea and lemonade on the coffee table if anyone wants some. Unless you'd rather have tea or coffee?"

"I'm good, Chelsea, thanks," Gretchen answered, as Tess and Leah filled their glasses with iced tea. Everyone took a seat in the living room, an air of anticipation hanging over them. Chelsea, seated beside Gretchen, could feel her sister's apprehension and gave her an encouraging squeeze on the shoulder.

Just as Chelsea opened her mouth to speak, Steven strolled into the room, whistling cheerfully with a glass of water in hand. He took one look at the serious expressions on all four faces, stopped mid-whistle, and his eyes widened.

"Whoops," he said, holding up his hands in surrender. "Didn't mean to interrupt what looks like...uh, some very intense sister business." He began to back away, one slow step at a time.

"Good instinct," Chelsea teased, stifling a laugh as Steven turned on his heels and practically tiptoed out, muttering, "I'll just, uh... find a safe corner somewhere."

The sisters burst into laughter, momentarily easing some of the tension. Gretchen looked at Chelsea, a small smile breaking through her nerves, and Chelsea nodded, encouraging her to go on.

"So," Chelsea began, steering them back on track, "before Steven and I leave, Gretchen has something important she wants to share."

Tess and Leah exchanged wary glances. Gretchen took a steadying breath. "I've been thinking... about what comes next for me. And I've decided I don't want to go back to Key West," she said. "I'd like to stay here on Captiva for a while, maybe even look for a place in the area."

Leah's mouth dropped open, and Tess's expression turned stormy.

"Wait, you're staying?" Tess asked, her tone tinged with disappointment. "Since when was that the plan?"

Leah folded her arms, frowning. "So, you're just going to leave Key West behind? You love it there, Gretchen! And now, just because you came here for Chelsea's wedding, you suddenly want to stay on Captiva?"

Gretchen glanced at Chelsea, her face tight with unease. "It's not a sudden decision. I've been feeling this way for a while but being here helped me realize I need a change."

Tess scoffed, crossing her arms. "A change? Gretchen, you always seem to need a change. First, it was leaving the island for Key West, and now it's this. You never stick with anything!"

Chelsea, sensing Gretchen's discomfort, stepped in. "Hold on," she said, her tone firm but calm. "Gretchen has every right to decide where she wants to be, just like we all do. And it's natural that she'd want to be close to all of us, but Key West doesn't fit the life she wants to live."

Tess rolled her eyes and shot Chelsea a look of irritation. "You always take Gretchen's side, don't you?" she muttered, her voice laced with resentment. "It's like no matter what, you're always there to back her up."

Chelsea's brow furrowed as she met Tess's gaze, surprised by the unexpected edge. "That's not true, Tess. I'm not taking sides. I just want Gretchen to feel comfortable sharing her decision with us. We're all sisters here."

Leah shifted uncomfortably, sensing the tension rising. "Tess has a point, though," she said, though her tone was gentler. "It does sometimes feel like you two are closer. And I think... maybe that's why this is hard for us."

Gretchen looked between them, a flicker of guilt crossing her face. "It's not about sides," she said quietly. "I just wanted to tell you both that I miss being near all of you. This isn't about Chelsea versus anyone else. It's about all of us being as close as we can."

Chelsea took a deep breath, softening her tone. "I understand where you're both coming from. But Gretchen hasn't had it easy either. She's been on her own, trying to figure things out after her divorce. Maybe if we all try to see it from each other's perspective, it'll help us understand why she's making this decision."

Leah's expression softened, though she still seemed a bit unsettled. "I guess... we just didn't expect this. We were getting used to our own lives, each in our own place."

Tess sighed, her posture relaxing slightly, though she still wore a hint of reluctance. "Fine, but I swear if you make this decision and then change your mind again, I'll never let you live it down."

Gretchen chuckled softly, some of the tension leaving her shoulders. "Fair enough. But I'm serious about this. I want to be here, near Chelsea. Besides, we're all still in Florida. I'd say that's far better than how things were growing up."

Chelsea grinned, squeezing Gretchen's hand in silent support.

"I think we all need to support Gretchen, just as I supported you all when you wanted to move to Key West."

Chelsea could tell she was getting through to Tess and Leah. Turning to Gretchen, she said, "I'm thrilled you'll stay at my place while Steven and I are on our honeymoon. It would be nice to know the house isn't empty, and heaven knows little Stella could use the company. Don't let her fool you. Just because she hides under the bed, she does love a cuddle now and then."

Gretchen's face lit up. "She's not the only one."

Chelsea laughed.. "I know you'll enjoy the house while I'm gone. Don't forget, Maggie and Paolo are just around the corner. You can always stop in to visit. Don't wait to be invited. I never do."

Tess smirked, glancing at Gretchen. "Well, I suppose that sounds like a pretty sweet setup. A cozy house on Captiva and Chelsea's spoiled cat? Maybe I should move in, too."

Chelsea laughed. "You're all welcome anytime, but for now, Gretchen's my official house-sitter."

Gretchen beamed, visibly relaxing at their plans. "Thanks, Chelsea. I'll take good care of the place—and Stella, of course."

Leah sighed, a smile finally breaking through. "Well, if you're going to stay, you'd better keep that invitation open. Tess and I will drive up as often as we can, just in case you change your mind again."

Gretchen chuckled, rolling her eyes. "Deal. I don't plan on changing my mind, but I won't stop you from checking up on me."

Chelsea looked at her sisters, her heart full as she watched them ease into this next phase of their lives together. "Good. Now I can head off to Hawaii without worrying about a thing. Just promise me you'll all try to get along."

They all laughed, and the last of the tension melted away. Chelsea hoped for the best but knew a future without her siblings fighting was an impossible dream.

# CHAPTER 20

*T*he gentle whisper of the waves and the crisp saltiness of the sea air filled Maggie with a deep sense of contentment as she stood on the back porch.

In the quiet morning, with only the rhythmic sound of the tide and the distant call of a seagull, she found herself breathing a little easier, savoring the peace that came with these rare, still moments.

She thought back on the past few days, feeling grateful. She'd shared private talks with her children during this Christmas visit, feeling close to each one in a way that warmed her heart. They'd spoken about everything—hopes, dreams, worries—but she realized now, as the family prepared to return to Massachusetts, she hadn't yet had a quiet moment with Lauren, and she wasn't done talking to Michael.

She'd call it mother's intuition but something tugged at her. Her son, Michael, whose life had taken such a challenging path, had always been one of her greatest sources of pride and worry. She wanted to say more to him without overstepping. The time seemed right, and so, she looked for him.

With a gentle sigh, she turned and walked back inside, where

Michael was gathering a few things before joining the others. She caught his eye and smiled, tilting her head toward the beach.

"Care to take a walk with me?" she asked..

Michael looked up, a bit surprised, then smiled. "Sure, Mom," he said, setting his things down. "I'd like that."

As they stepped onto the sand, Maggie tucked her arm through his, their footsteps blending with the gentle hum of the waves and the occasional gust of wind that swept across the beach. She was grateful for this moment, a chance to share a private, quiet time with her son before the bustling life of Massachusetts would call him away again.

For a while, they walked in silence, the only sounds coming from the gentle rush of waves and the occasional cry of a seagull. Maggie took a deep breath, savoring the peace of this moment. There had been so much joy and activity with Christmas and Chelsea's wedding, and it felt good to share this stillness with her son.

"I can't believe how grown up you are," she finally said, a soft smile playing on her lips. "Seems like just yesterday you were that little boy running around, pretending to catch the 'bad guys' in our backyard."

Michael chuckled, a warm glint in his eyes. "Yeah, those were the days. I was convinced I was Andover's best detective. I remember hiding behind every tree and corner, 'protecting' the neighborhood."

Maggie laughed, shaking her head. "Oh, I remember! You had that plastic badge and your toy walkie-talkie. You'd announce to anyone within earshot that you were keeping them safe."

Michael's face softened with nostalgia, his smile fading slightly. "I guess some things never change. Even now, I just want to keep people safe."

They continued walking, Maggie stealing glances at him, marveling at the man he'd become. She could still see hints of the boy he used to be—the determined gaze, the protective stance.

But there was also something new, something quieter and more grounded. He'd been through so much.

"I want you to know," Maggie began, her voice soft but steady, "how proud I am of you. Your dad would be, too."

Michael's steps faltered slightly, and he glanced down at the sand, his expression becoming more serious.

"I hope so. I was never certain he felt I made the right decision when I joined the police force. I guess he thought I wasn't living up to his example."

"You've done more than live up to his example, Michael. You've become a man he would be proud to know. And even though he couldn't be here, I believe he's watching over you."

Michael's jaw tightened, and he nodded, his gaze fixed ahead. "It's strange," he murmured, his voice barely audible. "Sometimes, in the toughest moments, I think of him. When things got really hard after the...incident, it was his face that came to mind."

Maggie squeezed his arm, her own heart tightening at the memory of what he'd been through. She had never felt so helpless as she did when she heard her son had been shot. Even now, two years later, the thought of it sent a shiver through her.

"You've come so far, Michael," she said, her voice thick with emotion. "I know it hasn't been easy. And I know there are still days that aren't. But you've shown so much strength."

He paused, watching the waves as if they held answers.

"It's still a struggle sometimes. Going back to work felt like reclaiming a part of myself, but there are moments when... when I'm not sure I can keep doing it. The therapy helps, but it doesn't erase everything."

Maggie nodded, letting his words sink in. She knew that some wounds ran deeper than physical injuries, and no amount of therapy or time could completely erase the scars of what he had endured. But she also knew her son—and the resilience that had carried him through.

"Your strength isn't about forgetting what happened," she said gently. "It's about living with it, accepting that it's a part of you now. And you're doing that, Michael, one day at a time. That's courage."

Michael took a deep breath, as if drawing in the encouragement his mother's words offered. "Sometimes I wonder what Dad would say," he admitted. "I mean, he went through his own battles. I wish I could have talked to him about all this."

Maggie felt a pang of sorrow but offered him a reassuring smile. "Your dad would tell you that he's proud of you. He'd remind you that it's okay to have doubts, to struggle. He wasn't a stranger to hardship, Michael. But he'd tell you to keep going, just like you are. Heaven knows, he wasn't perfect."

Michael's eyes misted over slightly, and he looked away, his voice rough.

"I'm not the only one with courage in this family, Mom. What you endured with him…I mean, I know some of what you went through, but not all of it. Initially, I was so angry at him, but I don't know…the anger isn't there anymore."

Maggie smiled. "That is something I do understand. I think all of us in this family have had our moments of anger, and disappointment. In the end, I think all of us chose forgiveness."

Michael nodded. "I think you're right, at least that's how it's been for me."

"Michael, I don't want you to feel the weight of this family on you."

Confused, he asked, "I don't understand. What weight?"

"I worry that you feel a responsibility to be the male head of the Wheeler family. I know your need to take care of people, and your siblings especially. I just want you to let that go. Everyone is happy, doing well, and as a family, we can support each other. Not one of us needs to carry that burden alone."

Michael chuckled. "Maybe you should take your own advice, Mom."

Maggie smiled. "That's different. I'm the mother. It's my job to worry about all of you every single day."

They walked on, and the waves rolled over their bare feet, grounding them in the moment. Maggie thought of all the times she had walked this beach alone, wishing her husband was there to see the family they had built, the man their son had become. She could only hope that wherever Daniel was, he could see it all.

"When you were a boy, you used to run along this beach like you were on some secret mission," she said, her tone lightening. "I'd be sitting here, watching, and thinking, 'That's my little protector.'"

Michael laughed softly. "I guess I've always been drawn to it. The need to protect."

"And that's who you are," Maggie said, her voice thickening with pride. "But don't forget—you're allowed to be protected, too. You don't always have to be the strong one."

He gave her a rueful smile. "I think you're the only one who ever gets to see that side of me, Mom."

"And I'm glad for that," she replied with a soft smile. "You're my son. You don't have to hide anything from me."

They continued walking, the soft sand giving way beneath their feet as they moved. Maggie felt the weight of the past years ease a bit with each step. She knew that no matter how much time passed, some memories would stay with them forever—but so would the strength they'd gained from facing them.

As they reached a quieter stretch of the beach, Michael turned to face her, his gaze warm and grateful. "Thanks, Mom. For everything. For being there, for understanding...and for believing in me, even when I didn't believe in myself. You've always been my rock...you, and Brea."

Maggie's eyes shimmered with tears, and she took his hands in hers, looking up at him. "It's easy to believe in you, Michael. You've shown me what it means to be brave, to keep moving forward. I couldn't be prouder of the man you are."

They stood together, watching the waves roll in and out, the world around them quiet and peaceful. Maggie felt a profound sense of gratitude, for this moment, for her son's resilience, and for the love that had carried them both through so much.

As they turned back toward the inn, Maggie looked over at him, a soft smile on her face.

"I know we'll have to say goodbye soon, but I want you to remember...no matter where you go or what you face, you're never alone. I'm always here, and so is your dad, in spirit."

Michael's arm slid around her shoulders, pulling her close. "I know, Mom. I feel it."

As they walked back toward the family waiting for them, Maggie felt a profound sense of peace. Every mother hopes her children will grow into strong, capable adults, standing on their own two feet. Thinking of her children now, Maggie felt a deep gratitude, confident she had done her best to raise them well. Whatever lay ahead, she knew they would face it with the love, resilience, and connection they had built together.

# CHAPTER 21

The dining room at the inn was filled with the inviting aroma of a warm lunch, courtesy of Iris and Maggie. Together, they had transformed the room, laying out a feast of savory and sweet dishes to celebrate one last gathering before the family members would head their separate ways the next day.

The chatter and laughter of Maggie's children and grandchildren filled the space as they admired the spread, each dish a reminder of home and the love poured into this final meal together.

"Is that cinnamon streusel coffee cake I smell?" Grandma Sarah asked.

"Maggie told me you used to make it for Christmas, so I thought I'd give it a try," Iris said.

Grandma Sarah smiled at Maggie. "You remembered."

"Of course I remembered. Some things you never forget. I panicked when I couldn't find the recipe. Thankfully, I found it stuck to the recipe in front of it in the recipe box."

Oliver stood near the doorway, his gaze drifting back to the table and, more so, to Iris, who was quietly finishing a few last touches in the kitchen. Maggie caught the glance, sharing a quick, knowing smile with Paolo as Iris set down a platter of fruit.

Oliver's attention didn't go unnoticed by the others, either; Grandma Sarah gave Maggie a gentle nudge and a smirk, whispering just loud enough for Maggie to hear, "That boy's got more than food on his mind, doesn't he?"

Maggie chuckled, not hiding her amusement. "He's got a lot on his mind, that's for sure. And maybe something, or rather someone, is keeping him here."

As everyone began to settle in for the meal, Maggie glanced around the room, feeling a surge of gratitude mixed with a bittersweet sadness. Her family was here, filling the inn with their energy, and even though it was hard to watch them leave, she knew these moments would carry them all through the next months apart.

Iris joined her at the head of the table, where Maggie had saved her a spot. She looked at Oliver, who was quietly helping Grandma Sarah get settled, his face caught between a smile and something deeper, something conflicted. Iris leaned close to Maggie, her voice barely above a whisper. "Do you think he's going to be okay? With his father, I mean...and Philippe."

Maggie placed a reassuring hand on Iris' arm. "I think he'll be fine. He's a strong man, and Captiva is home for him now. He knows what he wants, even if it's a hard trip to make."

They sat around the table as Oliver gave Iris and Maggie a brief, grateful smile as he took his seat. The food was passed around, and the family dove into their meal with laughter and the usual banter.

Beth, in her usual lively fashion, began recounting a Christmas story from years past, when she'd convinced Lauren to join her in a midnight beach walk that had nearly ended with them both being chased by a few overly curious seagulls.

"And you were screaming like a banshee!" Lauren protested,

laughing even as she shook her head. "I thought you were going to make me run all the way back to the hotel!"

Beth grinned, clearly relishing the memory. "Hey, I kept us moving! Admit it, you've never had that much excitement since."

Lauren groaned, rolling her eyes. "Not true, but I'm not about to let you talk me into another 'adventure,' especially one involving the ocean in December."

"Wait, I thought you all came to Captiva in the summer. You were here for Christmas?" Oliver asked.

Maggie nodded. "Just once. We stayed at the Tween Waters. I'm not sure what made Daniel and I come up with such a crazy idea. It wasn't the warmest December on Captiva Island either."

"That's why it was such a crazy idea to get in the water," Lauren said. "Thank goodness we've outgrown such nutty ideas."

"Oh, come on," Beth shot back, her grin widening. "One last night on the island! Why don't we all stay up, enjoy the tree, and maybe even go for a dip?"

A chorus of groans, chuckles, and cheers filled the room. Lauren shook her head, muttering to Maggie, "Mom, your daughter is insane."

Maggie laughed, looking around at her family with shining eyes. "Yes, she is, but I wouldn't change her for anything."

Through the laughter and storytelling, Maggie noticed that Oliver's gaze kept returning to Iris, who was doing her best to stay focused on the family conversation but seemed distracted, her own eyes drifting toward him whenever she thought no one was looking. Maggie saw the quiet worry there, the concern that this trip to New York might be more than just a quick goodbye. She knew Iris's fears well—there was always a chance that old ties could resurface and hold someone back, even when they wanted to move forward.

As the lunch came to an end and plates were cleared, Oliver stood up, glancing at his watch. "I should be going soon," he announced, his voice steady, though Maggie could sense the emotions just beneath the surface. Everyone's faces softened, the laughter replaced by quiet understanding as they gathered around him.

One by one, the family members came forward to hug him, offering him words of encouragement. Grandma Sarah pulled him into a tight embrace, patting his back with an affectionate sigh. "You go take care of your business, but don't linger too long. The snow's no place for a beach boy like you."

Oliver chuckled, his smile softening as he looked around at the group. "Thanks, Grandma Sarah. I'll keep that in mind."

Beth wrapped him in a bear hug, her eyes bright. "You'll be back before we know it, right? Don't get too used to the big city again. My mother and Paolo are spoiled with your cooking now. They'll be miserable if you don't return."

Oliver smiled, nodding. "I'll be back. Captiva's my home."

Maggie hugged him tightly, feeling her heart ache as she held him close. "Be safe, Oliver. Take care of yourself, and remember, you've got a family here who loves you."

He gave her a gentle squeeze. "I know, Maggie. Thank you."

As Oliver moved toward the door, Iris followed, lingering as he stepped outside. Maggie stayed close, watching them through the open door as the rest of the family chattered in the background, giving them a moment. Iris's hand rested on the doorframe, her expression a mixture of worry and something deeper.

"Are you sure you'll come back?" she asked softly, her voice barely above a whisper.

Oliver met her gaze, his own face softening. He reached out, tucking a stray strand of hair behind her ear, and held her hand for a moment longer than necessary.

"Captiva is where I belong, Iris. I don't want the life I left behind in New York. I promise, I'll be back."

They stood there in silence for a heartbeat, the unspoken tension thickening the air between them. Neither had acknowledged what simmered beneath their friendship, but it was there, lingering, waiting.

"Take care of yourself, Oliver," Iris said, her voice barely steady.

He nodded, giving her hand a final squeeze. "I will. And thank you... for everything."

Iris watched him as he walked away, her hand lingering on the doorframe even after he was out of sight. Maggie came up beside her, placing a comforting hand on her shoulder.

"He'll be back," Maggie murmured. "I have no doubt."

Iris nodded, her eyes glistening. "I hope so. It's just... New York has a way of pulling people back in. And there's so much history there."

Maggie squeezed her shoulder. "He left that behind a long time ago, Iris. Captiva is his home now—and so are we."

They walked back inside, joining the others as they settled around the living room, where the Christmas tree glowed softly in the corner. Beth, always one to keep the mood light, clapped her hands and raised her voice.

"All right, everyone, one last Christmas hurrah! Let's stay up all night, drink cocoa, and maybe even do that midnight swim."

"Oh, please," Lauren groaned, leaning back in her chair. "You can drag me out there when it's warm again."

But Beth's enthusiasm was contagious, and soon the whole room was filled with laughter and voices as they reminisced over past Christmases, shared stories, and clinked their mugs of cocoa and tea.

Maggie sat back, watching her children and grandchildren, her heart full of pride and love, though she couldn't deny the pang of sadness at knowing they'd all be gone tomorrow.

Grandma Sarah, sitting beside her, noticed the glimmer of tears in her eyes and patted her hand gently. "I know, honey. It never gets any easier, does it?"

Maggie wiped her eyes, smiling through the tears. "It's the

price I pay for moving here, I suppose. But I wouldn't trade it. These moments, even if they're brief, mean everything."

The night continued, laughter mingling with a few quiet tears and the occasional sigh as they enjoyed their last hours together, the family close, sharing warmth and love beneath the glow of the Christmas tree.

Maggie thought about Oliver on his journey to New York. He'd come to Captiva Island after a year-long sabbatical to focus on healing from the pain of loss, something he'd carry with him forever.

However, in a few short months, he'd become an integral part of her family. She could only hope that he felt the same and carried with him the memories of this day, and the promise that he would return to the life he'd chosen for himself.

Lauren had just put Daniel down for a nap when Maggie tiptoed into the bedroom.

"Is he asleep?" Maggie whispered.

Lauren nodded, and they both quietly walked out of the room.

"He's such a good baby, he never fusses. Olivia and Lily were the complete opposite," Lauren said.

"I remember," Maggie responded. "You used to call me all the time for advice on what to do when Olivia wouldn't settle down."

Lauren nodded. "I thought I was the worst mother in the world."

Maggie laughed. "Join the club. How about a cup of tea?"

Lauren smiled. "Uh-oh, does this mean you've got something you want to talk about?"

Maggie slipped her arm around her daughter's waist. "Can't I just spend a few quiet moments with my daughter?"

They made their way down to the kitchen and Maggie filled

the tea kettle with water. "How about we sit outside while we wait for the water to boil? There isn't a cloud in the sky today."

"Sounds good," Lauren answered.

Rubbing her lower back, Lauren sat on the swing. "I thought after the baby, I'd get a break from having back pain. It better subside soon or I'm back in the doctor's office."

"I didn't know you were having back pains?" Maggie said.

Lauren nodded. "All during the last two months of the pregnancy and it hasn't let up since."

"Well, I know it's hard when you've got to carry the baby but try not to pick up anything too heavy. You should see the doctor as soon as you get back."

Lauren nodded. "I'm looking forward to us being together tonight, Mom. It's been a long time since we all had a chance to just be...us, you know?"

Maggie nodded. "I know what you mean. The family is growing and we all have such busy lives. We need to always make time to come back together and remember the past. I think it helps guide us to where we each need to go. What's that saying? How do I know where I'm going if I don't know where I've been?"

Lauren laughed. "I'm not sure that's the exact quote, but I get the point."

"Well, I think the idea is to learn from the past," Maggie explained.

"You mean my past or *the* past?" Lauren asked. "I only ask because maybe you're trying to tell me that I need to learn from *your* past. Am I right?"

Maggie didn't want to argue with Lauren, but she could see her daughter understood her meaning. "Honey, since you were a little girl, everyone has said how alike you and I are."

Lauren sighed. "People have been telling me that my whole life."

"And it bothers you?"

Lauren nodded. "There are some things about me that are similar to you but I'm not you, Mom. I never have been."

Maggie smiled. "I know that honey. I just wanted to hear you say it. I was worried that you had this ridiculous legacy to uphold. That's nonsense, and nothing I want for you. Do you understand?"

Lauren's eyes watered, and Maggie worried she'd hit a nerve. Still, she was glad they were finally having this conversation.

"I'm incredibly proud of who you are, Lauren, and it's not because you're anything like me. I'm proud of the person you've become. You did that all on your own. Your father and I might have had some influence on you when you were little, but just like your siblings, you always have been your own person. I never want you to think I'd want anything else for you."

Lauren reached for Maggie's hand. "Thank you, Mom. I needed to hear you say that. I'll let you in on a little secret though. If I'm half the mother you are, I'd be so proud."

It was Maggie's turn to cry. She pulled Lauren to her and held her tight. When she pulled back she took a tissue from her pocket and wiped her eyes.

"You'd better get that tea before we're in a puddle on the floor," Lauren said.

Maggie laughed through her tears. "I think you're right about that."

# CHAPTER 22

$\mathcal{T}$he inn was quiet, the only light coming from the soft glow of the Christmas tree in the corner, of the room. Maggie sat comfortably on the couch, a steaming mug of cocoa in her hands, as her children gathered around her.

After Iris cleaned up in the kitchen, she went home and promised to be back first thing in the morning.

Leaving Christopher to enjoy the time with his siblings, Becca left to stay at her father's so she could spend time with her brothers and Ciara. Brea put the children to bed and Trevor took Noah, Sophia and little Maggie home, leaving Sarah to spend the time with her siblings. Gabriel and Jeff headed to bed after a few backgammon games.

Paolo struggled with Lexie, who had burrowed under a blanket, insisting she stay with the rest of the family.

"Looks like she wants to join your pajama party," he said.

"Come on, Lexie. Be a good girl," Maggie added.

Paolo attached the leash, pulling Lexie slightly to get the point across.

"Goodnight everyone. I'm going to take her out for one last

walk around the block." He kissed Maggie. "I'm headed to bed when I get back."

"Night, honey," Maggie said. "Goodnight Lexie."

The pup obediently followed Paolo out the door, leaving the rest of the family to settle in for the night.

Lauren curled up in an armchair with a blanket, Beth settled on the floor near the tree, and Michael and Sarah sprawled out on the floor. Christopher took his place at the end of the sofa, grinning as he looked around at his siblings and his grandmother, who'd made herself cozy in a nearby armchair.

"It feels like we're back in Andover," he said.

"Remember how we'd stay up like this after Christmas? Just the five of us in the living room, trying not to wake Dad."

Michael chuckled, shaking his head. "I think we woke him up more times than not. He'd come downstairs with that stern look, but he'd always end up joining us, didn't he?"

"Yeah," Sarah added with a warm smile. "He'd say something like, 'Can't you kids go to bed?' but within minutes, he'd be laughing and sharing stories with us."

Maggie smiled, feeling the familiar tug of bittersweet memories. Daniel had been gone for years, but in moments like these, she could almost feel his presence. And while she loved Paolo dearly, she knew her children cherished these memories of their father, and she was happy to share in them for their sake.

Beth sighed, looking around the room. "I remember that one Christmas when Dad tried to put together that huge playhouse for us in the backyard. It was freezing, and he was out there with that tiny toolset, muttering to himself."

Lauren laughed, covering her mouth. "Oh, yes! And he wouldn't let anyone help him because he wanted it to be perfect. We were all watching from the window, and he was out there in his old coat, trying to read the instructions by flashlight."

Michael smirked. "He had half the thing put together by Christmas morning, and then he told us it was Santa's fault the rest of it wasn't done, you know…because he was so busy bringing toys to other families."

The room erupted in laughter, each sibling recalling the sight of Daniel out in the snow, determined to build something that would make his children's eyes light up.

"That playhouse was so lopsided, it's a miracle it stood up for as long as it did," Christopher added, shaking his head. "But Dad was so proud of it. And we loved it."

Sarah leaned back against the sofa, her smile fading into a softer expression. "Mom, how did you handle all of us during those years? Five kids… it must have been chaos. I have three and there are days when I think I'm the worst mother in the world."

"You are," Christopher teased as Sarah threw a pillow at his head.

Maggie chuckled, reaching down to squeeze Sarah's hand.

"Oh, it was chaos, all right. But it was a beautiful kind of chaos. You were all so different—Lauren, always trying to be the responsible one, and Beth, my little daredevil." She gave Beth a playful wink. "Then Michael, the protector, and Sarah, my little dreamer… and Christopher, who could make anyone laugh. You all had your own little quirks."

"Lauren still tries to be responsible," Michael teased, earning a playful glare from his sister.

"Well, someone has to keep the rest of you in line," Lauren shot back. "I am the oldest after all."

Maggie shook her head, smiling as she watched them.

"You kept each other in line more than I ever did. I think it's why you were always so close. You were like your own little team."

Beth leaned forward, her eyes bright. "Mom, tell us a story about Dad. One we haven't heard in a while."

Maggie thought for a moment, letting memories wash over her.

"All right, let's see… Do you remember the time your father decided to surprise us all by cooking Thanksgiving dinner?"

Groans and laughter erupted from the group, and Christopher shook his head, covering his face.

"Oh, no. Please tell me you're not talking about the turkey."

"The turkey that looked like it had been run over," Lauren said, giggling.

"I remember that turkey," Grandma Sarah added as she entered the room. "It was then that I told you to never let that man in the kitchen ever again."

Maggie laughed, nodding. "Yes, that turkey. He was determined to make it himself, but he left it in the oven too long, and when he took it out, it looked like a rock. He tried to convince us it would taste fine if we just added extra gravy."

"Extra gravy couldn't save that thing," Michael said, rolling his eyes. "I remember him slicing it, and it was so dry it just crumbled."

Beth wiped tears of laughter from her eyes. "And he still insisted it was 'an acquired taste.'"

Maggie leaned back, her heart full as she watched her children laugh together, sharing memories that had bound them all, memories that seemed to grow warmer and brighter with time.

"I miss him," Sarah said softly, her voice breaking the laughter. "He had such a big presence. Sometimes I still expect him to walk into a room and start talking like nothing happened."

The group grew quiet, each one lost in their thoughts. Maggie reached over, gently rubbing Sarah's back.

"He's with us in moments like these," she said softly. "He lives on in every story, every memory, and every laugh we share. And I know he'd be proud of each one of you."

Christopher's expression softened, his eyes misty. "You really think so, Mom? I'd like to think that's true."

Maggie looked around at her children, feeling the pride swelling within her.

"I know so. He may not have said it often, but he was proud. And he'd be even prouder now."

Lauren took a deep breath, wiping at her eyes, but then she broke into a grin. "All right, enough sentimentality. Who remembers the time Beth decided to paint the living room bright purple?"

"Oh, no!" Beth groaned, hiding her face in her hands. "I thought we'd all forgotten about that."

"Forgotten? Impossible," Michael said, laughing. "I'm still traumatized from that purple paint. Dad came home, and I thought he was going to faint right there in the doorway."

"He was so quiet about it," Maggie added, laughing at the memory. "He just stood there, staring at the walls. I don't think he could find the words."

Beth shrugged, grinning. "Hey, I was experimenting with my artistic side."

"Artistic side, sure," Lauren teased. "But those walls were never the same again."

The laughter continued, but soon Grandma Sarah's voice cut through, full of mock sternness. "Well, while you're all reminiscing about little purple disasters, I've got some news myself. I'm going on a cruise."

The room fell silent for a moment before bursting into more laughter and questions. Beth's eyes widened. "Another cruise? Didn't the last one end with you getting a tattoo?"

"Oh, please, it was just a tiny rose on my ankle." Grandma Sarah waved a hand, grinning mischievously. "But this one's to Alaska. Can you imagine? The Northern Lights, the glaciers... maybe another tattoo, but this time, something with teeth. A bear, maybe."

"Oh, no," Lauren gasped, shaking her head in mock dismay. "Grandma, you'll come back with a whole polar bear on your arm!"

"Well, I'm sure not getting it on my ankle again," Grandma

teased. "But yes, Alaska. It's cold, but I've never let a little thing like weather hold me back."

The family shared amused glances, and Christopher gave his grandmother a thumbs up. "I'll bet you'll lead the conga line and the polar plunge."

"You can count on it," Grandma Sarah replied, a smirk tugging at her lips. "But I'll try not to break any bones. Just a little something to keep me on my toes—and to keep you all on yours when I tell the stories!"

Maggie shook her head in affectionate disbelief. "You never change, Mom. But I love that about you. Just promise you'll come back with *only* one tattoo this time."

"I make no such promises!" Grandma Sarah replied, lifting her mug in a mock toast. "Here's to new adventures—and here's to a family that never runs out of stories."

Maggie watched her children and her mother, and her heart swelled with happiness as the stories flowed, one after another, each bringing a fresh round of laughter or a sigh of nostalgia. She felt herself leaning into the joy of this moment, knowing these memories were part of the legacy she and Daniel had built together, part of the family they'd raised with love and laughter.

As the night wore on, the laughter and stories softened into a comfortable silence. Lauren stretched, stifling a yawn. "I suppose we should all try to get some sleep if we're planning to get to the airport in the morning."

Sarah looked around, her smile tinged with sadness. "I'm really going to miss you guys. I'm glad Mom and Grandma are close, but I miss my siblings so much. I hate saying goodbye."

"I know what you mean," Lauren said, falling to the floor and landing on Sarah's lap. "I have no idea how you manage without your big sister's advice."

"Very funny. Thank goodness I've got Mom to talk to."

"Yeah, but I won't make you drink tea if you come to me for advice," Lauren teased.

Maggie's face lit up. "What? I thought you all loved my tea."

Beth giggled. "Did we ever have a choice?"

Lauren sat up from Sarah's lap and reached for her mother's hand.

"I do...we do," she said looking at Beth.

"Honest, Mom, we do love your tea," Beth confirmed.

"I'm glad we got to spend Christmas together...and Chelsea's wedding was an added bonus," Michael added, his voice gentle. "And next time, we'll be gathering for a whole new reason." He glanced over at Christopher with a warm smile. "Can't wait to meet the newest Wheeler."

Everyone's gaze shifted to Christopher, who grinned proudly. "I think Becca's going into her seventh month so it won't be long. I've got to get working on the nursery."

Beth's face lit up with excitement. "I can't wait to meet the little one! A new baby in the family... it's going to be amazing."

Christopher chuckled, his eyes sparkling with excitement. "Becca's a bit nervous, but she's also really excited. And she'll have all of you to spoil the baby, I'm sure."

Maggie beamed, thinking about the new addition. "It'll be such a joy to welcome a new grandchild. And you know Paolo and I will fly up there when it gets close."

"Me too," Sarah said.

Lauren nodded. "I'll be around as much as you need. Becca already knows she can count on me."

Grandma Sarah cleared her throat, drawing everyone's attention with her signature smirk. "You know, I'll be back from Alaska by then—hopefully without any tattoos of arctic wildlife. I'll fly up too. You can count me in as the official baby-spoiler. After all, I've got years of experience."

Christopher laughed, reaching over to squeeze her hand. "Wouldn't have it any other way, Grandma. By the way, did you all see Finn and Jillian got married and didn't tell anyone?"

"You mean Crawford didn't know?" Beth asked.

Christopher shook his head. "Nope, and neither did Becca. She was just as shocked as her father was. I have no doubt she's giving her brother a piece of her mind right now."

"Not to mention, Jillian's sister Emma won't be too pleased about it either," Sarah added. "I expect a call from my best friend first thing tomorrow. I can't wait to hear what she has to say about it."

"Well, it's getting late. I suppose we ought to get some sleep. Tomorrow is going to be a long travel day," Lauren said.

As they started to rise, they exchanged hugs, each one lingering a little longer, knowing it would be months before they'd all be together again. When Christopher hugged his mother last, he pulled back with a grateful smile. "Thanks, Mom. This was the perfect end to the holidays."

Maggie nodded, tears in her eyes as she looked around the room. "Thank you all for staying up a bit. These moments mean the world to me. You all get to sleep, and we'll have something delicious for breakfast before you go."

One by one, they drifted to their rooms, leaving Maggie by the tree, bathed in its gentle glow. She stayed for a few moments and watched as Christopher pulled a blanket over his body and snuggled into the pillow on the sofa.

"Goodnight, honey," she said as she pushed his hair off his forehead.

"Night, Mom. Don't tell Becca, but it feels awesome to have the sofa all to myself. Ever since she's been pregnant, she hogs all the blankets."

Maggie laughed. "Your secret is safe with me."

Maggie switched off the small lamp by the front door, then moved through the kitchen, leaving only the stovetop light on as a soft glow for the night. Stepping outside, she walked onto the back porch, where the crickets' chorus nearly masked the faint sound of ocean waves rolling in. A gentle breeze stirred the wind chimes, and she caught snippets of distant voices carrying through the night.

Looking across the driveway, she saw the light glowing warmly in the window of the Carriage House. Paolo had left it on for her, as he always did, a quiet gesture of togetherness, even when they weren't side by side.

Tomorrow, her children would leave once again. Their departures were always the hardest part, a bittersweet ache she had come to know well. But now, she found comfort in knowing they would always return. Their love, laughter, and connection bound them to her, no matter the miles between them.

With a soft smile, Maggie crossed the inn's driveway, heading toward the Carriage House—toward her husband and the familiar comfort of home.

# CHAPTER 23

True to her word, Iris was at the inn long before anyone got out of bed. Trying not to wake Christopher as he slept on the sofa, she prepared breakfast and got the coffee pot going.

"Good morning, Iris," Maggie whispered as she walked into the kitchen.

"Morning, Maggie, did you all have fun last night?"

"It was wonderful. This Christmas was better than I ever imagined it would be. I thought I'd make my cranberry walnut scones this morning. I want to make enough for everyone, and maybe extra for them to take on the plane."

The screened door opened and Chelsea walked in.

"Good morning, Key Lime Garden Inn family. How is everyone today?"

"Hey, Chelsea, I wasn't sure if we'd see you today. Don't you leave for Hawaii today?" Maggie asked.

Chelsea filled a coffee cup and then sat at the kitchen island. "Nope, we leave tomorrow. By the way, Ciara told me she and Crawford would be by this morning to say goodbye to everyone.

I expect they'll show up early. I understand Becca stayed with them last night?"

Maggie smiled. "She did. I think she wanted to give Chris and the others some time alone, and I have to admit, last night was wonderful. We all sat around and talked about the past and it was so sweet listening to the kids share their feelings about Daniel. I'm so grateful we've had this Christmas together. And, everyone agreed your wedding was a lovely added surprise to their trip."

Chelsea smiled. "I'm glad. If you'd told me a couple of months ago that this is how we'd spend Christmas, I would have thought you crazy for even suggesting it…and now, here I am, a married lady about to go on my honeymoon."

Maggie mixed the scone ingredients and then dropped spoonfuls of the mixture onto the baking sheet.

"It's impossible to sleep with the smell of coffee," Christopher said.

"Good morning, Chelsea…Iris," he said as he kissed Maggie.

Looking over at the counter, Christopher's eyes grew wide. "Oh, are you making scones?"

Maggie smiled. "I am, indeed."

"Oh, man, I hope I get one right out of the oven and before anyone else comes downstairs."

"Too late!" Beth announced as she entered the kitchen.

"Morning, honey," Maggie said. "Iris is making eggs and pancakes, so no one should leave this place hungry today."

Slowly, the others came downstairs and made their way to the coffee pot.

"I'm glad you've got those coffee carafes, Mom. I don't think I could wait for another pot to brew," Michael said. "Is it me, or does everyone feel like they haven't slept?"

"I feel a bit groggy too," Lauren said. "I think it's because we stayed up so late."

"Not me," Gabriel announced as Jeff nodded and teased everyone about how he and Gabriel got a good night's sleep.

"Please, spare us the goody-two-shoes story. At least we had fun," Beth said.

"Oh, right. I had a blast trying to get the kids to sleep," Brea said. "You all don't know what you missed. "

Everyone laughed and Michael hugged his wife. "Thanks for handling all that."

"Good morning, all," Sarah said as she and Grandma Sarah joined the group. "I haven't slept here in years. I hope Trevor didn't struggle too much with the kids on his own last night. He just sent me a text that they'd be over shortly."

"Hey, everyone!" Becca called out as she came in through the front door followed by her father Crawford and his wife, Ciara.

"Hi, honey," Christopher said, pulling her into a hug.

"How'd you sleep on the sofa?" she asked.

Christopher shrugged. "Okay, I guess. It just wasn't the same without you," he said as he winked at his mother.

"I'll go upstairs and get my stuff. Are you all packed?"

"Mostly, but I'll come up with you," he answered.

After breakfast, the rest of the morning was busy with noise from her family running up and down the stairs preparing to leave. Before long, suitcases lined the entryway, and the sounds of last-minute packing and hurried conversations filled the air.

Grandma Sarah sat in an armchair by the door, her cane resting against her knee, watching her grandchildren bustle about with a bemused smile.

"You'd think they were moving cross-country rather than heading back to Massachusetts," she quipped, earning a chuckle from Maggie, who stood beside her.

"It always feels like a big move when they leave," Maggie replied softly, her gaze following each of her children as they organized bags and made quick trips to the car.

As the family gathered in the main room, Trevor arrived with Noah and Sophia, handing the baby to Sarah. "Someone misses her mommy," he said.

Sarah squeezed little Maggie and kissed the baby's cheek. "I missed you, too."

"Come on, kids, one cookie each," Lauren said, grinning as Grandma Sarah produced treats from a small tin.

"I swear you're spoiling them," Jeff said.

"That's what great-grandmothers do."

Amid the laughter and farewells, Chelsea wandered over to Maggie.

"You holding up okay?" she asked quietly.

Maggie nodded, her expression warm. "It's always a mix of things—sad to see them go, but grateful for the time together. And now I get to spend some time with you before you're off on your honeymoon."

Chelsea smiled, a hint of excitement and nervousness flashing across her face. "I'm glad I'll get to see you before we go, too. I'll definitely miss this place, even if it's only for a month."

"I thought it was for a couple of weeks," Maggie said.

Chelsea shrugged. "It was, but you know Steven. He likes to do things in a big way and wanted us to visit more than one island, so now we're away for a month."

Beth appeared at Maggie's side, wrapping an arm around her mother.

"You'll come visit soon, right, Mom? I mean, maybe not in the dead of winter," she added with a chuckle, "but before too long?"

Maggie hugged her. "Of course. I'm just a plane ride away, and it just might be in the dead of winter. Let's not forget Becca's due date isn't in warm weather."

The next round of goodbyes began as the family gathered their coats and bags, each child taking a moment to hug Grandma Sarah, who issued her traditional advice as each of them approached.

"Remember, Lauren, don't be too hard on your husband. Jeff deserves a medal for putting up with our crazy family."

Lauren laughed, giving her grandmother a peck on the cheek. "I'll keep that in mind, Grandma."

"And Michael," Grandma Sarah said, gripping his hand, "stay out of trouble, and keep an eye on that lovely wife of yours. You're lucky she puts up with you."

Michael grinned. "Yes, ma'am. I'll try to keep the mischief to a minimum."

The procession of hugs continued, each goodbye wrapped in laughter, love, and a tinge of bittersweet. Maggie stood back, her heart full, watching her children exchange hugs and jokes with each other and with their grandmother. She felt Chelsea's hand on her shoulder, offering quiet support.

Finally, it was time for the last goodbyes, with everyone gathered around the door. Maggie embraced each of her children in turn, trying not to cry.

When she hugged Lauren, she held her a little longer, feeling the warmth of her daughter's presence. "Don't forget what we talked about. You're an amazing mother and wife. Don't you ever forget that."

Lauren smiled. "I won't. Thanks, Mom."

Lauren hugged Sarah.

"I'm going to miss my little sister. Take care of Mom and Grandma."

Sarah nodded, squeezing her sister's hands. "Of course. You know I will."

They lingered a moment longer, sharing a smile, before the family began piling into their cars.

"Well, I've got to get home before I head to the Outreach Center. You okay, Mom?" Sarah asked.

Maggie smiled. "I'm fine, honey. You and Trevor get going. I understand Trevor is covering for Steven while he and Chelsea are on their honeymoon."

Sarah nodded. "Yup, he's going to be pretty busy the next month. I'll call you later?"

Maggie nodded. "Sounds good."

As the cars pulled out of the driveway and the inn grew quiet, Maggie felt the familiar ache of parting, but it was softened by the joy of seeing them all together, and by the promise of future gatherings. She looked over to Chelsea, who was still by her side.

"Well, it's just us now," Maggie said, her voice tinged with a mix of relief and sadness.

Chelsea smiled, slipping her arm through Maggie's. "Shall we take a walk? I think I hear the beach calling."

Maggie nodded, grateful for the company.

"I think that's a wonderful idea. Let's go."

Maggie and Chelsea made their way to the beach, the soft murmur of the waves greeting them. The sand was cool beneath their feet, and the sky was a gentle blend of blues and grays, hinting at the day ahead. They walked in comfortable silence for a few minutes, breathing in the salty air and soaking up the calm.

"It's been a while since we had a moment like this," Chelsea said, breaking the silence.

Maggie nodded. "Too long, really. I always treasure these little chances to just hang out and enjoy the beach. We're so lucky to live here. I always say that I love living in a place that people come to for vacation."

Chelsea smiled. "It's definitely Paradise. I'm glad you're here to see me off. Tomorrow feels so surreal—it's strange to think I'll be away for a whole month."

"You'll be back before you know it," Maggie replied, nudging her gently. "Besides, you don't want to wish away your incredible honeymoon. You and Steven are going to make lovely memories. I'm so happy for you." She added with a twinkle in her eye, "A month in Hawaii with Steven isn't exactly a hardship."

Chelsea laughed, her face lighting up. "I know, I know. Can you believe it? I've always wanted to go there, and now I am."

Maggie wrapped an arm around Chelsea's shoulders, giving her a warm squeeze. "I'm so happy for you, Chelsea. This new chapter—it's everything you deserve."

They strolled in silence again, each lost in her own thoughts. Maggie glanced over, sensing there was something else Chelsea wanted to say.

"Is there anything on your mind?" Maggie asked gently.

Chelsea hesitated, then nodded, her expression softening.

"Yes, actually. I'm worried about my sisters. I know Gretchen is making the right choice to move here from Key West. I never thought she fit in there, it's more about Tess and Leah."

Maggie's brows lifted. "Gretchen's taking good care of things, though, right? I thought you all resolved your disagreements?"

"Oh, absolutely, we did…I think," Chelsea said with a reassuring nod. "Gretchen has a good head on her shoulders. She'll be great and Stella will be fine with her. It's just… I'm more worried about Tess and Leah going back to Key West. Some of the things I've been hearing about their lives down there have me worried. Maybe I'm just overthinking it."

Maggie chuckled softly. "Right now, I think all you should be focused on is Steven and your honeymoon. Your sisters and their issues will still be here when you get back."

Chelsea relaxed a little, seeming to let go of her worries. "You're right. Thanks, Maggie. I needed to hear that. You know me. I'm pretty laid back unless we're talking about my sisters. But, you are absolutely right. For the next month, I'm done worrying about anything."

They walked along the shore, letting the rhythm of the waves fill the quiet spaces between them. After a while, Chelsea looked over, her face tinged with both mischief and curiosity.

"Isn't it funny how life works?" Chelsea murmured. "Neither you nor I ever planned to live on Captiva Island, and yet, now, I can't imagine either of us ever leaving. This island has brought me so much peace."

They reached a small tide pool, and Maggie bent down to trace a finger along the water's edge. "I think sometimes we're called to places, people, moments we don't understand until later. Captiva has become that for us—a place of healing, of new beginnings."

Chelsea nodded, her face reflecting the same sense of wonder.

"It's strange to think about all the twists and turns that led us here. And now, on the eve of my honeymoon, I feel like I'm starting another chapter, yet still so tied to Captiva."

"You are starting a new chapter," Maggie said softly, rising to meet Chelsea's gaze. "But no matter where you go, this will always be home. Captiva will always be a part of you, a part of us all."

After a moment, Chelsea sighed, a gentle smile on her lips. "I suppose I should get back. Still have a million little things to do before we leave."

Maggie chuckled. "That's always the way, isn't it? A thousand details just before a big trip. But remember, focus on having a great time. Enjoy every moment, and don't worry about a thing."

Chelsea hugged her. "I'll try. And don't let your mother convince you to adopt any wild ideas while I'm gone," she teased, pulling back with a grin.

"Oh, don't you worry," Maggie replied, laughing. "I think my mother is saving all her energy for Alaska. I don't think that state will ever be the same after she visits there."

Chelsea laughed and gave a small wave and turned back toward the inn, leaving Maggie standing by the water's edge. Maggie watched her go, feeling a profound sense of happiness for her best friend.

As Chelsea disappeared down the path, Maggie turned her face to the sea, the wind lifting her hair. She felt grateful—for

Captiva, for her children and grandchildren, and for Chelsea, who had found love again.

When she finally turned to head back, she looked at her watch and remembered she had much to do to get ready for the inn's guests scheduled to arrive the next day. Millie would arrive at the inn to help Maggie get the rooms ready, and she'd need to go over the menus for the coming week with Iris.

The Key Lime Garden Inn would soon be bustling with activity and excitement over Captiva Island's New Year's festivities, and there wasn't a minute to waste.

# CHAPTER 24

*O*liver shifted in the backseat of the taxi, the familiar pulse of New York City beating around him as he neared The Dakota building. The cab slowed as they turned onto Central Park West, the stately lines of the Dakota coming into view against the winter sky. The iconic building, with its ornate stone façade, iron railings, and looming gables, seemed both timeless and imposing, a fitting home for the man he hadn't seen in years.

As the taxi pulled up to the curb, Oliver felt a rush of conflicting emotions—a cocktail of resentment, guilt, and reluctant acceptance swirling through him. His father, Jacques Laurier, had always been a larger-than-life figure, a man whose principles were as unyielding as the walls of The Dakota itself. The rift between them had stretched over years, fed by his father's scorn for Oliver's chosen career, his brother Philippe's manipulations, and the shadows of betrayal that lay between them.

He stepped out, glancing briefly up at the building. It was just as he remembered, an aura of old-world elegance that couldn't be imitated. Oliver approached the doorman, who straightened at the sight of him. There was a hint of recognition in the man's eyes a brief flash of something like sympathy.

"Mr. Laurier," the doorman said with a slight nod. "We've been expecting you. Your brother let us know you'd be arriving today."

"Thanks," Oliver replied, taking a breath to steel himself.

As he stepped inside, the lobby's grandeur washed over him—a beautiful fusion of vintage and elegance, with dark wood panels, polished marble floors, and the quiet luxury of a place steeped in history. His footsteps echoed softly as he approached the elevator, each step carrying him closer to the reunion he both dreaded and felt compelled to make.

The elevator ride up was quiet, giving him a moment to gather his thoughts. He didn't want to dwell on his last conversation with Philippe, but it hovered in his mind nonetheless, each word and loaded silence between them replaying in his head.

His brother had flown in as well, another complication in an already difficult situation. Their relationship was fraught with competition and rivalry, two brothers who had loved and despised each other in equal measure under the weight of their father's expectations.

As the elevator doors slid open onto the private floor, he stepped across into the corridor. Nine rooms, each as grand as the last, spread throughout his father's residence, with massive windows facing Central Park, framing the trees and lights beyond. It was a place of privilege, but also one that held memories he couldn't shake, some good, but many cloaked in tension.

Philippe was waiting for him. His brother stood by the door, arms crossed, his sharp gaze assessing as Oliver approached.

"Oliver," Philippe said, his voice carefully neutral, though the corners of his mouth twitched in something resembling a smirk. "Long time no see."

"I see you didn't waste any time in getting here before me. I assume to get to Father before I could talk to him?"

Philippe sighed, pushing himself away from the wall. "He's been waiting to see you."

Oliver's jaw tightened, but he forced himself to stay calm.

Philippe's eyes narrowed, but he kept his composure.

"Believe it or not, I don't want this any more than you do," he replied, his tone sharper now. "But he's asked for you. So try to keep that in mind before you start throwing accusations around."

They held each other's gaze, the tension between them evident. There were so many things left unsaid—resentments that ran deep, words that had cut both ways, and a lifetime of rivalry and betrayal. But in this moment, with their father's health failing, the old wounds seemed both trivial and insurmountable.

Philippe glanced away first, running a hand through his hair. "Look, just… let's try to get through this with some dignity, all right?"

Oliver nodded, taking a deep breath as he steadied himself.

"Fine. Let's get this over with."

Philippe opened the door, gesturing for Oliver to follow him inside. The familiar scent of leather and polished wood greeted him, mingling with the faintest hint of his father's cologne.

The apartment was as grand as he remembered—massive rooms with soaring ceilings, filled with carefully curated art and elegant furniture. Sunlight streamed in through the floor-to-ceiling windows, casting a warm glow over the space and illuminating the sweeping views of Central Park and beyond.

They walked through the spacious rooms—past the sitting room, with its velvet armchairs and antique fireplace; the library, lined with bookshelves and crowned with a crystal chandelier; and finally, the hallway that led to their father's bedroom. Every detail in the apartment was a testament to Jacques Laurier's taste for refinement and control, from the perfectly polished floors to the meticulously arranged decor. It was a palace built on pride and principles, a place that seemed to demand respect even in the quiet moments.

At the door to the bedroom, Philippe paused, turning to look at Oliver one last time. There was a moment of hesitation, a flicker of something in Philippe's eyes that Oliver couldn't quite decipher—regret, perhaps, or maybe just exhaustion.

"He's weaker than you might expect," Philippe said softly, his usual bravado gone. "Don't let his pride fool you."

Oliver nodded, swallowing the lump in his throat. He didn't know what to expect, but he knew he couldn't back down now. The years of bitterness, the resentment and hurt—they all seemed to fade in the face of this moment, as he prepared himself to confront the man who had shaped so much of his life.

Pushing open the door, Oliver stepped into the room, his heart pounding as he took in the sight of his father. Jacques Laurier lay in a massive bed, propped up by a pile of pillows, his once-powerful frame diminished but his presence still imposing. His face was pale, his features softened by age and illness, but his eyes—the same steely blue that Oliver had inherited—were sharp and aware.

Jacques turned his head, his gaze landing on Oliver with an intensity that hadn't faded with the years. A faint smile played at the edges of his lips, though it was more of an acknowledgment than a greeting.

"Oliver," Jacques murmured, his voice raspy but unmistakably strong. "You finally decided to come."

Oliver moved closer, his emotions warring within him as he looked down at his father. This was the man who had once towered over him, whose approval he had sought and never fully gained. But here, in the quiet of the bedroom, with the weight of years pressing down on both of them, the power dynamic had shifted.

"Hello, Father," Oliver replied, his voice steady, though he felt anything but.

They held each other's gaze, the silence thick with words unspoken and emotions too complicated to name. For a moment, Oliver felt like the boy he once was, standing in his father's shadow, desperate to be seen, to be understood. But he was no longer that boy. He was a man who had built his own life, one that defied his father's expectations, and he wouldn't let himself be diminished now.

Jacques' gaze softened, a glint of something almost like pride in his eyes. "It's good to see you, son," he said quietly. "It's been... too long."

Oliver nodded, the knot in his chest loosening ever so slightly. He didn't know what the next words would bring or how this reunion would unfold, but in this moment, he felt the smallest glimmer of hope—that maybe, just maybe, there was still a chance to find peace.

"I'm so very sorry for your loss. I...I should have reached out. I'm sorry."

Oliver nodded. "It's in the past now, Father. There's nothing more anyone can do but try to move forward. That's what I've been doing...one step, and one day at a time."

Jacques coughed and motioned for the water on the night-stand. Oliver brought the glass close and positioned the straw in front of his father. After a few sips, Jacques waved the glass away.

"I wanted to see you one last time. I'm sure Philippe told you that I'm sick. I don't think he realizes just how sick I am, but I can say that I don't have much time left."

"I understand. Please, save your strength. You don't have to talk."

Jacques nodded. "Yes, I do. I wanted you to know that I've changed my will. You will be contacted soon by my attorney. I'm leaving most everything to you. Philippe will be taken care of, so don't worry about him."

Oliver was shocked. It never occurred to him that his father wanted anything to do with him, let alone leave him such a large inheritance. He shook his head. "No…no, you mustn't. I've told you before, I can't run the company. I don't want to. I have a life, one that I want."

Jacques shook his head. "You don't have to do a thing. Philippe will have enough power to run the company and be well-compensated for it, too. I want you to know that I love you. I always have."

Oliver struggled not to cry, but the tears threatened to fall anyway.

"You don't have to give me money to show me that you care. Telling me you love me is all I need. I love you, too. I've been just as stubborn as you have, I think."

"Take the money, Oliver. If nothing else, use it to build the life you want. Maybe open a restaurant or travel the world. Start a foundation in Katie's name. Do whatever you want. It would mean so much to me after I'm gone to know I've had some small connection to you and your future. Please, do this for me."

Oliver wanted to protest for so many reasons, mostly, because he knew the wedge between him and Philippe would only widen. But this was his father's death-bed wish, and he couldn't deny him that.

Oliver nodded. "Okay, I don't have a clue what I'll do with it, but I promise whatever it is, your name will be associated with it. It's the least I can do."

His father's eyes had closed in the middle of his answer, and Oliver couldn't tell whether he heard his response. He waited, and after a few minutes, his father opened his eyes.

"Thank you, son. Thank you for granting me this. Live your life and be happy."

Jacques Laurier closed his eyes one last time and was gone.

Oliver closed the door to his father's room, his mind still reeling from the encounter. Jacques' frail figure haunted him, a shadow of the man he remembered, and the weight of their conversation lingered heavily in his chest. He needed to find Philippe or someone to tell them his father had died, but his first instinct was to find fresh air.

He ran to the nearest window, opened it, and let the blast of cold, winter air hit his face as his tears fell. He stayed in that position for several minutes and then closed the window. He was ready to retreat, to find some air in the quiet hallways of the Dakota, when a familiar figure appeared from around the corner.

Sabrina.

She paused, a slight smile curving her lips as she took him in. Dressed in an elegant but subdued dress, she looked every bit the polished socialite. Yet behind the carefully composed exterior, Oliver could see the calculated glint in her eyes—the same glint he'd recognized all those years ago.

"Oliver," she greeted softly, her voice smooth and layered with just the right amount of remorse. "It's been a long time."

He nodded, keeping his expression neutral. "Sabrina."

She stepped closer, her gaze flickering over him with a mixture of curiosity and something else—an unspoken invitation, perhaps, but he wasn't interested in finding out. Still, she continued, undeterred.

"I heard you were coming," she said, tilting her head. "Philippe told me you were coming." Her eyes softened in a way that felt rehearsed, though she tried to make it look genuine. "I… I'm sorry for everything, Oliver. For the way things turned out between us. It wasn't how I wanted things to go."

He met her gaze, his face unreadable. "You wanted a life of wealth and influence, Sabrina. That's exactly what you got. Besides, it was a long time ago."

Her smile wavered, a brief flicker of frustration crossing her face before she recovered. She took a small step closer, her voice dropping to a softer, more sympathetic tone. "I heard about Katie. And... your boys. I can't imagine the pain of losing them. Truly, Oliver, I'm so sorry."

Oliver's jaw tightened, and he forced himself to breathe evenly, resisting the urge to walk away. The mention of Katie and their children stung, but he wouldn't give Sabrina the satisfaction of seeing him react.

"Thank you," he replied curtly, though he kept his voice polite.

Sabrina studied him for a moment, her gaze lingering as she seemed to search for a crack in his composure. "If there's anything I can do... I know it's been years, but we were close once. And sometimes, I wonder..." She trailed off, letting the implication hang in the air, her eyes flickering with a hint of flirtation.

Oliver narrowed his eyes, unimpressed. "Wonder what, Sabrina? How things would be if you hadn't chosen Philippe? Or if you hadn't decided that a man's bank account wasn't worth more than his integrity?"

She flinched, though she quickly masked it, smoothing her expression back into one of practiced sympathy.

"I made mistakes, Oliver," she said, a slight quiver in her voice, as if she were on the verge of being vulnerable. "I was young, impressionable. But that doesn't mean I don't regret what happened between us."

He crossed his arms, leaning back against the wall. "Regret doesn't erase choices. And we both know you're exactly where you want to be."

Sabrina gave a soft sigh, lowering her gaze as if considering his words.

"You think I'm happy?" she asked, her voice barely above a whisper. "With Philippe? We may share a house and a name, but there's no love between us. None at all."

Oliver raised an eyebrow, unimpressed by her confession.

"Maybe that's because you both only see people as stepping stones."

A faint blush crept into her cheeks, but she met his gaze, undeterred. "I used to think that way. But seeing you again... it reminds me of what we could've had." She reached out, letting her fingers graze his arm lightly. "Maybe we don't have to keep pretending, Oliver. We're both trapped in lives that are... unfulfilling."

He stiffened, stepping back from her touch. "I'm not trapped, Sabrina. I chose my life. And I may have regrets, but I'd rather live with them than go back to someone who values money over loyalty."

Her eyes darkened, a flash of frustration finally breaking through the mask of sympathy. "You're one to talk about loyalty. You were the one who walked away, who refused to fight for us."

He met her glare with one of his own. "There was no 'us' to fight for, Sabrina. You made your choice, and I moved on. I was happy with Katie, and we built a life that meant something."

She pursed her lips, her expression hardening. "And now she's gone, isn't she?" Her words were a whisper, cutting and deliberate. "You're alone. Just like I am."

The cruelty in her tone was unmistakable, and Oliver felt a surge of anger rising within him. He took a step closer, his voice cold and steady.

"Don't ever speak of her again, Sabrina. You don't get to use her memory to get what you want."

A flicker of fear crossed her face, but it vanished as quickly as it appeared. She forced a smile, though it no longer held any warmth. "It's a shame," she murmured, her voice brittle. "I thought maybe we could start over. That we could find something we both lost."

Oliver shook his head, his gaze unyielding. "The only thing I've lost is any trace of respect I had for you. I know exactly why you're here. You want me to tell Jacques to leave more to

Philippe, to make things easier on him. But I'm done playing games with you."

Sabrina's expression faltered, her carefully constructed mask slipping as she clenched her jaw. "You don't know anything about me, Oliver."

"Oh, I know plenty," he replied, his voice cutting. "I know that nothing's ever enough for you. Not love, not loyalty. And you'll never get that from me."

They stared at each other for a long moment, the air between them charged with unspoken resentment and bitterness. Finally, Sabrina straightened, her eyes cold as she regarded him.

"Fine," she said quietly, her voice laced with disdain. "If that's how you want it. But don't think Philippe won't make things difficult for you if you stand in his way."

Oliver's expression didn't waver. "Philippe's been making things difficult for me my whole life. I can handle it. But if you have any doubt about my opinion of you, let me say this. Knowing what I know now, I'd choose Katie all over again. I would choose to have only a few years with her rather than a lifetime with you."

Sabrina's lips pressed into a thin line, and without another word, she turned and walked down the hallway, her heels clicking sharply against the polished floors. Oliver watched her go, a sense of finality settling over him. The past, with all its betrayals and regrets, seemed to fade into the distance as he stood alone in the hallway, the echo of her footsteps growing fainter.

With a deep breath, he was about to turn away but stopped and called out to her.

"Sabrina!"

She turned to look at him with a confused expression. "What?"

"Find your husband, our father died five minutes ago."

# CHAPTER 25

helsea stood on her front porch, watching her sisters gather their things. Their final moments together were calm and without the usual drama Chelsea had come to expect. Tess was rummaging through her tote bag, searching for her keys, while Leah was securing the last of her luggage.

Gretchen stood off to the side, her arms crossed, a small smile on her face as she watched her sisters. She would be staying behind, holding down the fort at Chelsea's house while she and Steven took off for their honeymoon in Hawaii. It felt strange, this moment—the four of them together, but already starting to splinter off in different directions.

Chelsea broke the silence, her voice warm but tinged with a hint of sadness. "Well, I guess this is it. I feel like we just got together, and now everyone's scattering again."

Leah grinned, coming over to wrap her arms around Chelsea in a tight hug. "That's how it always is, isn't it? We gather, we laugh, we make memories, and then life pulls us back to where we came from."

Tess joined them, tucking her keys into her bag.

"Back to Key West, where the real adventure is," she joked,

nudging Leah with a wink. "I think the two of us need to keep things interesting while Gretchen plays house here."

Gretchen rolled her eyes, though her smile softened. "I'm just grateful Chelsea trusts me with her place. I'll take good care of it, I promise." She gave Chelsea a small, reassuring nod. "Stella and I are going to be best friends by the time you get back."

Chelsea laughed, picturing her independent cat, Stella, cautiously warming up to Gretchen over the course of the next month. "Good luck with her. She's picky, but I think you'll win her over eventually."

"By the way, I've already called a real estate agent to help me look for something permanent. So, who knows what I might find while you're gone."

"Well, we wish you luck. Come here and give us a hug," Tess said.

Chelsea smiled, watching her three sisters do their best to mend fences and get along. Just then, Steven came down the front stairs to join them.

"Steven, you take care of our girl here, or you'll have to answer to us," Leah added.

"Oh, you don't have to worry about that. If she'll let me, I plan to spoil my new wife."

Chelsea laughed. "I promise, I'll let you."

There was a brief silence as each sister took in the moment, knowing how rare these goodbyes had become as life took them in different directions.

Leah cleared her throat, glancing over at Tess before turning back to Chelsea.

"We'll miss you," Leah said softly. "And I hope this trip is everything you dreamed it would be. You deserve it, Chelsea. You've always taken care of everyone else—now it's your turn to be taken care of."

Chelsea's heart swelled, and she hugged Leah tightly again,

then Tess, feeling the familiar sense of connection that had carried them through every stage of their lives.

"Thank you, Leah. And Tess, you two better not get into too much trouble down in Key West," she added, smiling as she pulled back to look at them both.

"No promises," Tess shot back, grinning. "But we'll keep it within reason, at least until you get back."

The laughter faded, and Gretchen stepped forward, giving Chelsea a hug that lingered a little longer than the others. "I'll take good care of your home. And if Stella gets lonely, I'll make sure she has plenty of company."

Chelsea squeezed her tightly. "Good luck with that. She spends most of her time under the bed. It will be interesting to see how she handles this. It means a lot to me, knowing you'll be here. And just... take care of yourself too, all right?"

Gretchen nodded, her gaze steady and full of reassurance. "I will. And I'll be waiting for you to come back so we can catch up on all the honeymoon stories."

Tess and Leah shared a smirk, exchanging amused glances. "Oh, we'll want to hear those stories too," Leah teased, winking at Chelsea.

Chelsea blushed, laughing. "You'll have to wait for that. I'm not spilling all the details."

Tess gave her one last hug, a mischievous gleam in her eyes. "Well, we're happy for you, big sis. Steven's a lucky guy."

As they pulled back, Chelsea felt the bittersweetness of the goodbye settle over her again, the weight of each parting hug and shared smile. But there was warmth in it too—the kind of warmth that only family could bring, grounding her in the knowledge that, no matter where they were, they would always be there for each other.

With one last wave and a few shared laughs, Tess and Leah made their way to the car, leaving Chelsea, Steven and Gretchen standing together.

Chelsea sighed, watching the car pull away, before turning to Gretchen and giving her a hug. "All right, looks like the taxi is here for us."

Steven greeted the driver and together they put the luggage in the trunk.

"You two have a beautiful honeymoon, and don't worry about a thing. I've got everything here covered."

Chelsea and Steven got in the backseat of the taxi and waved as it drove down Andy Rosse Lane.

Maggie's phone buzzed softly on the side table, the screen lighting up with Oliver's name. She answered quickly, her heart sinking as she prepared herself for the conversation. She'd been awaiting this call, but a part of her had hoped, irrationally, that it might bring some relief.

"Oliver," she greeted, her voice warm but careful. "How are you doing?"

There was a pause on the line, one that stretched a beat too long. When he finally responded, his voice was low, carrying the exhaustion of someone who'd been holding a heavy burden alone. "It's been a long day, Maggie. My father passed this morning."

"Oh, Oliver," she whispered, leaning back into the couch, her heart aching for him. "I'm so sorry. I know it's been difficult."

"Thank you," he replied, and she could hear the strain in his voice, the weight of years spent in complicated family dynamics.

"He... it was peaceful, in the end. But there's so much left to do here. He had a lot of connections, and there's a long list of people who'll expect a formal farewell."

Maggie imagined the grand world Jacques Laurier had inhabited—New York's elite, the longstanding business alliances, and the reputation that Jacques had so meticulously cultivated. It was a world that had cast its shadow over Oliver his whole life, and now it seemed to be pulling him back in.

"Of course, of course," she said softly. "I understand."

Oliver exhaled a breath that sounded almost like a sigh.

"Philippe's made it clear he wants me to stay and help oversee everything. He's been in touch with the old business associates, getting the legal matters in order. There's... so much to handle." His voice trailed off, weighted with exhaustion.

She didn't respond immediately, sensing that he needed space to share his thoughts. There was a vulnerability in Oliver's tone that he rarely let show, a reminder of the man who had once confided in her during his time at the inn, away from his former life.

"It sounds overwhelming," she said gently, after a pause. "But don't feel like you have to take it all on yourself, Oliver. You've done a lot. Maybe let your brother carry the load a bit. I don't know him of course, but don't let him dump everything in your lap."

Maggie chuckled. "Listen to me. I sound like an over-protective mother."

"I know," he replied, though there was an edge of resignation in his voice. "But he was my father. And despite... everything, I feel a responsibility. Philippe's putting pressure on me, but it's probably nothing to the pressures I'm putting on myself. It's hard to just walk away."

Maggie's heart sank a little further. She knew how deep the pull of family obligations could run, especially with a history as tangled and complex as Oliver's with Jacques and Philippe.

"Take all the time you need, Oliver. Just remember, you have a life here too. You've built something for yourself, something that's yours."

He was quiet, and she wondered if he was grappling with the same fears she was—that perhaps New York would pull him in once again, that he might feel compelled to stay, to assume a role he had once rejected.

"I'll do my best, Maggie," he said finally, his voice heavy. "I'm not sure when I'll be back. It could be weeks—maybe longer."

She closed her eyes, the uncertainty gnawing at her.

"Whenever you're ready. We'll all be here, waiting for you."

He murmured a quiet thank you before they ended the call.

Maggie sat for a moment, her phone still in her hand, her thoughts swirling. She wanted to believe he would come back to Captiva, back to the inn and the life he'd started to build. But his voice had been laden with a resignation she hadn't heard before, a weariness that made her wonder if he would indeed return.

She felt a hand on her shoulder and looked up to see Paolo standing beside her, his expression concerned.

"Was that Oliver?" he asked gently, his hand squeezing her shoulder.

She nodded. "Yes," she replied, her voice thick with worry. "His father passed away this morning, and he's staying in New York to handle the arrangements."

Paolo nodded, a look of sympathy crossing his face.

"That makes sense. I imagine there's a lot to take care of."

"Yes," she agreed, though her heart felt heavy. "But it wasn't just that, Paolo. He sounded... different. Like he might not come back. New York has a way of pulling people in, and with his father's legacy and Philippe pressuring him, not to mention...the money. That kind of money he'll never get here. I just... I'm worried he'll feel he has to stay, or worst yet, he wants to stay."

Paolo wrapped his arms around her, offering the comfort she needed.

"I understand. But Oliver's his own person. He's not the boy he once was, trying to live up to his father's expectations. He's made a life here—a good one. Give him some time to sort things out."

Maggie rested her head against Paolo's shoulder, trying to take solace in his words.

"You're right. I just hope he remembers what he's built here and doesn't lose himself in that world."

Their conversation was interrupted by a soft shuffling sound, and they turned to see Iris standing in the doorway, her face pale and her eyes wide. She had a stack of dishes in her arms, and it was clear she'd overheard every word.

"Iris," Maggie said, her tone gentle but surprised. "I didn't realize you were still in here."

Iris set the dishes down carefully, her hands trembling. "I… I just heard. Oliver might not be coming back?"

Maggie hesitated, realizing how her words must have sounded to Iris, who had quietly harbored feelings for Oliver. "He's just handling things in New York for now. There's no need to worry."

But Iris' face fell, her expression one of barely concealed distress. "You don't understand, Maggie. If he stays in New York… I don't know if I'll…we'll ever see him again. He means a lot to the inn…to all of us."

Maggie stepped toward her, reaching out a comforting hand, knowing full well Iris felt more for Oliver than she could share.

"Iris, I'm sure he'll be back. He has a life here—a life he loves. You're part of that."

But the assurance did little to ease Iris' worry. She shook her head, taking a step back as tears filled her eyes.

"It's different in New York. There's so much there, so many expectations. What if he feels he has to stay? What if he thinks he doesn't have anything worth coming back for?"

The depth of Iris' words struck Maggie, and she realized just how much Oliver's presence had come to mean to her. She opened her mouth to speak, but before she could offer any more comfort, Iris turned and hurried out of the room, her footsteps echoing down the hallway.

Paolo sighed, rubbing a hand over his face. "Poor Iris. I didn't realize…"

Maggie nodded, watching the door through which Iris had disappeared.

"She cares for him more than she's ever let on. I wish I could say something to reassure her, but I don't know what Oliver's plans are."

They sat in silence for a moment, each lost in thought.

Finally, Maggie let out a deep breath, looking up at Paolo. "I just hope he realizes how much he has waiting for him here. The inn, his friends, and people who care about him deeply."

Paolo nodded, wrapping his arm around her again. "He's a good man, Maggie. Whatever decision he makes, it'll be the right one. All we can do is trust him."

Maggie nodded, though her worry lingered. In her heart, she knew that Oliver was facing a choice that would define the rest of his life—a choice between the past and the present, between family duty and the life he'd created for himself. She only hoped that, when the time came, he would choose the path that will lead him back to Captiva Island.

# CHAPTER 26

*T*he imposing stone pillars of the cathedral loomed high above, casting long shadows over the gathered crowd. Dignitaries, business magnates, and politicians mingled with family members and longtime friends, each clad in the somber attire befitting Jacques Laurier's stature. The entire affair had been planned meticulously, with every detail mirroring the formality and power Jacques had commanded in his life. For Oliver, it was almost surreal to witness.

Sitting in the church pew, Oliver felt both part of the scene and yet profoundly detached from it. His father's presence lingered in every corner of the vast cathedral, from the solemn organ music that echoed through the vaulted ceilings to the opulent arrangements of white lilies and roses adorning the aisles. It was a scene befitting a king, a spectacle of reverence and tradition that spoke to the man his father had been—formidable, respected, and feared.

The guest list read like a who's who of the global elite: European royalty, CEOs from the world's largest corporations, and several prominent political figures all sat in the pews, their heads bowed in tribute. Jacques had always been more than just a businessman; he was a symbol of power, a man whose influence stretched far beyond Wall Street. Yet, as Oliver looked out over the sea of faces, he couldn't help but feel that few of them had truly known him.

As the eulogy began, Oliver's gaze fell on his brother, Philippe, seated with Sabrina at his side. Philippe's expression was one of solemnity, his back straight, his hands folded neatly in his lap. Beside him, Sabrina dabbed delicately at her eyes with a lace handkerchief, though Oliver doubted the sincerity of her tears. She had known Jacques less as a father-in-law and more as a man who could elevate her own status, and her grief seemed calculated, almost performative.

The archbishop's voice filled the space, recounting Jacques Laurier's achievements with a reverence that Oliver found difficult to share. "Jacques Laurier was a man of vision," the archbishop intoned, his voice carrying a weight that reverberated through the cathedral. "A man who saw beyond the limitations of his time, who forged a path of success and power not only for himself but for those who came after him."

Oliver's jaw tightened, listening as accolades were heaped upon his father's legacy. To the world, Jacques Laurier was a paragon of success, a man whose legacy would live on for generations. But to Oliver, he was simply a father—flawed, distant, and often harsh. The love he'd withheld had left scars that no amount of wealth or praise could ever heal.

When the archbishop finished, Philippe rose, his steps measured as he approached the podium. His shoulders were squared, his expression somber but composed, and for a moment, Oliver saw a reflection of their father in his brother. Philippe had been molded by Jacques, shaped into the very image of the man who now lay in a casket before them. As Philippe began to speak, his voice steady and unyielding, Oliver felt a pang of sadness for his brother. Jacques' legacy had become Philippe's burden, a weight he carried with pride and resentment alike.

"My father," Philippe began, his voice clear and steady, "was a man of great ambition. He believed in the power of hard work, of discipline, and above all, in loyalty to family. He taught us to strive, to never settle, and to leave a mark on the world that would endure." Philippe's eyes scanned the crowd, his gaze lingering on familiar faces. "His legacy is one of resilience, of vision, and of strength."

Oliver watched as Philippe continued, each word polished, each sentence a tribute to the man their father had been. But beneath the carefully chosen words, Oliver sensed an undercurrent of bitterness, a resentment Philippe could never fully mask. His brother was Jacques' successor, the chosen heir to Laurier Financial Holdings, but that inheritance had come at a cost—a cost Oliver was all too familiar with.

As Philippe finished, a soft murmur of approval rippled through the congregation. He returned to his seat, his expression once again unreadable, and Oliver felt a moment of sympathy for him. Philippe bore the weight of their father's expectations, a burden that would shape him long after Jacques was gone.

Finally, it was Oliver's turn. He hadn't intended to speak, but as he rose, he felt an inexplicable pull—a need to honor his father in his own way, to find closure in the words he'd never been able to say.

He approached the podium, his steps slower, more hesitant than Philippe's had been. As he looked out over the crowd, he saw a few familiar faces—family friends, old colleagues, even some from his past life in New York. But his gaze returned to Philippe and Sabrina, both watching him with expressions that ranged from curiosity to mild surprise.

"My father and I... had our differences," he began, his voice steady but soft. "He was a man of strong convictions, and he lived his life with a sense of purpose that was, at times, difficult to understand. But as I stand here today, I realize that despite our differences, he gave me something invaluable—the freedom to find my own path, even if it was one he couldn't understand."

A hush settled over the congregation as he continued, his words unpolished but genuine. "My father taught me many things, some of them through words, others through silence. He showed me the power of resilience, of determination. And though we rarely saw eye to eye, I know he wanted the best for me, even if his way of showing it was... complicated, just as I know that he is at peace beside our mother, once more."

Oliver paused, gathering his thoughts, and took a steadying breath. "I am grateful for the lessons he taught me, for the example he set, and for the strength he passed on to my brother and me. His legacy is one I will carry with me—not in the way he may have imagined, but in my own way."

He stepped back, his heart heavy yet strangely lighter, as if a weight had been lifted. Returning to his seat, he felt Philippe's eyes on him, a brief moment of understanding passing between them. They may have chosen different paths, but they shared a bond that even their father's death couldn't sever.

The service continued, the organ music swelling as the congregation rose to pay their final respects. As they filed past the casket, Oliver's thoughts drifted to Katie and his sons, to Captiva, and the life he had carved out for himself far from the world of wealth and power. He knew now, more than ever, that he had made the right choice to leave this world behind, and he couldn't imagine returning to it now.

When the last of the guests had paid their respects, Oliver, Philippe and Sabrina remained, their father's casket before them, the silence settling heavily in the grand space. Philippe turned to him, his expression guarded but not unkind.

"He respected you, you know," Philippe said quietly, his voice tinged with something Oliver couldn't quite place. "He may not have shown it, but he did."

Oliver met his brother's gaze, nodding slowly. "I know. I think, in his own way, he wanted us both to succeed."

A faint, bitter smile crossed Philippe's face. "And now that he's gone, it's up to us to carry on that success."

Oliver said nothing, understanding the weight of those words. Philippe would continue the legacy, holding on to the business and everything their father had built, while Oliver would return to Captiva, to the life he had chosen—a life free from the constraints of Jacques' world.

As they left the cathedral, the city stretched out before them, bustling and indifferent, the sounds of traffic and voices filling the air. It was a stark contrast to the quiet, solemn atmosphere of the funeral, and Oliver felt a pang of relief, as if he was finally able to breathe again.

He turned to Philippe, his tone soft. "I'll be heading back soon. To Captiva, but we undoubtedly have to deal with the estate. How long do you think that will take?"

Philippe shrugged. "I wouldn't think it would take very long at all. Father made it clear that I would take over and you would live your life as you see fit. I don't expect anything will change."

It was clear to Oliver that Philippe had no idea what was coming. They were to meet with his father's attorney in a few days, and Oliver felt sick over what lay ahead.

Whatever he knew of their father's wishes, Philippe wasn't letting on, and that meant a storm was about to come down on all of them.

# CHAPTER 27

*T*he next two days, Oliver walked the streets of New York City, aimless but not entirely lost. The bustling streets spread out before him, a sea of movement and noise that never seemed to end.

Yellow cabs zipped past in constant streams, honking their way through traffic as pedestrians navigated around them with practiced ease.

He drifted along, letting his feet carry him while he took in the familiar sights, the towering skyscrapers that stretched up like monuments to ambition and wealth. There was a time when this activity energized him, but now the noise and fast-paced city life felt overwhelming.

He passed Rockefeller Center, its gleaming ice rink drawing in tourists bundled up against the chilly December air. Laughter echoed as couples held hands, children wobbled on skates, and everyone seemed engrossed in their own small worlds. A few blocks later, the enormous glass facade of the Apple Store loomed ahead, its entrance crowded with people streaming in and out, each on a mission. It was the pulse of the city—a vibrant, unstoppable rhythm that had once fueled him.

But now, that pulse felt distant. He felt like an outsider, an observer in a world he'd left behind. He continued to walk, his thoughts drifting to the years he'd spent under his father's shadow, striving to meet expectations he had never felt aligned with.

Growing up, the path had always been clear: follow in Jacques' footsteps, take his place in the family business, and uphold the Laurier name. Yet, he'd chosen a different path—a winding, uncertain one that had led him to the life he had now.

As he approached Central Park, he paused, looking out over the vast stretch of green against the concrete cityscape. In the distance, he could see the outlines of the Plaza Hotel and the shimmering surface of the lake beyond it. Captiva's beaches seemed so far from here, a world apart from the frenetic energy of New York. Captiva had given him something he'd never found here—a sense of calm, of being at home in his own skin.

He continued walking until he found a small coffee shop nestled on the corner of a quiet street. Pushing the door open, he was greeted by the comforting scent of freshly ground coffee and the soft murmur of conversations.

He ordered a coffee and settled by the window, watching as people hurried by, each one with their own destination, their own purpose. In the middle of all that chaos, he felt a strange sense of peace. Here, surrounded by strangers and the city's noise, he could almost lose himself in the anonymity of it all.

As he sipped his coffee, his thoughts wandered back to Captiva, to the life he'd built there. The inn, with its warm walls and familiar faces, felt like a sanctuary compared to the cold formality of his father's estate.

He thought of the mornings he spent at the inn, the scent of breakfast wafting through the kitchen, the easy laughter that filled the halls. It was a far cry from the life he'd known here, where every interaction was transactional, every relationship tinged with the expectation of gain.

His thoughts drifted, unbidden, to Katie, and a pang of bittersweet nostalgia washed over him. She had been his anchor during those turbulent years, the one person who saw past the Laurier legacy and loved him for who he was.

In Katie, he had found a partner, someone who encouraged him to pursue his passion for cooking, to embrace a life that felt true to him, even if it meant walking away from the family business.

Katie had been a wonderful mother, a quality he cherished even more deeply now, more than eighteen months after her passing. She had a gentle way of nurturing their boys, her patience endless, her love a steady, comforting presence that filled their home.

Even in the chaos of young children, she had managed to bring a sense of calm, a sense of order that allowed him to focus on his dreams.

Watching her with their children, he'd often been struck by her selflessness, her willingness to give of herself without reservation. She'd created a home filled with love, laughter, and warmth—a sanctuary for him, just as Captiva had become.

But Katie had also been strong, her support unwavering even in the face of his family's disapproval. She'd stood by him as he made his choice to break away from the Laurier empire, quietly shouldering the consequences that came with it. She had understood him in a way no one else had, seeing beyond the surface to the man he wanted to become. And when she'd passed, it was as if a piece of that vision had gone with her, leaving him adrift, uncertain if he could ever find that kind of peace again.

He let out a long breath, a wistful smile touching his lips. Katie had been irreplaceable, and no one would ever fill the space she'd left. But, as his thoughts wandered to Iris, he couldn't deny the warmth that flickered in his chest. She had her own quiet strength, her own gentleness, and, like Katie, a genuine love for life and people that had begun to draw him in.

He remembered the way Iris' face lit up over the smallest things—a new recipe, a story shared over dinner, or the simple joy of harvesting fresh herbs from the inn's small garden. She hadn't known him in the world he'd left behind, hadn't seen him as the heir of a powerful family, and he loved that. She saw him as he was now, without expectations, without the weight of his family's legacy looming over him.

The two women were worlds apart in his life's timeline, yet they were both gentle souls who'd shown him different paths to happiness. Katie had been his first true love, someone who'd believed in his potential and given him courage.

Iris... she was becoming something else, something unexpected. He didn't know if he was ready to name it, but he knew it was real and unforced, growing quietly between them.

He recalled one evening at the inn when they'd lingered in the kitchen long after closing, swapping stories over coffee, neither one in a hurry to leave. Iris had laughed at something he'd said—a rich, genuine laugh that had filled the quiet space—and he'd felt a strange warmth bloom in his chest, a feeling he hadn't known in years.

Now, sitting in this bustling New York coffee shop, he realized just how much he missed her, how much he missed that life. Captiva was home in ways he hadn't fully appreciated until now. There, he was more than just Jacques Laurier's son; he was himself, free to live as he chose. Iris had become part of that life, part of the comfort he felt there. She was woven into his days, her laughter, her company, and her friendship an unspoken anchor he hadn't even known he'd needed.

A sharp jolt from the street outside interrupted his thoughts— a horn blaring as a cab swerved around a bicyclist—and he blinked, pulling himself back into the present. The city's chaotic energy surrounded him, but he felt detached, as though a wall stood between him and the life that had once been his reality. Here, ambition, money, and reputation ruled, but in Captiva, none of that mattered. It was a place of peace and simplicity, qualities that had become precious to him.

For a fleeting moment, he wondered what Katie would think of Iris, and he felt certain that she would approve. They shared the same kindness, a genuine love for life and for the people around them. It comforted him to imagine Katie's silent blessing, as though she'd somehow guided him toward Iris.

With a final sip of coffee, Oliver felt a quiet resolve settle over him. He was certain now, more than ever, that his future belonged in Captiva.

Whatever the next few days held, whatever turmoil the will might unleash, he would face it all knowing where his heart lay. And when it was all over, he'd return to the island, back to the life and the people who had come to mean so much to him.

As he gathered his things and left the coffee shop, a strange, unshakable calm filled him. He knew who he was and where he wanted to be.

# CHAPTER 28

*T*he heavy oak doors of his father's office loomed ahead, familiar yet imposing, and Oliver took a deep breath before stepping inside.

His father's presence still lingered here—the scent of polished wood, faint traces of cigar smoke, and the quiet orderliness of the room, as if Jacques Laurier might reappear at any moment, surveying his kingdom. Rows of leather-bound books lined the walls, and the grand mahogany desk commanded the center of the room, its surface meticulously organized, with not a single object out of place.

As Oliver entered, he saw Philippe already seated in the leather armchair beside their father's desk, his posture tense, his gaze locked forward. Sabrina was beside him, her hand resting lightly on his arm, her expression calm but watchful. She glanced at Oliver as he entered, her eyes lingering on him just a moment too long, and he returned her gaze with a blank expression, unwilling to give her any reaction. He found his own seat, keeping his distance from both Philippe and Sabrina.

Across from them, at the desk, was Mr. McMurphy, their father's longtime lawyer. A man in his sixties with graying hair and a somber face, McMurphy was known for his discretion and meticulousness, his loyalty unwavering until the end. Today, his demeanor was more serious than usual, and he gave Oliver a brief, respectful nod before organizing the documents spread before him.

"Thank you all for being here," Mr. McMurphy began, his voice formal yet gentle. "I know this is a difficult time, and I appreciate you gathering to go through Jacques Laurier's final wishes. Your father, as you both know, was a man of order. He left very specific instructions regarding the distribution of his assets and control of his business."

Philippe shifted in his seat, glancing over at Oliver, a hint of impatience in his expression. Oliver noticed the tightness around his brother's mouth, the way his hands gripped the armrests a little too hard. The tension between them was palpable, unspoken words and years of rivalry hanging heavy in the air.

McMurphy adjusted his glasses, taking a moment to ensure he had their attention. "Jacques Laurier was very clear about how he wanted his legacy to be handled. He left substantial financial holdings, real estate properties, and, of course, the family business. I will read his specific allocations and instructions now."

Sabrina's eyes flickered with interest, her gaze sliding from the lawyer to Oliver and then to her husband. She sat with her back straight, her expression a blend of politeness and barely concealed curiosity. Oliver suspected she knew more than she let on, but he kept his focus on Mr. McMurphy, determined not to let Sabrina's presence distract him.

McMurphy cleared his throat, beginning with the formal language of the document. "To my eldest son, Philippe Laurier, I bequeath full control of Laurier Financial Holdings. Philippe, you will have the final say in all business matters and continue as CEO, upholding the family name and tradition."

Philippe's posture relaxed slightly, and a faint smirk appeared on his face, though he kept his gaze straight ahead. The business had always been his focus, the one thing he could control and shape in his own image. Oliver knew that to Philippe, this was a victory. His brother's shoulders squared, as though he'd received the validation he'd always craved.

McMurphy continued, his tone unchanging. "In addition to control of Laurier Financial Holdings, you will also inherit a portion of your father's personal estate, to the amount of twenty-five million dollars."

Philippe's smirk faded, replaced by a look of confusion. Oliver could see the calculation in his brother's eyes, the realization that their father's wealth far exceeded twenty-five million dollars. Philippe's gaze shifted to McMurphy, waiting, clearly expecting more.

McMurphy didn't falter. "Now, to Jacques Laurier's younger son, Oliver Laurier. Jacques specified that, in light of Oliver's decision to pursue his own career outside of the family business, he wished to support Oliver in his chosen path. To that end, he has left you a sum of three-hundred and fifty million dollars, along with ownership of the family estate in Connecticut and the vacation property in the Hamptons."

A sharp intake of breath escaped Philippe, his face growing pale as McMurphy's words sank in. He shot Oliver a glare, barely masking his anger, his hands gripping the armrests even tighter. "What?" he demanded, his voice low but seething. "Three-hundred-fifty million?"

McMurphy looked at Philippe, his expression carefully neutral. "That is correct, Philippe. Your father felt it was important to recognize Oliver's independence and provide him with a secure future."

Sabrina's gaze darted between the brothers, a flicker of surprise and perhaps envy crossing her face. She glanced at Philippe, whose jaw was clenched tight, the fury in his eyes barely concealed.

"Of course," McMurphy continued, "both of you will retain

partial ownership of the family's real estate investments, and Philippe, you will have the authority to make decisions on their management."

Philippe leaned forward, his voice a hiss. "You're telling me he left Oliver more than fourteen times what he left me, his eldest son? The one who actually stayed in the family business?"

McMurphy's tone remained calm, though there was a faint hint of firmness as he replied, "Your father was very deliberate in his decisions, Philippe. He appreciated the sacrifices you made for the business, which is why he entrusted it entirely to you. However, he also recognized the value in supporting Oliver's independence."

Philippe scoffed, his eyes narrowing as he glared at Oliver. "Independence," he muttered, barely audible but loaded with disdain. "Right."

Oliver felt his brother's eyes boring into him, and he met Philippe's gaze with a calm he didn't quite feel. The inheritance was far more than he'd expected, and a part of him still struggled to understand his father's reasoning. Jacques had never been openly supportive of Oliver's career as a chef, often dismissing it as a waste of potential, something beneath the Laurier name. And yet, here he was, leaving Oliver a fortune that would secure him for life, as if in some final, unexpected acknowledgment.

Philippe's hands clenched into fists, and he shook his head, a bitter smile twisting his mouth. "Unbelievable," he muttered, his gaze now fixed on McMurphy. "So he gives me the business, the responsibility, and Oliver gets… everything else?"

McMurphy offered a measured response. "I assure you, your father made his decisions with great thought, Philippe. His intention was to honor each of you in different ways."

Sabrina placed a hand on Philippe's arm, her fingers tightening slightly. "Philippe, it's not worth it," she murmured, though her tone was far from soothing. "You have the control, the legacy. Isn't that what matters?"

Philippe looked at her, a flicker of frustration crossing his face before he turned his glare back on Oliver. "I hope you're happy," he said, his tone dripping with sarcasm. "You get your precious freedom, your millions, and yet somehow, you're still the one who comes out on top. Isn't that just perfect?"

Oliver kept his expression neutral, unwilling to give his brother the satisfaction of seeing him rattled. "This wasn't my decision, Philippe," he replied quietly. "I had no control over what he left us."

"Oh, spare me the act," Philippe snapped. "You waltz in here, the golden child who left it all behind, and now you get to reap the rewards for doing nothing."

Oliver felt a flicker of anger, but he forced himself to remain calm. "I didn't ask for this," he said, his voice steady. "If it means that much to you, Philippe, we can discuss other arrangements. But I won't apologize for my choices."

Philippe laughed bitterly. "Arrangements? Please. Do you think I want your pity?"

Sabrina's gaze lingered on Oliver, her expression unreadable, but there was a glint in her eyes that made him uneasy. "Maybe it's best if we all take some time to let this settle," she said smoothly. "We've all had a difficult few days."

McMurphy cleared his throat, interrupting the charged silence. "I understand this is an emotional moment, but your father's wishes were clear. My duty is to honor those wishes. If there are any questions or clarifications needed, please feel free to contact me."

Philippe's jaw tightened, and he pushed himself up from the chair abruptly, ignoring the lawyer's polite offer. "This is a farce," he muttered, heading toward the door, Sabrina following closely behind.

Oliver remained seated, watching his brother's retreating figure. He felt the weight of the inheritance, of his father's decision, settling on him, mingling with the conflicting emotions that had surfaced since he'd returned to New York. This city, with its skyscrapers and sprawling estates, represented a world he had left behind long ago—a world he'd fought to escape.

He rose slowly, nodding to Mr. McMurphy in acknowledgment before leaving the room. The hallway was quiet, but as he made his way toward the front, he caught a glimpse of Philippe and Sabrina, their voices muffled but unmistakably tense. Sabrina's gaze flicked toward him as he passed, a faint smile playing at her lips, though it lacked any warmth.

As he stepped outside, the cool city air hit his face, and he took a deep breath, letting it wash over him. He knew he had everything he needed to leave New York behind, to sever his ties with the family business and the complicated web his father had left for them all. And yet, Philippe's bitter words echoed in his mind, unsettling him more than he'd like to admit.

The world of wealth and expectation that he had escaped was now sitting in his lap, intertwined with a family legacy he'd never wanted to uphold. The fortune, the real estate, even the bitter looks from Philippe—it all felt like a chain linking him to a past he'd fought to leave behind.

A shadow passed over the doorway as Philippe and Sabrina exited the building, their hushed conversation dying as soon as they spotted him standing by the curb. Philippe shot him a sharp look, but Oliver didn't acknowledge it. Sabrina, however, let her gaze linger a bit too long, her eyes skimming over him with a strange mix of curiosity and interest. He knew her motives were anything but pure, and he wasn't about to fall into the trap of old flames and false promises.

"Planning to go back to your little inn on Captiva now that you've got your payday?" Philippe sneered, unable to resist one last jab.

Oliver met his brother's gaze, his voice calm and unyielding. "Yes, actually. I have people there who mean something to me—people I want to see again."

Philippe's mouth twitched, a trace of bitterness evident as he replied, "Must be nice. Enjoy your freedom, Oliver. Some of us don't get that luxury."

With a last cold glance, Philippe turned on his heel and strode off, leaving Sabrina standing awkwardly beside him. She looked at Oliver, an apology on her lips that he knew was as shallow as the pity she offered.

She gave him a small, rehearsed smile. "Take care, Oliver. Maybe someday you'll reconsider staying in New York. It has its charms."

"I doubt that," Oliver replied evenly, turning away.

Without another glance, he started walking down the street, his mind already back on Captiva and the life he'd built there. The inn, his friends, the peaceful rhythm he'd found—those were real, untainted by the poisonous legacy his father had left behind. In that moment, he knew that no amount of wealth or status could ever make up for the simplicity and contentment he'd carved out for himself on the island.

As he walked, his thoughts drifted to Maggie, Paolo, and the others at the inn. They were likely all busy with the usual post-holiday bustle, but he knew they'd be there waiting, ready to welcome him back without questions or judgment. Captiva felt more like home than this place ever had, and as the city lights began to blur around him, Oliver felt the weight on his chest begin to lift, replaced by a sense of purpose.

New York could keep its riches, its power games, and its grudges. He had all he needed waiting for him on Captiva. And this time, he knew, he wouldn't be looking back.

# CHAPTER 29

*M*aggie closed the office door gently, letting the sounds of the inn fade into the background. She settled into her chair, pulling her journal from the drawer, its worn leather cover a comforting touch under her fingers.

She opened it, flipping past previous entries filled with lists, reminders, and bits of daily life, until she reached a blank page. Taking a steadying breath, she began to write, her words flowing in a way they hadn't in a long time.

*December 30th*

*It's been a whirlwind few weeks, and tonight I finally have a moment to sit down and let it all sink in. I can hardly believe how much has happened in such a short time—Christmas, Chelsea's wedding, and now a new year beginning. The inn has been buzzing with life, family filling every corner with laughter, stories, and that wonderful chaos I love so much.*

*Christmas felt more special this year. Having all the children here, watching them gather around the tree with their own little ones, brought back memories I thought I'd tucked away. How many years has it been since they were the ones eagerly tearing open gifts, their eyes wide with excitement?*

*And now, here they are, grown with children of their own. I never imagined my heart could hold so much pride...and yet, there's a bit of a bittersweet ache too. My children have all found their places in the world, their lives rich with experiences and love, and as happy as I am for them, there are moments when I miss the days when they were all mine.*

She paused, reading over her words, feeling the familiar pang of a mother's nostalgia. But she didn't linger on it for long. Instead, she let her pen continue, her thoughts drifting to the most recent memories.

*Chelsea's wedding was a beautiful celebration. Watching her, radiant and full of hope, was like looking at a piece of my own heart. She's been through so much and seeing her find happiness with Steven filled me with so much happiness. They are so well-matched, and I can see the ease and laughter between them. That little glimmer in her eye, the one that had dimmed for so long, was back. I couldn't ask for anything more than that, for her to feel cherished again, and to have someone who sees her strength, her heart, the way her family does.*

*The house feels a little quieter now that everyone's gone back. Even my best friend is away on her honeymoon. But there's comfort in this quiet, a kind of peace that lets me sit with my thoughts and truly take it all in.*

*I'm grateful for every moment, and as the years pass, I find myself valuing the small things even more—the touch of a hand, a shared laugh, the way family seems to wrap itself around you just when you need it most.*

Maggie tapped her pen against the journal, a few stray thoughts tugging at her mind. She thought of the many faces that had filled her days, but one in particular lingered, a face she hadn't expected to feel so much worry for. Her hand moved across the page again.

*And then there's Oliver. Oh, how my heart worries for him.*

*These past weeks have been so hard for him. His brother showing up, losing his father, going back to New York, facing all the complicated family ties he left behind...it's like he's been pulled back into a world that once held him captive, and I fear for what that might do to him. He found something here—a kind of freedom, a chance to be himself without all the expectations and judgments that come with the Laurier name. And yet, part of me worries that he might feel obligated to stay there, to fulfill whatever role his family expects of him.*

*It pains me to think of him trapped in that life again, surrounded by the weight of wealth and legacy, as though that's all there is to his story. I see so much more in him. He's got a heart that wants to give, to create, to build something of his own. I've watched him pour himself into this place, into his cooking, into friendships that mean more than any inheritance ever could. I want him to remember that he has a choice—that he's not bound by anyone's expectations, that he can build his own life here, with people who genuinely care about him.*

*I wonder if he knows how much he's become a part of our family. I see it in the way Paolo looks at him, in the way Iris lights up when he's around, and in the way even little Lexie follows him with that curious look in her eyes. He belongs here, but he needs to see that for himself. I can't make that choice for him, and I wouldn't even if I could. I just hope he finds the courage to choose happiness, to choose a life that fills him with peace.*

Her pen paused, a faint smile touching her lips as she thought of Iris. There was a quiet strength in her, a resilience that had drawn her to Oliver from the start. Maggie had noticed it, had watched them grow closer in ways both subtle and profound. She continued to write.

*Iris... I see so much of myself in her. She's strong, kind, and far more resilient than she gives herself credit for. I don't think she realizes how much Oliver means to her, or maybe she does and just won't let herself believe it. She's been through her own struggles, and I think she's learned to protect her heart a bit too well. But I can see it in her eyes when she looks at him—she's found something she didn't even know she was searching for.*

*If he does come back, I hope they both allow themselves to be open to whatever this could be. I've seen enough to know that love often blooms in the places we least expect that sometimes the right person finds us when we're too busy guarding our hearts to see it. And maybe they'll find their way to each other.*

Maggie set her pen down, rubbing her hands together thoughtfully. She let her mind linger on the faces that had filled her days—the laughter, the conversations, the love that seemed to flow so effortlessly among them all. The inn was more than just a place of work; it had become the very heart of her life, a place that held her family's memories, her hopes, and, in some small way, a piece of her soul.

Taking a deep breath, she returned to her journal.

*I don't know what the future holds for any of us, but I know that we're all a little stronger when we're together.*

*I'm so glad the children talked about Daniel. The pain of our difficult marriage is now long gone, and I can appreciate what we built together. He'd be proud of our children, of the lives they've built, of the people they've become. And I think, somehow, he'd understand the choices I made, even if it meant a different kind of happiness than we once planned.*

*As for Oliver, I'll keep a candle burning for him, in my own way. He's one of us now, whether he realizes it or not. And when he's ready, when he finds his way back, he'll know that he has a place here, just as much as any of us. Life has its way of unfolding as it should, and if I've learned anything over these years, it's that sometimes, all we can do is open our hearts and trust.*

Maggie closed the journal, a sense of peace settling over her. She placed the book back in the drawer and leaned back, letting herself bask in the quiet. Whatever lay ahead, she knew she had everything she needed—family, love, and a place to call home. And that was more than enough.

Iris sat on the edge of the garden bench, clipboard in hand, watching Lexie dart between the flower beds, a tiny whirlwind of energy. Paolo's Chihuahua puppy had a knack for finding trouble wherever she went, nibbling on blooms and leaving paw prints on freshly planted soil. Paolo chuckled as he watched her antics, occasionally reaching down to scoop her up, only for Lexie to wriggle free and tear off into the garden again.

Trying to focus, Iris flipped through the week's menus, her mind drifting more than she liked to admit. She'd poured herself into work over the past week, hoping it would drown out the thoughts that kept circling back to Oliver. Despite her best efforts, his absence lingered in her mind like an ache. New Year's Eve was just around the corner, and she couldn't shake the fear that he wouldn't be back to ring it in with them.

She took a deep breath, forcing herself to focus. "Paolo," she said, scanning the list, "I think we should do the sesame-crusted tuna for the open house. It's light, fresh, and it always seems to be a crowd-pleaser."

"Good choice," Paolo agreed, his attention momentarily diverted from Lexie's antics. "And maybe a vegetable risotto to balance it out?"

"Perfect," she replied, jotting it down. But even as she wrote, her mind wandered, and she couldn't help but imagine Oliver's reaction to the menu. He'd probably throw in his own twist— maybe a coconut glaze or a garnish of edible flowers he'd somehow sneak in from the garden. That was Oliver: unpre- dictable, passionate, and always surprising her.

Paolo seemed to sense her distraction. He peered over his glasses at her, a knowing smile tugging at his lips. "You're thinking about him, aren't you?"

Iris' cheeks flushed, and she ducked her head, pretending to study the clipboard. "I'm just... hoping he's doing all right, that's all."

"Ah, but you worry he won't come back," Paolo said softly, his tone laced with sympathy. "It's natural, Iris. He's got a lot to handle in New York, and sometimes old places have a way of pulling people back in."

She nodded, swallowing the lump in her throat. The rational part of her knew that if Oliver truly wanted to be here, he would be. But doubts whispered that maybe Captiva had only been a temporary escape for him—a brief interlude from the life he'd been destined for. She had to accept that she might have imagined something more between them than there really was. It was silly, she thought, to assume a bond had formed just because of a few shared laughs, late-night talks, and... well, feelings she couldn't deny.

"Maybe I was reading too much into things," she murmured, forcing herself to meet Paolo's gaze. "I need to get my head back in the game and just focus on the inn, on the guests, on what I'm here to do."

"Good plan, but don't be too hard on yourself," Paolo replied, patting her shoulder. "Life has a funny way of sorting itself out when we least expect it."

Lexie bounded up to Iris then, interrupting the moment by dropping a stray garden glove at her feet, her tiny tail wagging furiously. Iris laughed, grateful for the distraction, and gave Lexie a gentle scratch behind the ears.

"Well," Iris said, standing up, "we'd better get these menu plans finalized. Guests will be expecting a wonderful spread for the open house, and I intend to deliver."

Paolo laughed, raising his hands in mock surrender. "As if I'd expect anything less from you, Iris. Now, go give Maggie a hand if she needs it. I'll see what Lexie's got in mind for my garden beds."

Iris left the garden and headed inside, glancing one last time at the vibrant flowers and leafy herbs, the signs of life that had become so much a part of her world here. The inn had a warmth that went beyond its cozy decor or sun-dappled walls. It was the people—their quirks, their shared stories—that made this place feel like a true home.

She pushed open the door to the office, finding Millie going over the bookkeeping and bill-paying. Millie muttered something about tax deductions and Maggie came out of her office to see if she could help her.

"Iris!" Maggie's face lit up as she caught sight of her. "Come to rescue us from the tax monster?"

"Not quite." Iris laughed, leaning against the doorframe. "I think I'll leave that to the professionals. I just came to see if you need anything for the New Year's open house."

"No, I think we've got everything under control," Maggie replied, her eyes twinkling. "Millie's just making sure every penny's accounted for, as usual."

Millie shot Maggie a playfully indignant look. "Someone has to make sure we stay afloat! And with all the food you two are cooking up for the open house, we need every penny we can get."

Iris laughed along with them, her mood lifting. The inn felt like a refuge, a place where life continued in steady rhythms, regardless of the uncertainties outside its walls. She resolved, right then and there, to put her worries about Oliver to rest. Whatever happened, she'd be all right. She had her work, her friends, and the knowledge that she'd made a life for herself, independent of anyone else.

As the afternoon rolled on, she moved through the inn, checking on details for the open house, organizing the pantry, and making sure the kitchen was in perfect order. If Oliver did return, she wanted everything to be in top shape. But even as she focused on these tasks, a quiet sadness lingered, an unspoken ache she tried her best to ignore.

Later, just as she was organizing a stack of trays, the kitchen door creaked open. She didn't bother looking up, assuming it was Paolo or Maggie. But then she caught the faint, familiar scent of aftershave—a scent that had, unknowingly, etched itself into her memory.

She froze, heart pounding, and slowly turned around. There, standing by the pantry door, was Oliver, his gaze sweeping over the kitchen with a look of focused concentration. He didn't say anything, just moved quietly to one of the cabinets, opening it and starting to rearrange the shelves as though he'd never been gone.

For a moment, Iris couldn't breathe. She blinked, half-convinced she was imagining him. But there he was, solid and real, his presence filling the room like it always had.

"Oliver..." she whispered, her voice barely audible.

He glanced over his shoulder, a soft, almost shy smile touching his lips. "Didn't think I'd leave the cabinets this unorganized, did you?"

Before she could respond, footsteps echoed down the hallway, and moments later, Maggie, Paolo, and Millie bustled into the kitchen with Lexie following behind. They stopped in their tracks, their expressions morphing from shock to pure joy as they took in the sight of him.

"Oliver!" Maggie exclaimed, her face breaking into a broad smile. She hurried over, pulling him into a tight embrace, her laughter mingling with unshed tears. "We thought you'd be stuck in New York forever!"

"Not a chance," he murmured, his arms wrapping around her as though he, too, had missed this place more than he could put into words.

Millie clapped her hands together, her grin wide. "Look at you, back just in time for the open house! This place hasn't been the same without you."

Even Paolo, normally reserved, stepped forward and clapped a hand on Oliver's shoulder. "Good to have you back, my friend."

As the group reunited around him, Iris lingered at the edge, watching the scene with a mix of relief and disbelief. She felt the sadness that had hung over her these past days lift, replaced by a warmth she couldn't deny. Oliver was here, he'd come back, and it felt as though the world had righted itself once more.

Oliver's gaze found hers across the room, his expression softening. In that moment, surrounded by friends, she felt the unspoken understanding pass between them—a shared acknowledgment that this was where they were meant to be.

She looked at Maggie who smiled and winked at her. Iris wiped a small tear from the corner of her eye. Oliver was home… and so was she.

# CHAPTER 30

*M*aggie's mouth dropped open, and for a moment, she could only stare at Oliver in shock. "Three-hundred and fifty million dollars? Are you kidding me?"

Oliver shook his head, a small, bemused smile on his face. "Nope. My father's parting gift, I guess. As sad as it is, I think it was his last message to me."

She leaned back, letting the number sink in. "I can't even wrap my head around it," she murmured. "So what are you going to do with it all? I mean, Oliver…you could do anything—travel the world, start your own restaurant, live however you want."

Her voice softened, the weight of her words lingering between them. It suddenly occurred to her that the inheritance might be the thing that would take him away from the inn for good.

"I'm just surprised that you'd want to stay here, cooking for the inn, when there are so many other options."

Oliver took a deep breath, his gaze thoughtful.

"I know it might seem strange," he began, "but this money, it feels… complicated. My father's wealth was always tangled up with expectations, with what he thought was important in life.

There are no expectations now, instead that's been replaced with responsibility. I feel the money now represents a chance to show that something good could come out of tragedy and trauma."

Maggie studied him, nodding as she sensed there was more he wanted to say.

"There's something I've been thinking seriously about," he continued, his voice gaining a quiet strength. "I want to create a foundation—in Katie's name and in honor of my boys. Their lives were cut short, but their memory deserves something meaningful. I thought maybe I could help people affected by the floods in Miami, people who've gone through real loss and trauma. Many have yet to recover, and I think it will take years without the funds to help."

Maggie's heart swelled at his words, and she reached across the table, placing a comforting hand over his.

"That's a beautiful idea, Oliver."

He smiled, gratitude in his eyes. "Thank you, Maggie. I think…it's the only way this money could feel right to me. To use it for something good, something they'd be a part of."

She nodded, sensing his relief, his sense of purpose. But as she glanced back at him, she felt a glimmer of curiosity. "And what about you?" she asked gently.

He laughed softly, shaking his head. "I don't need anything but to live my life on my terms. No salary either. Cleary, I don't need it. I don't need more than what I have here. This place… it's become home. You, Paolo, everyone here on Captiva—you've all become my family. When I'm here, I don't feel like I have to be anyone other than myself."

Her smile softened, her heart touched by his sincerity. "Well, that's settled, then. You're one of us now."

Oliver hesitated, his expression taking on a new warmth. "There's…someone else," he began, glancing down as if gathering his words carefully. "Someone I'd like to spend more time with, and I hope you won't mind."

Maggie's eyebrows rose, but she felt a knowing smile spread across her face. "Ah," she said, leaning forward, her eyes twinkling with understanding.

"That wouldn't be a certain chef, would it?"

A faint blush crept up Oliver's cheeks, and he looked away, but not before Maggie saw the glint of affection in his eyes.

"Iris..." he admitted quietly, "...she's become important to me. I hadn't planned on feeling this way, but I think... I think there's something real there. I just didn't know if I'd be able to come back and say it."

Maggie's smile widened, warmth filling her heart. "Oliver, I think you might be the last one to notice it. We all saw it, even if you couldn't." She gave his hand a reassuring squeeze. "She cares about you too. Maybe now you both have the chance to see where it leads."

He met her gaze, and for the first time since he'd returned from New York, Maggie saw a deep sense of peace in his eyes. It was as though he'd finally let go of the weight he'd carried for so long, a freedom that she could feel radiating from him.

"Thank you, Maggie," he said, his voice barely a whisper. "For everything. For giving me a place to heal and a place to belong."

Her own eyes misted, and she patted his hand with a gentle laugh. "We've just been waiting for you to realize that for yourself."

They sat together in comfortable silence, a new chapter dawning for both of them, woven with family, healing, and the promise of something beautiful yet to come.

The soft whisper of waves lapped against the shore as Maggie, Paolo, and little Lexie strolled along the beach. The air was warm with a gentle breeze that tousled Maggie's hair, filling her with a deep sense of calm. Lexie trotted ahead, her tiny paws leaving prints in the sand, her nose twitching as she sniffed the salt-tinged air.

Paolo reached for Maggie's hand, lacing his fingers with hers as they walked in comfortable silence. It felt like the perfect moment to reflect on the days behind them and look forward to what lay ahead.

"It's been quite a year, hasn't it?" Paolo murmured, glancing over at her, a soft smile on his face.

She nodded, a smile tugging at her lips. "It has. Full of surprises, laughter, and memories we'll carry forever."

She took a deep breath, her heart swelling with gratitude. "We've been blessed, Paolo. The inn has flourished, we've had all the kids here for Christmas, and Chelsea's wedding was... oh, just perfect. And, I'm feeling healthy and strong. I can't ask for anything more."

Paolo squeezed her hand, his gaze affectionate as he looked out over the ocean. "I think the new year holds even more for us, Maggie. It feels like this family is continuing to grow."

Maggie laughed softly, casting a glance toward the inn, imagining the rooms filled with children's laughter, with the next generation making their own memories.

"It does, doesn't it?" she said, her voice filled with warmth. "And don't be surprised if, after Becca's baby arrives, Beth ends up pregnant too. I think Gabriel's father coming back has made her think about family in a whole new way."

Paolo chuckled, nodding. "That wouldn't surprise me at all."

The thought of her family growing brought Maggie a sense of peace she hadn't known in years. As she watched Lexie dash through the sand, a feeling of gratitude settled deep within her, like the roots of a tree, grounding her in the here and now. This was her life, a life filled with love, laughter, and the constant blessing of family.

They walked a little further, the sound of the ocean mingling with their thoughts. Maggie felt the future unfolding in her mind

—more family gatherings, more celebrations, more love to fill the rooms of the inn and spill out onto this very beach.

They stopped to watch Lexie run in and out of the water. Maggie leaned her head on Paolo's shoulder.

"Whatever this year brings, I know we'll face it together," she said softly, her words carried away by the breeze.

Paolo pressed a gentle kiss to her forehead. "Always."

"Can we stay right here for a bit? I want to watch the sky change colors."

Lexie scampered by their side, leaving footprints in the sand as the sun dipped below the horizon. A new chapter awaited, but for now, this moment was enough.

THE END

# ALSO BY ANNIE CABOT

**THE CAPTIVA ISLAND SERIES**

Book One: KEY LIME GARDEN INN

Book Two: A CAPTIVA WEDDING

Book Three: CAPTIVA MEMORIES

Book Four: CAPTIVA CHRISTMAS

Book Five: CAPTIVA NIGHTS

Book Six: CAPTIVA HEARTS

Book Seven: CAPTIVA EVER AFTER

Book Eight: CAPTIVA HIDEAWAY

Book Nine: RETURN TO CAPTIVA

Book Ten: CAPTIVA CABANA

Book Eleven: CAPTIVA COTTAGE

Book Twelve: CAPTIVA MOONLIGHT

Book Thirteen: CAPTIVA BOOK CLUB

**THE PERIWINKLE SHORES SERIES**

Book One: CHRISTMAS ON THE CAPE

Book Two: THE SEA GLASS GIRLS

# ABOUT THE AUTHOR

Annie Cabot is the author of contemporary women's fiction and family sagas. Annie writes about friendships and family relationships, that bring inspiration and hope to others.

With a focus on women's fiction, Annie feels that she writes best when she writes from experience. "Every woman's journey is a relatable story. I want to capture those stories, let others know they are not alone, and bring a bit of joy to my readers."

Annie Cabot is the pen name for the writer Patricia Pauletti. A lover of all things happily ever after, it was only a matter of time before she began to write what was in her heart, and so, the pen name Annie Cabot was born.

When she's not writing, Annie and her husband like to travel. Winters always involve time away on Captiva Island, Florida where she continues to get inspiration for her novels.

# ACKNOWLEDGMENTS

With each book I continue to be grateful to the people who support my work. I couldn't do what I do without this team. Thank you all so much.

Cover Design: Marianne Nowicki
Premade Ebook Cover Shop
https://www.premadeebookcovershop.com/

Editor: Lisa Lee of Lisa Lee Proofreading and Editing
https://www.facebook.com/EditorLisaLee/
Beta Readers:
John Battaglino
Nancy Burgess
Michele Connolly
Anne Marie Page Cooke

And to the readers who love these books so much they convinced me to write four more books in this series for 2025.

Made in the USA
Columbia, SC
26 June 2025

59881036R00137